INTO

THE

MIDNIGHT

VOID

By Mara Fitzgerald

BEYOND THE RUBY VEIL

Beyond the Ruby Veil
Into the Midnight Void

INTO
THE
MIDNIGHT
VOID

Mara Fitzgerald

LITTLE, BROWN AND COMPANY

New York Boston

To my parents

Little, Brown and Company
Hachette Book Group
1290 Avenue of the Americas, New York, NY 10104
Visit us at LBYR.com

First Edition: January 2022

Little, Brown and Company is a division of Hachette Book Group, Inc.
The Little, Brown name and logo are trademarks of Hachette Book Group, Inc.

The publisher is not responsible for websites (or their content) that are not owned by the publisher.

Library of Congress Cataloging-in-Publication Data
Names: Fitzgerald, Mara, author.
Title: Into the midnight void / Mara Fitzgerald.
Description: First edition. | New York : Little, Brown and Company, 2022. | Series: Beyond the ruby veil ; 2 | Audience: Ages 12 & up. | Summary: Emanuela has used her magic to rule the six cities of Occhia absolutely and without mercy toward those who 'disrespect' her, while her enemy Verene controls the resistance, just as they agreed—but now everything is going wrong, the 'omens' are out of control, and since Emanuela has already killed the old rulers who might have explained the deeper secrets of magic, she and Verene will have to work together in order to keep all the cities from collapsing into chaos.
Identifiers: LCCN 2021021273 | ISBN 9780759557758 (hardcover) | ISBN 9780759557772 (ebook)
Subjects: LCSH: Magic—Juvenile fiction. | Good and evil—Juvenile fiction. | Signs and symbols—Juvenile fiction. | Fantasy. | Young adult fiction. | CYAC: Fantasy. | Magic—Fiction. | Good and evil—Fiction. | Signs and symbols—Fiction. | LCGFT: Fantasy fiction.
Classification: LCC PZ7.1.F5732 In 2022 | DDC [Fic]—dc23
LC record available at https://lccn.loc.gov/2021021273

ISBNs: 978-0-7595-5775-8 (hardcover), 978-0-7595-5777-2 (ebook)

Printed in the United States of America

LSC-C

Printing 1, 2021

ONE

I'VE BROKEN HIM.

And I haven't even done anything yet.

All I did was stand here, waiting quietly as the man was dragged before me. My guards dropped him unceremoniously at the foot of the cathedral steps. He lifted his eyes, beheld my form, and in an instant, he was sobbing like a baby.

It's been going on for about ten seconds. But it already feels like an hour.

"I didn't mean it, Highest Lady Emanuela," the man manages to choke out. "I didn't mean it."

"Oh, so you're not even going to try and deny it?" I say. "Good. We can get this over with quickly."

"I didn't mean to insult you," he insists. "I simply had too much wine at the party, and I mixed up my words."

"And what were your words again, exactly?" I say.

The man hesitates, trembling, his eyes on the stairs. "I didn't mean it—"

"What were your words?" I say, sharper.

The man's bottom lip wobbles treacherously. He looks around at the assembled crowd. They're huddled at the edges of the cathedral square, watching the proceedings in wide-eyed silence.

All of my prisoners have this exact same moment of desperation. They hope that, against all odds, someone is going to leap out of the safety of the throng and help them. This man's clothing is finely stitched, his jacket a rich shade of green and the gold buttons polished within an inch of their lives. He thinks people will care about him because he's wealthy. If not that, then surely his mother, or his best friend, or paramour will come to his defense.

They're not coming. They never do.

"I didn't mean it—" the man tries again.

"Guard?" I say.

One of my guards, who's standing stiffly at the man's side, unfolds a sheet of paper and begins to read.

"All I'm saying is that it's strange. Our old ruler lived for a thousand years, and now she's just gone? What gives this girl the right to take over and change everything? Why does she hide behind all those veils? And why is she so short? If you ask me, she's nothing but an ugly child pretending to have magic. She can't actually make us any water. It will dry up soon, and she'll be unmasked as the murdering fraud she is. You'll see."

Silence.

The man kneeling on the ground has gone extremely still.

"Anything else you'd like to add?" I say.

Apparently not.

I gesture at the guards, and they pick the prisoner up.

"Wait!" The man comes back to life, flailing uselessly in

their grasp. "Please, Highest Lady Emanuela. I'm sorry. I'm sorry. I don't want to die."

"Well, you should have considered that before you disrespected me," I say.

And then he's gone. The guards drag him, sniveling and pleading, around to the back of the cathedral. Another guard in a red coat approaches from the edge of the crowd and bows to me.

"That was the last of them, Highest Lady Emanuela," he says.

The entire crowd holds their breath, waiting for me to declare that I'm satisfied. For one long, delicious moment, I stay silent and let them imagine what could happen if I'm not.

"Very well," I say finally.

I turn and march up the cathedral steps, my long red cloak streaming behind me. The people gathered around the square don't move. They won't move until I pull the double doors shut. Then, they'll go back to their lives, and they'll wait for the next appearance of the mysterious Highest Lady Emanuela. And, if they're smart, they won't go around telling people that I'm an ugly child.

I proceed through the dim foyer of the cathedral. Two guards are poised at the entrance to the inner chamber, waiting for me on either side of the tall arched doorway.

"The prisoners are ready, Highest Lady Emanuela," one of them says.

I sweep past them without a word of acknowledgment. This building used to be the center of life in the city called Auge. They had worship and weddings and every single holiday celebration here. They spent almost as much time in it as they did their own houses. But now, the cathedral belongs to me.

The room has been emptied out. In the center, sitting alone on the black-and-white tile floor, is an enormous glass tank shaped like a dome. The prisoners of the day—about twenty in total—are trapped inside. As always, they're scrambling for freedom, clawing at the door the guards have bolted shut. The man I just had arrested is kicking futilely at the thick wall. When they see me coming for them, the frenzy only intensifies.

As I stop before the tank, my guards shut the doors to the inner chamber with a dull thud. Highest Lady Emanuela always does her magic in private.

I say nothing to my prisoners. I simply reach up and start to pull aside the veils covering my face.

All the clamor inside the tank stops. The prisoners turn to watch, transfixed in spite of their terror. I haven't looked in a mirror in a long time, but I know I'm very pretty, with tiny sharp features and chin-length hair that I cut to perfection myself. And then, of course, there's the thing everyone notices first—my viciously dark eyes.

Things used to be different in these cities. People died for something they couldn't control. They got a silly little mark on their skin, called an omen, and they were forced to hand themselves over to their ruler. She locked them in her tower and killed them slowly, draining their blood through a little needle in their neck. They wasted away for days, feeling every drop of life being squeezed out of their body.

I changed all of that. I control who lives and dies now. People who respect me are rewarded. People who don't are shoved into this glass dome for execution. I'm not like their old leader. I don't put them through long, agonizing deaths alone in a cell.

I allow them to die on their feet, surrounded by their fellow misguided citizens.

And as a little treat, the last thing they ever see is my face.

I blink, and my magic floods into my eyes, cold and hungry. My new vision strips away everything else about the people in front of me, leaving the only piece of them it wants—their blood. Just like that, the prisoners have become nothing but intricate, pulsating webs of veins.

They barely even have time to scream. A moment later, they're all gone, exploded out of their skins, and the inside of the dome is soaked with blood.

"That's what you get," I inform them.

And then I'm gone, waltzing through a side door without looking back.

I make my way through a familiar maze of narrow halls, winding up pitch-black staircases. The veil outside is approaching the dark red of evening, but I don't bother to light any lanterns. I'm used to the dark.

The cathedral has four spires, one at each corner. I've claimed the one at the top right as my personal quarters. It's a small, unassuming space—aggressively neat, the way I prefer it. On one side of the round room is a small red love seat. In the middle is my sewing table, draped in swathes of vivid red fabric, a half-completed gown on a mannequin. And over by the window is my desk.

This doesn't look like a living space that could sustain a normal human, with all their normal human needs. Because it's not.

I approach my desk, pulling off my crown and depositing it

carefully in my tank of pet spiders. I let them weave fresh webs among the thorns each night to achieve that perfect, shimmery effect. Then I sit down, and for a moment, against my will, my eyes go to the darkening veil outside. It's hard to ignore. At the top of this spire, the noise of the streets below is far away, and there's nothing but the two of us—the girl that looms over the city, and the veil that looms over the girl.

To everyone else, the veil is a presence as constant and inevitable as air. It stretches above our heads, surrounding our manors with a glowing presence that turns red in the day and black at night. My people used to say it's where our souls dwell before we're born, and it's where they return when we die. Everyone in every city believes, more or less, the same thing. We live our little lives until the veil puts omens on our skin. When the omens cover us, we die, and we have no control over any of it.

When I took over, I told people that we weren't going to let our omens have so much power over us. I told them that the first mark isn't the death sentence they used to believe, and that some people live for years before their omens spread and kill them—a fact their previous ruler conveniently glossed over so she could terrify everyone into giving themselves up to her tower. The people were uneasy at first, but a few months later, they'd all seen the truth of it for themselves. My favored citizens—the ones who are wise enough to show me respect—see this for the gift it is. Now, in Auge, they happily walk around with omens exposed, even going out of their way to show them off if they're feeling bold. The old wives have come up with ways to divulge meaning from their location—they claim people who get marked on the face first are the luckiest, and so on and so on. When someone's omens do spread, as they always will, they're in their own homes, going out on their own terms.

I've made things so much better for so many people. Right now, somewhere in the streets below, there could be a little girl sitting on her bed, staring at the red mark that just appeared on her skin for no reason at all. Now that I'm here, she doesn't have to die.

And the best part is that I'm just getting started. The old rulers devoted themselves to keeping things exactly the same for a thousand years. Their lack of vision was tragic—not to mention dull—but fortunately, that's all over with, and a much worthier successor has taken their place.

I finally light my lantern, and I turn my attention to the map on my desk. It shows the eight cities, arranged in a ring, barely overlapping with their neighbors. In the center of the cities is the veil. Outside of the cities is the veil. Everything except us is the veil.

There are two cities I've left unlabeled. I never look at them. I only bother with the six I control. I make a little tick mark next to Auge to indicate today's successful visit.

As I set down my pen, I become aware that the hairs on the back of my neck are standing on end. Someone else is in the room. And they're right behind me.

There's only one person in the six cities who can sneak up on me like this. It takes skill to move through the darkness as easily as I do.

I hastily fiddle with my outfit, making sure it's perfect. When I stand up and turn around, I make a show of being casual about it, but my heart is thrumming.

"Fancy seeing you here," I say.

"Oh, believe me," the intruder says. "I don't fancy it."

There's one very important thing that sets me apart as the ruler of the six cities. I have magic, and it makes me dangerous and immortal and untouchable. It creates water from blood and keeps my people alive. It's a power that no one else has.

No one else, that is, except the girl in front of me.

Beneath my veils, I smile. It's always nice to see an old enemy.

Two

LAST YEAR, VERENE AND I WERE IMPRISONED TOGETHER. And we spent every day fighting over napkins.

The bundles of food always came at the same time. I figured that out because I had nothing to do but count the minutes, so I did. It didn't surprise me—Verene's brother was the one sending the food down to the very bottom of the catacombs, and he'd struck me as the sort of person who was devastatingly punctual.

The predictability made it an event. As the moment drew nearer, Verene and I would pace on opposite sides of our small iron cell. Right before, we would stand poised in our fighting positions. And the second the food fell from above and hit the floor, we attacked.

Our cell was pitch black, so the fight was always a messy affair. We scrambled at the bundles, and at each other. We let the bread and carefully packed bowls of pasta fall by the wayside, because all we really wanted was the rectangle of fabric they were wrapped in.

Not long into our captivity, my mortal enemy had accidentally blurted out her whole escape plan—to make a rope long enough to hook around the latch at the top of our cell and climb out. It wasn't that I didn't have my own brilliant ideas for getting out of a smooth, tall cell made entirely of iron. I just decided that stealing Verene's plan sounded like more fun. Mostly because of all the napkin fighting.

"Stop biting me!" Verene shrieked, writhing around underneath me.

"Stop taking my napkin," I said—clumsily, as my teeth were still clamped onto her wrist.

"You are—" She slapped at my face. "The most vile—disgusting—appalling—"

I yanked the napkin out of her hands and retreated to my side of the cell, victorious. In the middle, Verene was still panting.

"I'm going to bite your finger off tomorrow," she said.

"I look forward to you trying," I said.

I tied my new napkin onto my budding rope and wrapped the whole thing around myself in a pathetic attempt at a blanket. It was always cold in our cell, but it felt especially cold right after one of our fights. Verene was soft and warm, even when she was furiously whacking me in the head.

She crawled back over to her side of the cell, and I heard her fussing with her own rope. I settled in for another day-long wait. Verene and I didn't talk between our fights. We schemed in silence.

"Do you know what I've realized?" she said.

"That your efforts to escape before me are futile?" I said. "Finally."

I could tell she was glaring at me, even in total darkness. We were just so powerfully connected in that way.

"I've realized that I don't know anything about you," she said.

I fiddled with the end of my rope, making sure the knots were perfect. "I think I've been pretty clear about who I am."

"Yes, I know that you're a terrible person who only cares about yourself," she said. "But you know much more about me. When you invaded Iris, you saw my whole life."

"Oh, are you referring to your cathedral, which I burned down?" I said. "Or your housekeeper, whom I murdered? Or the entire city, which I turned against you?"

"Yes, I'm referring to all of that." Her teeth were obviously clenched. "It's not fair." She paused. "Tell me something about you."

"Hmm," I said. "No."

"What is your family like?" she said. "What is your city like? Why did you leave it and come to Iris? You still never told me. Not really."

And then it all flashed through my head—the city of Occhia as it had once been, full of dutiful people with a great love for tradition, and elaborate superstitions, and very strong opinions about food. But almost immediately, all the memories in my head vanished, replaced by an image of our cathedral as I'd last seen it, filled with nothing but blood and the crumpled remains of clothes.

"Why do you care?" I said viciously.

Even from across the cell, I felt the way Verene withdrew.

"I don't," she said.

She'd obviously remembered who she was talking to. We

both went back to our usual silence, preparing for the next napkin fight.

But after that day, the food bundles stopped coming. At first, I assumed I'd dozed off and gotten my counting wrong. I didn't dare admit that out loud, though, so I just waited. And waited. Finally, after endless hours in the darkness, Verene spoke up.

"Theo knows that I don't actually need to eat like a normal person, now that I have magic," she said. "He must have decided it wasn't worth the effort anymore. He said he was going to leave me down here until he had a better way to keep everyone safe from me, so...he can spend as long as he wants figuring out what that is."

"Well, that's more than I got from my accomplice," I said without thinking.

Then we both went quiet, because we realized what we'd just done. We'd gotten so good at not talking about the boys who'd sent us away. I didn't even think about mine most days, because I didn't let myself. I refused to remember, and I refused to wonder. But all it took was one slip—one moment where I wasn't actively fighting against it—and he was back in my head.

"You told me once that Alessandro wasn't your paramour," Verene said, her voice cautious. "So what was he to you? Really?"

I couldn't believe she was trying to breach this wall between us—a wall the two of us had built with all our stealing and stabbing and merciless ploys to destroy each other. If I wasn't going to talk to her about my city, I certainly wasn't going to talk to her about this.

"He was my accomplice," I insisted.

"No," she said. "No, Emanuela. Don't lie. I saw the way you looked at me after I . . . well. You know what I did to him."

She cut out his eye. I saw him bleed, and I heard him scream, and I wasn't fast enough to stop it.

"You looked at me like all you wanted was to see me dead," she continued.

"Isn't that how I always look at you?" I said.

"This was different," she said. "He meant something to you. You were working together. But obviously, things went wrong, and that's why he put you down here."

She'd already seen more than I wanted her to, clearly. So I decided that, in the safety of the darkness, I could tell her one thing about myself. Just one.

"He was my best friend," I said.

She didn't even acknowledge the words. But I knew she was listening. And it felt worthwhile, somehow, for her to know something about me and the boy I tried so hard not to think about. There was no one else left alive to know about us.

The silence stretched on again. We were both used to silence at this point. We were used to waiting, so we did. And still, the food didn't come.

"So?" Verene said finally.

"So?" I said.

"We do have a weakness, even with our magic," she said. "We'll still die if we get a mortal wound. That's the one thing that will bring our omens back."

"Are you asking me to mortally wound you?" I said. "Again?"

"No," she said. "I'm just saying . . . if there are no more napkins coming . . ."

Then we'd have to fight over the ones that we already had.

I wasn't concerned about my ability to defeat her. Verene always put up a good fight, but at the end of the day, I knew which one of us was more ruthless. It was time to finally rid myself of her and climb out of the prison on my own. I imagined doing just that—finding my way out of the catacombs on my own, creeping into a foreign city on my own, and taking down the ancient rulers on my own.

Then, on an impulse I didn't entirely understand, I found myself picking up my rope and crawling across the cell.

"What are you doing?" Verene demanded. "If you come any closer, I swear I'll—"

She flailed around in a wild attempt to defend herself, and I shoved my rope into her hands. She went still.

"We could tie them together," I said. "Then it might be long enough."

"Sure," she said. "And then we'll climb out holding hands, I suppose? I'm not going to fall for this, Emanuela. How many times have I told you that I know exactly what sort of person you are, and I'm never going to forgive you for the things you did to me? All you want is to take the cities for yourself."

"And what do you want?" I said.

"To save them from the rulers, of course," she said.

"You want to become their hero," I said.

She hesitated, just for a moment, and I wondered if she was thinking about the same moment I was—the moment in Iris when her people, who had worshipped her like a saint the day before, turned and fled from her in terror. It didn't take much. They loved Verene because she said she would do anything for them. But people who say they want that from a girl are lying. Because when they actually get it, they're terrified of it.

"Yes," she said. "That's what I've always wanted."

"And what if we could both get exactly what we want?" I said.

There was a highly suspicious silence from her direction that made my heart start pounding. I felt almost like I'd just asked her to court me—which made the moment the closest I'd ever get to actually doing such a preposterous thing.

"I'm only entertaining this because I'm tired of being in this dirty cell," she said. "But . . . what do you mean?"

Now, in the dim light of my quarters, Verene holds out an expectant hand. I reach back and fumble with my top desk drawer, then pull out a bottle of red wine and hand it to her. My stash is almost out, so I make a mental note that tomorrow, when I use the catacombs to cross between cities, I'll have to make a detour to the wine cellars near the greenhouse. Verene claimed this drawer of mine for herself months ago. Now, it's full of hair ties and little jars of the black powder she's taken to smearing around her eyes, and somehow, I've become responsible for providing her refreshments. I'm only tolerating this invasion of my personal space because now I have an easy way to poison her whenever I please.

She pops the loosened cork and takes a swig, then ducks around me and sits down on my desk, crossing her long legs. She looks exactly the same as she usually does, dressed elegantly in black. Her long curls are loose and so perfectly ethereal they're practically floating around her head. The soft light from the desk lantern makes her brown skin glow, and behind her black, rose-covered mask, her eyes are sparkling.

She's truly unbearable to look at. I don't know how I've put up with it for this long.

"I cleaned up your mess," she says.

She's referring, of course, to the glass tank downstairs filled with blood. Verene insists on being the one to transform it into water, so that she can feel productive.

"How was your day?" I say. "Let me guess—you kissed some babies and made an impassioned speech on a street corner?"

"I'll tell you one thing I didn't do," she says. "Murder someone for mispronouncing my name."

"She's lucky I didn't take her whole family for that offense," I say. "What's your update? Any rumblings amongst the commoners that I should know about?"

Verene takes a slow sip of her wine, and her eyes dart over my veils. She's the only person in our six cities who's seen my face and lived to tell the tale. Every time she looks at me, I'm reminded of that uncomfortable fact.

"Tomorrow is our anniversary," she says.

"Our … what?" I say.

"It will have been a year since we first met in Iris," she says. "You didn't remember? I, for one, will never be able to forget the day my life was ruined by the human embodiment of malevolence."

My stomach twists itself into sudden knots. I don't look at calendars. I just let time pass, trying to not even count my monthly bleedings. I don't want to know how long it's been since—

No. I can't think about it. I won't think about it. I swallow hard, glad my face is shielded by three layers of gauzy fabric.

"You're giving me a gift then, I assume," I say.

"I want to interrupt your trials," she says. "For a rescue mission. A dramatic one."

I stiffen. "That's not how our arrangement works."

"That's exactly how our arrangement works," she says. "You get to rule the cities, and I get to rule the hearts of the people. That's what we agreed on."

"And you're *supposed* to stay away from my cathedrals," I say. "Unless you want your little rebel groups to find out that the two of us are conspiring to make sure we rule every square inch of these cities—"

"The Garden of Resistance is getting restless, Emanuela," she says. "We've been under your thumb for a long time. And they hate you a lot—almost as much as I do, which is saying something. They want to do more. Just let me swoop in and rescue a couple of prisoners from you. That will keep them happy for a while."

And, of course, it will remind all her followers how great she is. Verene and I are completely different, but we do have one thing in common. No matter what we have, we always want more. That's why we started out taking one city and quickly decided we needed to take all six. That's why she's built an elaborate rebellion movement that's always trying to outdo themselves with bigger and bigger demonstrations. That's why I never go a single day without holding a trial somewhere. We have the cities firmly in the palms of our hands. But we could always hold them a little tighter.

"Fine," I say. "Go ahead. Interrupt my trials."

Verene eyes me for a moment. "You're not going to try and stop me?"

"You'll just have to wait and see," I say.

She smiles. She has a bright, wide smile—sparkling, like the rest of her. But there's a little edge of mischief to it. It's such a subtle thing, and I bet her devoted followers don't see it. But I do.

Her smile is the most unbearable thing about her. It makes me sweaty. So very sweaty. It doesn't seem right for an immortal being like myself to sweat this much.

"I can't wait," she says.

She drains the last of her wine and slides off my desk, heading for the door. And just as quickly as she appeared, she's gone.

Three

IT's THE MIDDLE OF THE NIGHT, THE VEIL INKY BLACK AND the streets below silent. By now, Verene is surely back on the outskirts of the city—where she sleeps in a bed with a dozen of her drunken rebel friends, I assume. I don't ask for the details of her life, so I wouldn't know.

With our magic, the two of us don't technically need sleep. But after months without it, I feel the absence, carving out a horrible aching pain in my head and my limbs. That's why I'm lying on my love seat, staring at the ceiling and telling myself that tonight will finally be the night I manage to drift off.

First, I think about the tight black pants Verene has taken to wearing, and how good I would look in them. That keeps me occupied for quite a while. Then, I think about my map of the eight cities, and the careful paths I've drawn through the catacombs to travel between them. Then, I think about the prisoners I murdered today.

And then I'm thinking about my people. My real people.

The people of Occhia, dead in the cathedral. I see their blood. I taste it, too. I hear their screams.

And before I can stop myself, I'm thinking about him.

I see my best friend, exactly as I last saw him. Ale was standing in the middle of the cathedral, his mamma's blood splattered on his face. He was staring at me like he couldn't comprehend what I'd just done.

I couldn't comprehend it, either. But I've had a whole year to relive every second of the day I accidentally murdered everyone in my city—everyone except the boy who used to be my best friend.

My stomach seizes up, and I fling myself off the divan and retch. Nothing comes up except a horrible trail of spittle. Nothing ever comes up, because I don't eat.

I used to love eating.

I'm on my knees, somehow, shaking madly. I force myself to breathe until it comes a little easier. Then, I get to my feet and hobble over to my sewing table. I put one of my cloaks on. I add the veils to cover my face, and I drift to the window, seeking the cool night air and the reassuring sight of a place where everything is under my control.

The city of Auge stretches out below me, with its pristine half-timber manors and charmingly narrow streets. There are lights still on in a few of the manors, and I catch a glimpse of two of my guards patrolling. There's only one rule in my city— that people respect me. A lot of these houses belonged to the same nobles for a thousand years, but they don't anymore. I let my most loyal citizens get the best spots.

Parliament has all but collapsed. They say I'm too *disruptive*. But the way things were needed to be disrupted. Also, the men of Parliament need water from me, too, so at a certain point, they had no choice but to stand down.

It's possible that, in my early days of ruling, I made a few unwise choices. For example, perhaps it wasn't the best idea to arrest the only workers who knew how to repair the intricate system that waters the greenhouses. But I'm learning. Next time, I'll have new workers trained first.

This is my city now. They all are. I've saved everyone from dying in a tower, and they'll never be able to forget that. They'll never be able to forget me.

But as I lean on the windowsill, admiring my domain, a small, persistent thought creeps into my head. It's the same thought I have every time I return to this particular cathedral.

I've done so much. But I could be doing more.

I turn away from the window, and slowly, my eyes drift up to the trapdoor in my ceiling. Almost against my will, I find myself walking over to pull it down—a fussy process, because I have to stand on a chair to reach. The ladder unfurls, and I look up into the darkness. The hole in my ceiling should be unassuming, but instead, it reminds me of the catacombs. It feels like something ancient that shouldn't be intruded upon.

I shake myself, and I intrude, climbing the ladder with confidence. Inside the attic, I fumble for the lantern on the wall. The flame springs to life to reveal a woman in a red gown, chained up in a corner, a bag placed firmly over her head.

"Guess who?" I say.

The woman is silent.

It wasn't hard to capture the old ruler of this city. It wasn't hard to capture any of them. The mysterious women in red gowns had been all-powerful and uncontested for a thousand years. They didn't expect two girls to crawl out of the cata-combs and abruptly put a stop to that by throwing potato sacks over their heads. The rulers were all solitary creatures, spending their nights alone in their little quarters at the top of their towers. This one was playing the harp when we found her. We smashed it up and made her listen to the whole affair. We were feeling a bit petty, on account of all the people she's killed.

Verene and I were bursting at the seams to interrogate these women. We already know one of their biggest secrets—that their blood magic isn't innate, but acquired through a gruesome ritual. We thought we had the perfect leverage to get them to tell us everything else—everything about magic, and the eight cities, and the veil, and why it all has to be this way.

That's what we expected.

That's not exactly what we got.

"I know what you're wondering," I say. "Where are my spiders? Shall I go fetch them and allow them to say hello? Or are you finally ready to talk?"

The ruler draws in a breath, and I tense in anticipation.

"There is no other way," she says in her throaty Augen accent.

It's always the same. Sometimes, when I can't sleep, the words run through my head over and over.

There is no other way.

I don't respond right away. I wait, letting my breath even out, because I refuse to sound irritated when I speak.

"I've already made another way," I say. "The cities don't need you. They need blood magic—my magic. If you're not in the mood to talk, that's fine. I'll just come back later—because I'm immortal now, too, in case you've forgotten."

I turn to go.

"Do you think that's what makes a ruler?" she says. "Do you think that's all there is to the magic? Blood and water?"

I stop short.

This is the first time in a year the ruler has said anything new. Carefully, I turn back to her.

"If not that..." I say. "Then what?"

"Our power is tied to our cities," she says. "Our power protects our cities in ways you will never understand. And you—a random little girl who happened to stumble upon the ritual—cannot replace us."

"A random little girl?" I echo softly. "Is that all I am?"

"You are, in the eyes of the veil," she says. "And those are the only eyes that matter."

A chill goes down the back of my spine.

"What does that mean?" I say.

"It means there is no other way," she says.

I think, abruptly, about the omen that used to be on my hip. The veil marked me with that omen when I was only ten years old. I still don't know why it happened. I still don't know why the veil makes the choices it makes. But she does.

I want to grab the ruler and shake her until she gives me answers. I want to dump spiders on her until she explains herself. But I'm very aware of the fact that I have to think like an immortal now. She's been locked up here for almost a year, and she barely seems fazed. This has to be handled delicately.

Besides, I know enough. I made my omen go away with the ritual. And it hasn't come back. It will never come back.

"I'm afraid I just don't believe you," I say. "I know you're upset that I'm ruling your city without you. It's hard to believe that you could be so easily forgotten, isn't it? But you have been. The only ruler they know now is Highest Lady Emanuela."

"So you've figured everything out, then?" she says.

"Yes," I say.

"You've figured out how to control your magic?" she says. "Really control it?"

My entire body flushes hot, then cold. I blink, and even through my veils, I see the ruler's blood. She's reduced to a spiderweb of veins in the corner.

Everyone looks the same when all you can see is their blood.

"Ah," the ruler says. "That's what I thought." She pauses, and when she speaks again, her voice is almost gentle. "If you let me out, I can teach you—"

And then she's gone.

My magic did it again.

The only thing it knows how to do.

Slowly, I leave the attic. I grab the bucket of water by my bed and carry it upstairs. And I start to clean up the bloody mess I've made, because I have to hide the evidence.

Verene can control her magic. I don't know how she figured it out. All I know is that one day, she was sitting on my desk, drinking her wine, and she said, "Guess what I've realized? We can turn our monthly bleedings into water. Mine was all over the bedsheets this morning, but that will never be a problem again."

"I prefer to just roll around in the blood," I said. "It reminds me of when I stabbed you to death."

But my mind was racing, overcome by the idea that she could do something like that. I've never been able to do anything like that. Every single drop of blood I try to control explodes in my face—literally.

The first person I tried to practice on was the ruler of Oga. I killed her. Then I tried to practice on the ruler of Suil. I killed her, too.

I kept trying. I couldn't stop myself. They kept telling me in their cold, unknowable voices that there was *no other way*, and I kept needing to show them how wrong they were. Before I knew it, five out of the six were dead.

Now the last one is, too.

Hours later, when the mess is finally gone, I leave the attic and close the trapdoor behind me. I shove the bloody rags under a pile of fabric next to my sewing table, then straighten up and push aside my veils to peer around the room, convinced that the next time my accomplice sets foot in here, the truth will be written all over the walls.

Verene can't know about this—any of it. We agreed I would be the one to interrogate the rulers, because I'm the one who likes making spiders crawl all over people.

She can't know that they're all gone, and we're never getting any answers from them.

She can't know that every time I catch myself staring at her for a second too long, I become treacherously close to bursting every last one of her veins.

She can't know that I'm somehow, always, even more dangerous than she is.

Her wine bottle from earlier is empty, sitting abandoned on the sewing table. I pick it up and trace an anxious finger over the embossed label.

If Verene knew the truth, she wouldn't want to be in an

arrangement anymore. She would want to fight like the enemies we are. All these evenings together in my quarters, schem-
ing about what to do next... that would all be gone. She would
come after me tirelessly, and it would be our most violent fight
of all. One of us would die. And this time, it would stick.

I look down at the wine bottle. I think about the little red
mustache that got smeared onto Verene's upper lip after one too
many sips, and I press the bottle to my own mouth, suddenly
convinced that the warmth of her is left behind, and that I'll be
able to feel it.

When I realize what I'm doing, I toss the bottle onto the
sewing table and back away. I return to my divan, throw my
veils over my face, and curl up on my side to stare at the dark,
empty room.

Verene will never find out the truth. It will never come up,
because we don't need the rulers. They had no answers. All they
had was lies. They claimed there was no other way, but there is.
I am the other way.

Because this is what I wanted.

Because this is all I have left.

FOUR

By the next afternoon, I've traveled to the city of Glaz, and I'm ready for the day's trials. I emerge into the foyer of their cathedral, dressed in a fresh cloak and veils, and briefly look over the notes my guards have left me. Most of today's prisoners are people who were caught gossiping about me in the market, along with several members of the Garden of Resistance who staged a very dramatic demonstration that involved making a life-size doll of me and throwing it off a roof. I'm sure watching that was the highlight of Verene's week.

I push open the front doors of the cathedral and emerge into the rich red light of the veil. In an instant, the people gathered all along the edges of the square drop to their knees.

The first time I saw the watercrea wield such power in Occhia, all I could think about was how nice it must feel to bring everyone in the city down with one move. It still feels nice. It does. I'm just impatient to move on to the other bits of the trials, like whatever worthless display Verene is preparing.

"Rise," I say.

They do, and a nervous ripple goes through the crowd as my guards bring the first prisoner forward. It's an older man with a touch of gray in his hair. When he looks at me, I feel his resolve wobble, but he stays standing.

"Well?" I say. "Anything to say for yourself?"

He swallows hard. "I do not deny my charges. I'm ready to meet my creator if it means my blood will provide for the city."

These are the worst cases—the religious ones who think I'm disturbing their higher order, and that praying as they're shoved into my glass tank will save them. I want them to fight back. When their lives are on the line, people should always fight back.

"You said…" I glance off to the prisoner's right side. "Guard, what did he say?"

My guard dutifully starts to read off his notes. *"I think we should just go back to the old way. I'd rather let the veil decide my fate than leave it in the hands of some girl—"*

"Stop!"

The crowd gasps as Verene runs into the square, her curls billowing. That didn't take long. Verene is nothing if not charmingly impatient. Not that I'm charmed.

She stops a few feet away from the prisoner, and my guards tense, recognizing her rose-covered mask.

"Who are you?" I say.

"We are the Garden of Resistance," she announces. "And we're not going to let you take any more prisoners today. You've arrested these people for disliking you? Well, no one dislikes you and your reign of terror more than me. So what do you say to that?"

A dozen of her followers from this city—she's built this exasperating movement everywhere we go—are rustling on the sidelines, ready to be called into action. I hope Verene picked her least favorites, because they're all about to die. The chance to make such a crushing blow to her rebellion is too good to pass up. And of course, since I don't sleep, I've had plenty of time to think of an elaborate way to do it.

"Guards," I say. "Bring out the torches. Let's set the Garden of Resistance on fire and see how well their pretty flowers do against—"

And then I feel it.

It's the lightest touch on my hip. It feels like an invisible finger just reached out and poked me.

I know what it is. I've felt it before. It's what the people of Occhia called the hand of God.

It's what it feels like to get an omen on your skin. It's what it feels like to be marked for death.

But I imagined it. Of course I imagined it. My magic protects me from omens—it protects me from everything but mortal wounds.

"Highest Lady Emanuela?" my guard says, and I realize I've been silent for too long.

Verene is frozen, too, her face confused. She has no idea what to do if I'm not actively trying to ruin her.

I try again. "Bring out the—"

There's a second touch on my hip.

Then a third.

I've never had three omens on my skin before. I've never let it get that far.

But then, a moment later, I have four.

And then they're coming so fast that I can't keep count. The marks are spreading down my thigh. They're curling around to my backside. They're climbing up my stomach and covering my chest.

This isn't real. This is too cruel to be real. This is exactly how every nightmare I had as a child played out, with my omens attacking and snuffing me out like a candle before I fully realized what was happening.

My legs give out of their own accord, and I'm dimly aware of the crowd gasping as I tumble down the steps. But as I get onto my hands and knees, I'm too preoccupied with my own skin to care. My hands are covered in smudgy red marks already.

If the omens cover me entirely, I'll die. That's how it works. I'm going to die in the exact same way everyone else does. And in a few seconds, all these people will be standing here, staring at the crumpled red clothes that used to be me, and the first thought they have will be that maybe I wasn't so extraordinary after all.

I lift my head, and the first person I see—the only person I see—is the older man I was about to sentence to death.

Well, he said he was ready to give his blood for the good of the city.

I throw myself at him. In an instant, I'm on top of him, and my fingers are digging into his eye.

The last time I did the ritual, it was on my own papá. Back then, it was an experiment born out of desperation. I'd been taunted by the omens on my skin for long enough, and I'd discovered the secret to making them vanish—a secret the rulers had kept for a thousand years—but I still wasn't entirely sure it would work. And I wasn't entirely sure I could jab my fingers into someone else's eye socket and rip their eyeball out. But now, I know exactly what I'm capable of. I already have the man's eye in my hands, and I'm covered in his hot blood. As the omens crawl up my throat and pepper my chin, I throw aside my veils and shove the eye into my mouth. I chew and swallow so fast that I nearly choke, and it's down, already churning in my stomach.

For a moment, all I can do is breathe. I lie half on top of the wailing man, because I don't have the strength to move. I brace my blood-soaked hand on his stomach, and I stare at the red smudges on my skin, and I wait.

All at once, the omens halt. Then they disappear.

Every last one.

I'm still here. I'm still alive.

But I know, without a doubt, that was the closest I've ever been to death. If I had been alone at the top of my cathedral, like I usually am, that would have been the end of me.

Only then do I notice that there's a hand next to mine. Someone else is leaning on this bleeding, writhing man, too.

I lift my head and find myself looking right at Verene's masked face. This is the closest I've been to her in a long time. She's breathing hard, so hard I can feel her breath on my mouth, and her dark brown eyes are filled with a raw terror that looks exactly like the raw terror I just felt.

There's blood dribbling down her chin.

I look back at the man underneath us. He's not just missing one eye. He's missing both. I was so frantic I didn't even notice I had company.

"What happened?" I choke out. "Why did . . . ?"

She starts to answer. But then, at the same time, we both realize how very quiet it is.

When I look up, I expect to see that all the people at the edges of the square have disappeared. I'm certain that every last one of us just got bombarded with omens, and now there's no one left.

But they're all still here.

And they're all staring at us. They're staring at my face, which is uncovered in public for the first time. They're staring at the bloody and mangled man underneath me. And the members of the Garden of Resistance are staring at their beloved leader, who just ripped someone's eye out and ate it in unison with the tyrant they all despise.

My first thought is that we can explain this. We have to explain this. We can't lose control of this city.

I can't lose control. Not again.

One of my guards moves, quick and abrupt, like he's turning to run. He doesn't get very far. A second later, he explodes into a shower of blood.

It was me.

Of course it was me. It's always me.

It's just that sometimes, my magic is so quick that even I can't keep up with it.

I throw my veils over my face, despite the fact that there's no point, as the cathedral square descends into chaos. The people are running for their lives, desperately cramming themselves into the streets as everything devolves into a mess of fear and confusion.

The last time I used my magic in a crowd, it spiraled just like this.

And then Verene's hand is on my wrist, pulling me up, and the touch of her fingers is such a shock that I find myself unable to resist. We run up the steps and into the cathedral. She lets go of me and slams the double doors shut, deadbolting them aggressively, then whirls around. All of a sudden, we're alone in the dark foyer, facing each other and breathing hard.

Verene pushes up her mask. Her face is glistening with sweat. The dramatic black powder around her eyes makes her look particularly furious.

"What...was...that?" she says.

"I—" I don't have the words. My mind is still caught up on the screaming outside.

"That wasn't funny, Emanuela!" she says. "How dare you try and take my magic away. How dare you make me do the ritual in front of all those people—"

"I didn't do anything," I say.

"Of course you did!" she says. "It was some scheme of yours, when all I wanted was to look heroic for a second—"

"I didn't do anything!" I yell. "My magic almost went away, too!"

Verene goes quiet. I can feel her struggling to make out the details of my face through my veils, and I try not to think about that moment in the square when my eyes met hers, totally uncovered. I could have killed her by accident. She's lucky I didn't.

"So you have no idea what happened?" she says.

I'm silent, because I don't want to admit it.

She turns away and walks for a side door.

"Where do you think you're going?" I say.

"To strangle the ruler of this city until she gives us answers, since you're obviously not strangling her hard enough," she says.

All at once, the cold realization sinks into my skin.

I think, maybe, I do know what happened. At the very

least, I know that last night, one of the eight original rulers was still alive. And now, none of them are. But before she died, she said something about how she protects the cities in ways I don't understand.

I could tell Verene about this little mistake of mine.

Or, I could...not.

I decide to go with the second option. I follow Verene up to my quarters and into the attic, where I find her standing over a pile of clothes that used to be a ruler. Verene and I are both well aware of the fact that the immortal women in red are, in fact, rather mortal. But I know why Verene is staring at the red gown like she's willing it to mold back into the shape of a woman. It never gets any easier to accept the fact that someone can vanish in an instant. Even someone with magic.

"Oh, did I forget to mention that I killed all the rulers months ago?" I say. "I was bored of them."

Verene gives me a sideways look, and I hold my breath.

"Very funny, Emanuela," she says.

She turns and climbs back down the ladder.

This is proof that somewhere, deep down, Verene thinks I'm clever. Because a clever person would never let our precious hostages die—maybe a couple of them, just for fun, but certainly not all six. A clever person would never want to end up in a situation where we desperately need answers and have no one to turn to.

I return to my room to find Verene at my desk, pulling out a bottle of wine. She takes a long drink, and when she lowers the bottle, I can see that her hands are shaking.

"Everyone saw me do the ritual," she says, her voice flat.

"They also saw me," I say.

34

"Yes, but they already know you're evil," she says. "Now they know … well, now they know exactly what I'm capable of."

"You shouldn't have been hiding it anyway," I say without thinking. "Where's the fun in that?"

Verene pauses halfway to taking another drink. She gives me a cold look that very much makes me regret my words.

"I wasn't *hiding it*," she says. "I was choosing not to show it to my followers."

"And what, exactly, is the difference between—"

"Do you think I want this to be my whole life?" She gestures around. "Stuck in the cathedral because everyone else is scared of my magic? I was trapped in a cathedral for my entire childhood, in case you forgot. But I don't have to live like that now. I can live among the people, and they love me, because I'm a good—"

"If you say you're a good person, I'm going to puke up the eye I just ate," I say.

Verene throws her empty wine bottle onto the floor. Despite my best efforts, I jump at the noise.

"I am a good person," she says viciously. "We're in an arrangement, Emanuela, but we are not the same. Don't forget that."

"I never said we were," I say coolly. "I would never insult myself like that."

She takes a step closer to me. Then another. Then, she gets so close that I come dangerously close to kissing the ruffles on the front of her shirt, and I'm forced to crane my neck to look her in the face.

It's not like I ever forget how tall she is. But sometimes, especially when she has blood on her chin and murder in her eyes, our aggravating height difference feels slightly weightier.

"So you really don't know what's happening?" she says, deliberately. "You didn't do something that could have caused it? Anything at all?"

If we both tried to use our magic, right now, I wonder which of us would be the fastest.

"No," I say.

"Then we can't stay here," she says. "We have to go to another city. We have to hope that whatever just happened didn't reach the other rulers, and that they're still around to talk."

Her voice has gotten quiet. There's something very unnerving about her voice when it's quiet. It reminds me of the first time she threatened to kill me. That was a year ago. She told me that sometimes, it's good for people to die.

"Fine," I say.

For a moment, Verene says nothing. I hold her gaze through my veils, unblinking. Just as my eyes are starting to water, she pushes past me and marches for the door.

I glance around. I don't have any particular attachment to this room. It looks just like my rooms in the other five cathedrals. I rotate between them so often that I frequently forget which city I'm in. There's very little sign of all the months I've spent here—just a bunch of half-finished cloaks on the sewing table.

I slip over to my desk and open the lid on my tank of pet spiders. If I'm gone for a while, they'll have to fend for themselves. I grab my map of the eight cities and slip it into my pocket, and I follow Verene out the door without another look back.

FIVE

THE WORST PART OF RULING SIX CITIES IS THE CATACOMBS.

When Verene and I first clawed our way out of our prison, we were at the very bottom of the labyrinthine halls. We found our way out through sheer luck—and sheer immortality. It took us so long that it would have killed any ordinary person. We spent another month mapping out easy, relatively straightforward paths between each of our six cathedrals. Now, we never stray from them.

And we spend every walk being ever so slightly paranoid and jumpy.

Verene stops abruptly. "Did you see that?"

I stop, too. We stare at the dusty ground in front of us, but when nothing materializes out of the shadows, we keep walking. We're side by side in the narrow hall, with only our two flickering lanterns for company.

"Happy anniversary, by the way," I say.

"Ugh," Verene says.

"I was just thinking," I say. "Our anniversary means that

it's also been a year since we've actually seen the vide. Do you miss it? Do you think it misses us?"

"You know I don't like talking about the vide," she says.

"Then let's talk about me," I say. "I—"

"We haven't seen the vide because we hold on to these lanterns," she says. "The vide doesn't like iron."

She sounds like she's mostly reassuring herself. Verene was the one who first discovered the vide, a mysterious shadowy being that dwells in the catacombs. In fact, three years ago, it was the one trapped in that cold iron cell, not us. Verene freed it—by accident—and when she discovered that it would accept her blood in exchange for favors, she kept it around.

She used it to bring her city water. But then, her brother used it to send her away. Ever since then, she's been rather bent on avoiding it. It was never her friend—it can be controlled by anyone who knows how, and her brother definitely knows how.

"Do you think it knows we're in its domain, though?" I say. "Do you think it's following us right now?"

"It better not be." Verene raises her voice, glancing around suspiciously.

I've successfully steered her down the slight diversion from our usual path. She hasn't noticed yet, because every hall in the catacombs looks the same, and because all her attention is focused on keeping her feet moving as fast as possible.

A few minutes later, we approach a wooden door. Our normal path would let us out in the bowels of the cathedral, near the underground well. This door, as I can see already, has faint red light peeking through the cracks. The light of evening.

I act like nothing is amiss. I walk slightly slower, letting

Verene go first. She's so eager to get out that she barges through the door. Then she freezes, staring at the alley in confusion.

"Wait," she says. "We must have gone the wrong way—"

"Verene!" A girl passing by in the street spots her instantly. "What are you doing in the catacombs?"

This is going even better than I'd hoped. I knew that if I steered Verene onto the streets of Oga, the neighboring city where everything is still normal, the Garden of Resistance would spot her eventually. But of course, Verene is so famous that she can't take a single step without being noticed.

These friends of hers haven't seen her cut out someone's eye. They still think that she's a living saint. And as soon as Verene realizes it, she'll scramble to keep it that way. She'll leap out of the catacombs, so they won't find her with me, and then she'll have to struggle through all her adoring followers to get over to the cathedral.

And I'll already be gone. Because I know there are no answers to be found in this cathedral. I'll let Verene chase after rulers who are no longer alive. I'm going to solve this the way I solve everything—alone.

The girl who called out to Verene is coming into the alley. There's a whole group of the Garden of Resistance behind her, and I see Verene tense. Any second now, they're going to spot me lurking in the shadows.

I start to back away, but then, Verene does the last thing I expected. She reaches back and grabs my arm, thrusting me forward into the alley.

The others gasp, scattering back.

"Don't worry!" Verene grabs my veils and rips them off. "She's with us. She's a decoy."

"A decoy?" one of the girls says. "For what?"

"For our biggest mission yet," Verene says vaguely. "Anyway, what are we doing tonight?"

"Oh, we have a demonstration in the works," the girl says. "Come on!"

And then they're surrounding us. They start to usher us away, chattering excitedly, but I'm still frozen, trying to process the fact that my face is uncovered, just like that.

"That was a brilliant save on my part, wasn't it?" Verene says into my ear. "Take off your sinister outfit. You need to blend in."

She starts to pull my cloak off me. I grab it back automatically.

I can't take off my cloak. My cloak is what separates me from the ordinary people. I can't just stand here and pretend to be one of them. This isn't where I belong.

Verene reaches over and starts to undo the knots herself. Her fingers brush my collarbone, and I jerk away, overwhelmed.

"Get off me," I say loudly.

The followers surrounding us all stop. They stare at me.

They've never seen the face of Highest Lady Emanuela. But they've definitely heard her voice at the trials.

"Isn't she convincing?" Verene says cheerily.

But the look she gives me is full of death.

Fine. I'll play along. But only because I know that if I get rid of these people in front of Verene, then it's going to be a whole thing. Once she and her best friends start throwing darts at a sign with my name on it, I'll be able to sneak away much more easily.

I smile. "I've been practicing my impression of our all-powerful ruler."

"Well, it's very good," a nearby boy says. "You've even captured her strange accent."

"Oh?" I say. "You think Highest Lady Emanuela's accent is strange? How many languages do you speak?"

Verene puts her arm around my shoulders. It's such an alarming gesture, coming from her, that I find myself going stiff. She smells, as always, like the most delicately sweet flower.

"Take us to the demonstration," she demands.

Her followers lead us out onto the street. I yank free of Verene to hastily recover my veils from the ground. I pull off my cloak and bundle it all under my arm. I'm left in my simple—but flatteringly low-cut—black blouse. I'm also wearing tight black pants that may or may not have been inspired by Verene's attire. I feel completely naked, though. I'm very glad that I'm in the middle of a huddle, so that I can observe the city in little peeks and glances.

The eight cities used to be very orderly places. People went about their lives in predictable patterns—worship at midday, tea and coffee in the afternoon, and dinner parties with the same group of nobles at night. Everybody did what they were supposed to do. They did whatever work their family told them to do, and married whomever their family told them to marry, and when they got their first omen, they went straight to their ruler's tower without a word of protest.

The city looks a lot more interesting now. There are some manors that are shut tight and boarded up, like they're keeping out intruders. There are some with the doors wide open, overcrowded with servants and nobles who all seem to be mingling. We pass by a food delivery cart that's being swamped by eager children. Then we cross through an art market where a fight has broken out over a piece of pottery.

My guards are somewhere among it all, listening for anyone who's disrespecting me. But as long as people follow my laws, they can do anything else they want. Servants don't have to work their dull jobs. Nobles don't have to marry the dull boy their parents picked. I told people that they could do anything, and it seems they've listened. And they have me to thank.

Then we turn another corner, and we find the real party.

The Garden of Resistance has set up a bonfire in the middle of the street. They've strung up garlands of black roses between the roofs of the nearby manors, and there's a whole crowd of Verene's followers, drinking and bouncing around to the song of a nearby violinist.

"Well?" Verene says under her breath. "What do you think, now that you've seen it for yourself? A bit more pleasant than your operation, isn't it?"

"Ugh," I say. "Do they ever leave you alone?"

"No," she says proudly.

"Who needs a family when you have a hundred drunk sycophants following you around the streets, I suppose?" I say.

I know, instantly, that it was a mistake to bring up her family—or current lack thereof. When I dare to glance over at Verene, I see that she's gone stiff, the elegant line of her jaw turned tense.

I was trying to needle her, of course. She'll be suspicious if I suddenly become a pleasant companion. But I probably shouldn't have chosen this moment to poke at that particular bruise. There's just something about being around Verene that makes my worst impulses hard to resist.

"The Garden of Resistance *is* my family," she says, her voice tight. "And they treat me better than my family ever did. Not that I expect you to understand."

I swallow hard. "And I'm so happy for—"

"Verene is back!" someone nearby yells.

A dozen heads whip in our direction, and all at once, we're swarmed. I'm caught in the crush of people as they all scramble to get their hands on their beloved leader. I'm propelled closer to the bonfire, squirming angrily against the crowd. Somehow, my veil and cloak slip out of my hands, and I scramble to grab them back, but they've disappeared in the tangle of legs.

"Bring her to the front!" someone says, and then Verene is ripped away from my side. A moment later, she emerges above the heads of the crowd, standing on a stool. They've decorated her with a cloak made of roses, and somebody with quick hands has dabbed on black lip salve that looks frustratingly good. A boy is dutifully polishing the catacomb dust off her boots.

The noise of the party dies down, and all eyes turn to their leader. I'm not going to pretend I don't understand the appeal. Standing silhouetted against the roaring flames, tall and beautiful and proud, Verene certainly looks like the answer to everyone's problems. She lifts her chin and instantly launches into a speech, like she's been prepared for this all along.

"We're here to take a stand against Highest Lady Emanuela," she says. "Because she's evil, and she's ruining our great city."

The people clap like that was the most profound thing they've ever heard.

"We want to make a new way to live," Verene says. "A better

way. We don't want to be trapped under her hateful thumb for any longer."

This is the part where I should have been able to take advantage of Verene's distraction and slip away. Unfortunately, she seems determined to deliver this entire speech directly to me, because she hasn't taken her eyes off my face.

"She has so much power over us all," Verene says. "And all she does with it is cause pain and suffering."

And she still hasn't taken her eyes off my face. I smile, to make sure she knows that I graciously accept all these compliments she's paying me.

"But you know what?" Verene says. "In a way, I feel sorry for her. I really do. It's important to have compassion for everyone—even Highest Lady Emanuela. I feel sorry for her because I know that she has no one in her life who cares for her. Imagine sleeping alone at the top of the cathedral every night. No wonder she's the way she is."

I feel my smile falter, just a bit, but I fix it firmly back on. Verene should know by now that it takes a lot more than this to get under my skin. And she should know that I sleep alone at the top of the cathedral because I'm the only one who deserves to be above it all.

"I would never want to be like her," Verene says. "I would never want to be so vile and soulless and—"

Abruptly, a girl in the crowd reaches out and takes Verene's hand, which seems rather presumptuous, even for a sycophant.

"You're nothing like her, Verene," she says. "You're perfect."

The others murmur their agreement. It's nauseating.

"Oh, I don't know about that..." Verene says modestly.

The strange girl climbs up onto the stool with Verene. Which seems extremely presumptuous.

"You've given up everything for us," she says. "For the city. And we love you. We'll follow you anywhere. Anything you ask of us, we'll do."

She slithers her hands under Verene's cloak, grabbing her around the waist.

This is my chance to escape. But instead, I'm just standing here, staring at Verene and this strange girl who's suddenly climbing all over her. Verene doesn't look surprised by what's happening, but she seems to be holding herself oddly, unnaturally still, like a doll. But as soon as I have that thought, Verene smiles her most benevolent smile. She reaches over and toys affectionately with a token around the girl's neck—a token of a black rose, I realize.

"I love you, too," she says. "I love all of you!"

The Garden of Resistance members scream. They all pull black rose petals out of nowhere and throw them into the air.

And then Verenc and the strange girl are kissing. The delighted Garden of Resistance produce even more rose petals, tossing them onto the two girls and into the bonfire behind them. It occurs to me, then, that this girl is some sort of paramour of Verene's. And everyone already knew this. Everyone except me.

Well, I don't care. And I'm not surprised. Verene is undoubtedly the most stunning girl in this city, and everyone loves her and thinks she's flawless, just as she intended. I bet they all throw themselves at her. I bet it's hard to choose from all the potential suitors. I bet she has a different girl in every city, and when she gets home from her meetings with me, they're waiting at her bedside to fawn all over her.

I blink.

And the girl Verene is kissing explodes in her face.

Verene topples off the stool, unbalanced by the sudden loss. She lands in the puddle of blood.

I'm already slipping away through the crowd, my heart pounding in my ears. I scared myself with how quickly I just did that.

But I don't regret it. There's one rule in this city. People have to respect me. And I felt disrespected by that girl.

I skirt through the darkening streets, looking for an entrance to the catacombs. I came here to get rid of Verene, so now I have. There's no way she's escaping that little mess easily.

At least, that's what I think, until I turn a corner and find her standing in front of me.

I stop short. Verene is absolutely covered in blood. If there were people on this street before, they've cleared out at the sight of her.

Verene says nothing. She just looks at me. A drop of blood slowly forms at the top of her nose, then falls.

"Yes?" I say, like she's appeared in my parlor for a nice cup of coffee.

She remains silent. I just wait, knowing that I'm about to get reamed out, and that the only thing I can do is embrace it.

"Let's go," she says.

"Go where?" I say.

She looks at me like I'm being purposefully dense. "To the cathedral. To talk to the ruler."

I hesitate. I want her to address the fact that I just exploded her paramour in her face. I want to know exactly how much that girl meant to her and exactly how upset she is about her death. But I can't ask. I have no reason to ask. I don't care about things like that. Especially not when it comes to Verene.

"Let's go," I agree carefully. "But this time, I'm leading the way, since you seem to have forgotten how to navigate the catacombs."

Without another word, she walks off. So I resign myself to finding another way to get her off my tail, and I follow her.

We retrace our steps to the catacomb entrance we used before. At one point, Verene stops without explanation, picks up her foot, and stares intently at the bottom of her black boot. When she puts it down, I realize she's turned the blood on it to water. That will make it harder for the Garden of Resistance to follow her footprints in the dark—and occasionally, I can hear them on the distant streets, yelling her name. I try to look like this is something I, too, would have thought of, because I, too, use my magic for such things all the time.

Soon enough, we find ourselves underneath Oga's cathedral, emerging into the underground well. It's a small, dark room, mostly taken up by a large hole in the ground. Above it is a glass tank. The old ruler used to fill that with blood, collected slowly from her tower. I had the system in all my cities modified so that, once Verene transforms the blood in my glass domes into water, she can drain it into the tank, ready to be used. Since I haven't taken any prisoners recently in Oga, the tank is empty, but the well itself should still be half-full. I always leave my people generously supplied.

I walk past the well, headed for the steps that lead up to the cathedral. But when I glance back, I realize that Verene isn't following me. She's standing at the edge of the well, staring into it. She looks lost in thought.

I clear my throat. "Are you coming, or are you going to—"

"My maman didn't tell me any special secrets about her magic," Verene says. "I wasn't the favorite. But I still grew up with her. I know things about how she lived. Things that ordinary people wouldn't know."

There's a reason I don't talk about Verene's family unless I'm trying to needle her. It's because Verene doesn't talk about them, either.

"And?" I say delicately.

"She never left the city center," she says. "When we were children, we would go and visit Papa's family." She pauses. "I mean, I'm not really surprised she didn't go with us, because they were a bit scared of her. But..."

Verene has barely said a single word to me about her papa. The only thing I know about him is that he died when she was twelve, and in the aftermath, she went on a rampage of rebellious acts that lasted for years. I found that out by snooping in her maman's diary. At the time, the snooping felt both justified and entertaining. Now, it occurs to me that Verene still doesn't know that I know she once lit her bedroom on fire in a fit of rage and grief, and I feel strangely... uncomfortable about it.

"I remember Maman telling us we wouldn't always be able to travel like that," Verene continues. "She said that when we had our magic, our family would have to come visit us in the cathedral."

"So...?" I say.

"What do you think that was about?" she says. "Did the other rulers tell you anything similar? When you were interrogating them for an entire year? I noticed that you haven't said anything about what you learned during all those interrogations."

I hear the cold, flat tone in her voice, and know instantly that I'm in danger. I've been in enough fights with Verene to tell when things are about to go sideways.

"Well—" I say.

But she's already seized my body with her magic. It seeps into every one of my veins like cold fingers, holding me at her mercy.

She shouldn't be using her magic on me. Because she knows, of course, that I can retaliate with equal skill. But she doesn't seem worried about that right now. She lifts me up into the air, and my lantern falls out of my hands, hitting the dirt with a dull thud.

Verene drags me forward until I'm hovering over the well. And then she drops me.

Six

WATER.

The moment I hit the well, all I feel is water. It's cold and unforgiving, pulling me down and pouring into my throat, into my chest, overwhelming everything.

And then, abruptly, it stops. I feel myself being pulled free, and then I'm up, hovering in front of Verene again and dripping wet.

"You're acting suspicious," she says. "There's something you're not telling me about the rulers. What is it?"

I don't speak. I can't speak. She's taken hold of every vein in my body. I see her realize it, too. Tentatively, the feeling creeps back into my throat and the lower half of my face.

She's so good at controlling her magic. She has so much finesse. It's like she's been practicing for a thousand years.

"What are you suggesting?" I gasp out. "That I would lie to you, my dearest accomplice—"

She drops me in again. I thrash helplessly, trying to find any sort of groove in the wall that I can hold on to, but there's nothing. My chest burns with the pain.

Verene pulls me out again.

"Emanuela," she says. "I think you know what's going on here."

I don't speak, because she hasn't given me the ability to speak. I just stare at her in what I hope is a defiant way, although I can't feel my face, so I can't be sure.

"You have the same magic I do, right?" Verene says. "So why don't you save yourself? Why don't you control the water?"

She drops me again.

And I try. I do. But when I look at the water around me, it just explodes into the air, and the water below me rushes up to take its place.

It's not enough. It will never be enough.

Once more, Verene pulls me out.

"You really did kill all the rulers," she says in disbelief. "Didn't you? You've been pretending that you know how to use your powers, but you don't. All this time, you've been alone with me, and you never told me. You've been..." Her eyes dart over my body. "Looking at me, constantly. You could have killed me at any second. And now, the rulers are all dead, and something bad is happening with our magic, and we have no idea how to fix it. And it's your fault. Isn't it?"

She loosens her grip on my mouth and allows me to speak.

"Really, it was the rulers' fault for being so uncooperative," I say.

Her eyes burn. "We've already lost one city, Emanuela. What are we going to do if it happens again, and again, and we lose all the others?"

"We don't need the rulers, or any leftover bit of their magic," I say. "We can find another way."

"But what if it turns out there is no other way?" Verene says, a tremble in her voice.

As soon as she says the words, something inside me snaps.

"There is," I say. "Because I can't live like this forever."

For a long moment, Verene is silent. She blinks, and I feel myself fall for a second, but then she catches me again.

"What do you mean?" she says, and there's a hint of uncertainty in her voice. "You like ruling the six cities. You...you wanted to be the most powerful, and you are—"

"I wanted to be different," I say. "And I'm not. Not really. I take blood and turn it into water. I live alone at the top of the city, and I don't have anything. Or anybody. Do you know what the rulers told me, when they were alive? Every single one of them kept telling me that there's no other way, and they seemed so sure about it. But if that's true, then I don't know what to do. Because I don't want to go back to the way things were yesterday—even if it's the only option. I want..."

I trail off, suddenly terrified. I'm never this straightforward with her. This isn't how we talk to each other—like two people who are truly in on our schemes together.

"You want more," Verene says.

"Yes," I say, breathless.

She says nothing. She does nothing.

"There must be more," she says finally.

"There must be," I agree.

"But we'll never know what it is," she says. "Because you killed the only people who could have told us. What are we supposed to do now? Pretend like things are normal, knowing that at any second, we might have to do the ritual again, and we might ruin our reputations in another city? We only have five left. And you know how easily they can fall."

No. I refuse to believe I've broken the cities this badly. I refuse to believe that it all depended on the magic of eight women in red gowns. They were ordinary, once, before they did the ritual. They can't possibly be so much more special than me.

I can still change things. The rulers said their magic protects the cities—which means mine can, too, and it can do it even better than they did. My magic just must not be strong enough yet. But I'll make it strong enough. I'll find a way.

"I still have plenty of ideas," I say. "And I know which one to try first."

Verene gives me a wary look. "What is it?"

"It's interesting, isn't it?" I say. "That we get power from eating the eyes of a normal person? Something about their eyes is enough to make us magical." I pause significantly. "What do you think would happen if we ate the eyes of someone who already had power?"

A slow, cold horror creeps across Verene's face. But a moment later, her features become set with determination.

"The last thing you need is to become twice as powerful," she says. "I'm the only one who could handle it."

"We'll see about that," I say.

She yanks me over to her and sets my feet on the ground at the edge of the well. Abruptly, her magic lets me go, and I crumple over as all the weight returns to my bones. I hit the floor on my hands and knees, dripping puddles onto the cold ground. I try not to be too obvious about the fact that I'm desperately relieved as I suck in air.

"You don't really think this is a fight you can win, do you?" Verene says. "You can't use your magic on me. Not if you want my eyes intact. But I can use mine on you all day long."

I hear the tiniest thrill in her voice. She's excited. Of course she is. Out in the cities, Verene pretends not to have magic. She never gets to play with it.

And I'm excited, too. I'm excited to finally dispose of her and rule on my own. I knew there was a reason I was keeping her around, and I've found it.

I reach into my boot and whip out a throwing knife. An instant later, I'm on my feet, and it's landed in Verene's shoulder.

When she yelps in pain, I feel it in my stomach. My first instinct is that I don't like the sound at all. My second instinct is to remind myself that Verene almost just killed me by tossing me in the water—the way I once did to her in Iris, poetically. We've never fought with any mercy before. There's no reason to start now. In fact, I would say there's less reason to start now than there ever has been.

I'm already sprinting for the steps up to the cathedral. That knife was my only weapon, and I need to get to better ground. I emerge into a back hall, Verene's footsteps right behind. Outside, the veil has darkened to black, and there's barely any light.

That's perfect for me. I fumble along the wall until I find an alcove. Hung up on the wall is a heavy silver platter, probably lovingly etched with Oga's favorite saints. I rip it free. By the time I turn around, Verene is in front of me. I can feel her presence more than I can see it. I swing the platter just as she dives at me, and we end up on the floor of the alcove, scrambling desperately at each other. She's getting blood all over me, hot and sticky. Somehow, she manages to get me pinned underneath her.

"Thanks for giving me a knife," she says.

I throw up my arm to protect my eyes, instinctively, and Verene jabs the knife right into it. I gasp at the searing pain, and she tries to stab me again, but I manage to hit the knife out of her hands. It disappears somewhere into the darkness. Verene's weight rolls off me, and I hear her footsteps moving away.

I crawl out of the alcove and stand up just as she finds a lantern on the wall and turns it on. For a moment, all I see is her, covered in blood and staring at me with cold, deadly eyes.

I turn and run wildly, disappearing back into the shadows. Verene follows me, turning the lanterns on as she goes. I've lost track of where I am. I shove my way through a random door, and the inner chamber opens up in front of me, huge and cavernous in the dark. My footsteps echo loudly as I race for the other side.

Behind me, Verene turns on a lantern by the door. And then I feel myself... stop. I'm frozen in place, my blood totally under her control. She walks closer, her steps light. She moves around to stand in front of me, never taking her eyes off my face.

"Come on, Emanuela," she says. "Can't you think of any way to fight back? Or am I just too powerful?"

There's a hungry gleam in her eyes now. This is our first proper fight in a long time. No one gives her a fight like I do.

But... I've never tried to fight her when she has magic. And I don't have a way out of it. Not in this moment. I'm stuck here, staring at her, unblinking.

I see Verene realize it, too. And all I can do is wait for the next attack.

But then she backs up. She lets me go.

I don't question it. I run at her, tackling her viciously to the floor. We wrestle with everything we have, and I get her on her back, my arm across her throat. It's the perfect position to strike at her eyes. If I'm fast enough, she won't be able to stop me.

But when she meets my gaze, I feel myself hesitating.

Verene's magic seizes me. She throws me backward, and I go flying. I hit the huge glass dome in the middle of the room and crumple to the floor, landing painfully on my ankle.

Verene is already on her feet, stalking toward me. I stand up and fumble along the wall of the tank until I find myself backed up against the door my guards use to deposit the prisoners.

"What would you like me to tell the Garden of Resistance, after you're dead?" I say. "Oh wait—I'm not going to tell them anything. I'm just going to execute them all, and then there will be no one to call you a martyr. Wasn't that your biggest fear in Iris, when I almost killed you? That you would die alone, without a huge audience to know how noble your death was?"

She charges at me, just as I knew she would. That's a bit of a sensitive subject. I roll away, opening the door as I go. Verene stumbles, losing her balance, and I lunge back and kick her into the glass tank. I slam it shut after her, sliding the dead bolt across.

She whirls around, pressing her hands against it desperately. She leaves bloody prints behind.

"How are you going to take my eyes if you lock me in here?" she says, muffled and furious.

"Oh, I have my ways," I say. "There's not a single hole in this tank, and you'll never pry up the drain cover without using the outside mechanism. You'll run out of air eventually. But don't worry—you won't die right away. You'll pass out first, and then I'll be there."

She goes still. Her eyes meet mine, wide and fearful. But an instant later, she wipes the fear away, replaced with something dark and empty.

"So," she says flatly. "This is how it is."

"This is how it's always been," I say. "What else did you expect?"

For a moment, the two of us just look at each other.

There was nothing to expect. There's nothing between us. We're enemies, and we knew our arrangement would only last for so long. We knew that, one way or another, it was always going to come to this.

I don't know what I'm waiting for her to say. But I feel like I'm waiting for something.

"You'd better hope I never get out of here," she says, so quietly that it sends a chill down my spine.

Those weren't the words I wanted. But they're the only ones that make sense. I know that.

I back away, and I retreat into the shadows, leaving her behind.

SEVEN

I GO STRAIGHT UP TO MY QUARTERS, WHERE I PUT ON A
fresh cloak and veils. Then, I return to the ground floor of the
cathedral. It's an annoying detour, especially because I'm still
hobbling on my injured ankle, but I have no choice. I need to
speak to my guards, and I won't do it with my face uncovered.

At the back entrance of the cathedral, I find the two guards
at their station. They're sitting on the floor, playing a card game
that appears to involve wagering little pamphlets that are almost
certainly lewd. When they see me, they quickly leap to their feet.

"Highest Lady Emanuela!" one guard stammers, trying to
hide the pile of wagers. "You're back. We don't normally expect
you to make an appearance in the evening—"

"You." I point at him. "Patrol around the inner chamber
and shout if you see anyone trying to escape. And you." I point
at the other. "Come with me."

My guard dutifully follows me back through the cathedral
and up to my quarters.

"Stand outside," I say.

"Yes, Highest Lady Emanuela," he says, looking nervous. I never bring guards near my quarters.

I open the door a crack and slip inside. I don't want him getting a peek.

This room in Oga looks exactly like all my other rooms in the other five cities. I cross over to my desk, peering out the window for a moment as I light the lantern. The city seems small and quiet from here, all the noise a distant muffle. The people haven't all gone to sleep yet—lanterns are still burning, from the closest streets to the greenhouses at the very edge. I don't spot the massive bonfire of the Garden of Resistance, though. The mood was probably ruined when I exploded one of their own in front of them.

I think about all the members of the Garden of Resistance who saw my face. They might have figured out I wasn't a decoy after all. I'll have to do something about that, but the thought exhausts me. My arm is bleeding from Verene's quick work with that knife, so I wrap it in a bit of spare fabric from my sewing table and sit down at my desk.

And I keep counting the minutes. I know approximately how long it will take for Verene to run out of air in the glass dome. I've gotten very effective at timing my trials so the prisoners are still alive when I need them to be.

My eyes go to the drawer where Verene keeps her wine and hair ties. I quickly tear my gaze away.

I don't feel bad about this. I don't. Verene would do the same to me if she got the chance. And I won't miss her. I'll find another beautiful girl to tangle with, and it will be even better than the way I tangled with her.

As soon as I have the thought, I know it's a lie. I've seen all eight cities. No one in them compares to her.

But I can't just let her out. For one thing, she'll attack me and gouge my eyes out of my head. But, more importantly, then I'll have to explain why I'm doing it. And she'll know, somehow. She'll know what I think about when I'm alone, lying on my love seat and unable to sleep. She'll know that I think about the cute little face she makes when she's about to sneeze, and the soft way her body curves when she leans over my desk to look at my maps. She'll know that I think about how perfectly we fight—a give and take that's so natural it's like we can read each other's minds—and wonder what else we could do to each other.

She can't know any of that. Because it's mortifying. I'm not some ordinary girl who can just fancy another girl. I get fluttery inside when I think about being powerful and leaving my mark on everything I touch, not when I think about the way she plays with her hair.

She has to die. I'll take the power from her eyes. And if that doesn't help the cities, I'll find something else that will. I'm not going to stop. I'm never going to stop—

Someone pokes my arm, pointedly. I jump. I can't believe the guard had the nerve to follow me in here. But when I turn to look, I find no one.

There's another poke. And another. I feel the invisible touches creep down my arm, and when I lift it, I find a red smudge on the back of my hand. The omens spread out to cover my fingers, as quickly as if I've dipped my hand in paint.

It's happening again.

I was really, really hoping it wouldn't. But I'm not unprepared.

I leap up and run for the door. When I open it, my guard leaps to attention. "Highest Lady Emanuela—"

He's halfway through bowing when I grab the front of his coat and throw him into my room. I tackle him to the floor, and he's so surprised all he can do is let out a little whimper.

One very bloody minute later, I'm shoving his eye into my mouth. I pull away from him, sitting on the floor. I swallow the last of it down and stare at my red-smudged hand, waiting for the omens to stop. There's always a breath where it feels like they won't. But they always do.

So I wait.

And I wait.

And the omens just keep crawling up my arm. They spread across my chest to my other shoulder.

"Hmm," I say.

I'm not going to panic. I merely attack the injured guard and help myself to his other eye. That, surely, will be enough. I sit back.

And I wait again.

And the omens keep coming. They crawl down my other hand at a silent, steady pace. They don't seem to care one whit about the fact that I'm now vibrating with my need for them to stop.

"No," I hear myself saying. "No!"

And then I'm running. I tear out of my quarters and down the spiral stairs.

I wish I hadn't gone all the way up to the top of the spire. I wish this wasn't such a long run, and that my ankle wasn't injured and failing me. By the time I unlock the front doors of the inner chamber and burst inside, I can feel the omens all over my stomach.

Verene is on her feet, scrabbling at the walls of the tank.

Even in the dim light of the single lantern we turned on, I can see the omens on her face.

"Emanuela?" she yells. "Emanuela?"

She can barely make out my form in the shadowy doorway.

"It's not working," I hear myself say.

"What?" she says.

"The ritual." I raise my voice. "It's not working."

Verene goes still.

My omens crawl up to my neck.

"Why not?" she says.

I don't know. I can't know. Because the rulers are gone, and the rulers protected us in ways I don't understand.

"Because something is wrong," I say.

The moment the words leave my mouth, there's a loud boom.

It shakes the whole cathedral, and I topple over and hit the tile floor. The building keeps shaking, relentlessly, like nothing I've ever felt.

It's falling apart around us. I'm certain that's what must be happening. This cathedral has stood for a thousand years, but now, all of a sudden, it's decided to collapse. And it's my fault. Somehow, it's my fault.

"Emanuela!" Verene is still trapped in the dome, struggling to get to her feet. "What's happening? What did you do?"

I don't know.

I don't know what I did.

I didn't mean to.

Behind me, I hear the front doors of the cathedral crack open. I turn around to see the second guard. He's escaping, trying to run for his life.

I chase after him. Maybe I just need more eyes than I

normally do. Maybe that will stop this. I follow him out the doors and onto the front steps, trying desperately to snatch at his red coat.

And then I hear the screaming.

I don't know where, exactly, it's coming from. It seems to be coming from everywhere. It sounds like the whole city is screaming. The manors are shaking, too, I realize as I look down onto the streets. People are stumbling out of doors and climbing out of windows, seeking refuge and finding none. Once they get to their feet, they grab one another and start running, frantically.

It takes me a moment to notice that there's a pattern to the running. Every single person is moving toward the cathedral. It's like they think I'm going to protect them. What they don't know is that I'm covered in omens and terrified, because maybe I could eat all their eyes, and it still won't be enough to save myself.

Then my gaze travels farther out toward the edge of the city, and I realize that the people aren't running toward me. They're running away from something.

The buildings at the edge of the city are…gone. They've disappeared into the black of the veil, their lanterns snuffed out. I stare and stare, and I still can't figure out why the greenhouses have suddenly vanished.

But the darkness is only growing. And growing. I watch manor after manor melt away, in neat rows, like they're being painted over with thick black paint.

The ground shakes harder. The roaring around us grows louder. And the people keep running for the cathedral, screaming and crying in terror.

All at once, I realize what I'm looking at.

I turn around and hobble back into the inner chamber. My injured ankle is getting worse, but that's the least of my concerns.

"What is it?" Verene is screaming the moment I draw close enough to hear her. "What's happening to the cathedral?"

"It's not the cathedral," I say. "It's the veil."

"What do you mean?" she says.

My next words don't sound real, even to my own ears. "The veil is coming down on the city."

Verene goes very, very still. Her face turns gray.

"We have to…" she says. "We have to run. Emanuela, we have to run. We can get everybody into the catacombs and—let me out of here!"

She pounds on the glass, but I barely even register the noise. There are omens crawling down both of my legs, but I almost don't feel them anymore. I don't feel much of anything. Just a sudden sense of calm.

This isn't going to happen. Because I'm here. I'm not going to let the veil destroy the city. I'm not going to let us all die.

I walk toward the glass tank. Verene sees me coming, and she stops pounding on the glass, her eyes uncertain. She can't tell if I'm coming to take her eyes, or escape with her, or both. I don't even know. All I know is that I'm going to do something, and it's going to work.

Then I fall over. I try to get back to my feet, and I can't. My ankle has given out.

"Verene," I rasp. "Pull me. With your magic."

She doesn't even hesitate. I feel the cold fingers of her power creep into my veins, and I don't try to struggle against it. We can do this together. We can do anything together.

Then, the cathedral rumbles so violently that I find myself rolling across the floor. I hear the loud, horrible sound of shattering glass, and when I look up, the tank has collapsed into huge, treacherously sharp pieces.

Verene is somewhere underneath them. But I can't see her.

"Verene—" Her name comes out of my mouth in a single, frantic breath.

There's no movement from underneath the remains of the tank.

The screaming behind me gets louder. People are pouring into the cathedral, scattering into the back halls in search of places to hide. Behind them, the city is so dark I can't even see it anymore. All I see is the veil.

My omens are down to my ankles.

I didn't mean to do this.

I can't die. I don't want to die.

Not like this. Not at all.

With a furious roar, the veil bursts into the cathedral.

It happens whether I want it to or not. And I'm alone.

EIGHT

EVERYTHING IS WARM.

I'm huddled on my side, wrapped in blankets, drifting awake from a very good sleep. And for a moment, I swear that there's someone sitting beside me. I feel his presence, unassuming and soft around the edges and utterly reassuring. Everything feels fine. In fact, it feels perfect—exactly the way it was meant to be.

But when I open my eyes, I'm baffled by what I see. I'm lying on a black-and-white tile floor. It's dusty and bright, and there's a strange red hazy quality to the air that I've never seen before. It smells like blood. No—I'm the one who smells like blood.

That simple fact brings it all back.

I sit bolt upright. I'm still in Oga's cathedral chambers, and it's an absolute wreck. Little bits of the dark columns and the high ceiling are lying crumbled all around me. I'm not wrapped in blankets, like I thought—I'm still wearing my red cloak and veils, and they're stained with blood.

I look down at my hands. All of my omens are gone.

Bewildered, I look around again, and I find the remains of the shattered glass dome in the middle of the room.

I leap to my feet. "Verene—"

I run over just as a large piece of glass shifts, and Verene emerges, getting shakily to her feet. Her black clothes are still stained with blood, like mine, and they look a bit sliced up. There are little shards of glittering glass caught in her curly hair. But she's very much alive, and as far as I can tell, she's not even injured.

The moment our eyes meet, I stop short.

I shouldn't be happy that she's alive. In fact, I should be very annoyed.

"You said the veil was coming down," she says accusingly.

"It was," I say, my voice faint.

"So it stopped?" she says.

"Apparently," I say.

"Is this a trick?" she says.

"Me, trick you?" I say. "The very concept is unthinkable."

Verene blinks, slowly, her eyes still on the dirty floor. Then, without warning, her head snaps to me. The rage on her face is so sudden that even I'm taken aback. Before I can get a word out, Verene leaps out of the glass ruins and tackles me to the floor.

"What did you do?" she demands.

"Why does it always have to be something I did?" I say, squirming. I'm being bombarded with her sweet-smelling, glass-covered hair. "You were the one who tossed me into a well and—"

"What did you do to my magic?" she says.

I stop. "It's gone?"

"Yes, it's gone," she says. "And give me one reason why I shouldn't get it back, right now, before you do whatever it is you're planning."

I blink up at her, cautiously.

Nothing happens.

Verene claws at my face, and I yelp, fighting against her. "Verene! Mine is gone, too!"

By the time she comprehends my words, the two of us are tangled awkwardly on the floor, both her arms looped around my neck. Her grip loosens, and I slither free.

"Prove it," she says.

I hold out my hands. "Here I am, not exploding you."

She narrows her eyes, apparently unconvinced by my innocent face.

From the front of the cathedral, there's the faint sound of voices. We both jump and turn to see a cluster of people—the ones who took shelter in here. They're cautiously pushing open the cathedral doors, which have fallen shut.

I know what I expect to see outside—nothing. Oga disappeared in front of my eyes, swallowed into the veil. But from here, I can see the square and the first couple streets of manors, and they all look mostly untouched. They're sitting quietly in the hazy red light. The people lying scattered all around are coming to, starting to lift their heads.

It doesn't make sense. No one should have survived what happened to us.

There was a moment there, right at the end, when I was absolutely certain that I didn't survive. I felt it in every inch of my body. It felt like... I don't even want to think about it. I won't think about it.

Apprehensively, Verene and I get to our feet. We wait for the last of the people to filter out of the doors, and then we approach cautiously.

From a distance, I thought the city looked normal. And it does.

But it also very, very much does not. There's one thing that has changed, and it's a thing so big that the moment I step into the cathedral doorway, it's the only thing my eyes can see.

Something has appeared beyond the edge of Oga. There are still the greenhouses, arranged in a neat ring, marking the whole outer boundary of the city. Beyond the greenhouses, there used to be nothing but the veil.

Now, there are towers. Lots and lots of towers.

They're bright red, stretching up into the air, so high that I can't see where they end—which seems impossible. There are hundreds of them, clustered together like so many unfathomably huge needles.

They make the cathedral Verene and I are standing in look tiny. They make all of Oga look like a city for dolls.

Everyone on the streets is very still, staring at the towers, too. When my gaze sweeps to one side, I find even more to stare at—a black cathedral with dozens of spires, much like ours. At first, I think this has also suddenly sprouted into existence. Then I realize that it's the cathedral of Glaz, the neighboring city.

Slowly, slowly, I take the whole thing in. The eight cities have always sat right next to each other, forming a circle. But we've never been able to see one another. The veil was always in the way.

Somehow, the veil seems to have lifted. It's all here. It's all exposed. And right at the center of us—where I thought there was nothing—there are these strange red towers. Like an unseen ninth city that has suddenly decided to make itself known.

Very calmly—if I do say so myself—I back up into the shadowy foyer of the cathedral.

"So," I say. "Let's review what just happened. The rulers all died—"

"You killed them, you mean," Verene says.

"And then we started getting attacked by omens, even though our magic was supposed to protect us from that," I say.

"And then you locked me in a glass tank to suffocate," Verene says.

"And then, we got attacked by omens again, and not even the ritual could save us," I say. "And then, the whole veil attacked the city—all of the cities, apparently. And now everything is red and hazy and...?"

"You left out the part where you killed Gisele," she says.

"Who's Gisele?" I say.

"She *was* my paramour," she says.

"Oh dear, you're right," I say. "Let's stop everything and hold a three-day funeral for dear Gisele."

Verene glares at me. "I'm not saying she was the love of my life, all right? I'm just saying that you should feel bad that she's dead."

This admission feels like an enormous victory. I try not to look too pleased.

"Here's my question," I say. "Why would there be a hidden ninth city? And why can we suddenly see it when we couldn't before?" I pause, apprehensively. "And why does it seem like it has to do with the—"

"Emanuela?" Verene says. "Are those … your guards?"

I follow her gaze into the distance.

While everyone else in the city still seems stunned, there's a small clump of people moving down one street with purpose. They're wearing fine white coats, bright against the dark manors and green streets of Oga, accented with deep red cravats.

"That's not what my guards look like," I say. "Are they the Garden of Resistance trying to poorly imitate my guards?"

The cluster of people stops. One of them helps a woman clutching a baby to her feet. She exchanges a few words with them.

Then she points at the cathedral.

Verene and I fling ourselves out of the doorway.

"Do you think they're looking for us?" she says in a hushed voice.

I think the answer to that is pretty obvious. Quickly, I run into the inner chamber. I slam the doors and lock them before Verene can follow me.

"Emanuela!" she says, muffled. "Get out here and help me fight them!"

"I'll let you weaken them first," I call.

I'm not going in one of those towers. I may not know exactly what they are, but I've seen enough of the cities to know when someone is trying to lock me up.

I back up, satisfied that I've bought myself a few moments to think, and I bump into something. It feels solid and sturdy, but rather fleshy. It feels, in fact, like a person.

I start to turn around. But this intruder has already thrown a bag over my head. They pull it so tight around my face that I can't breathe. I struggle viciously, clawing at their gloved hands and kicking at their knees. The two of us fall to the floor, and I manage to twist free. I rip the bag off my head and throw it aside.

My attacker is dressed in a hooded black robe, their face completely covered with a similarly blank black mask. They're already rolling to their feet, grabbing the bag and coming at me again.

I scamper back. "Who are you? You can just talk to me instead of trying to subdue me. You'll certainly live longer that way."

They keep coming, faster now.

I sprint over to the glass tank and dig in the ruins, very aware that the tapping of the attacker's footsteps on the tile floor is getting closer and closer. At the last second, I find a shard that's the perfect size. I whirl around and plunge it into my attacker's gut.

They stop, bending double and clutching at the wound. But a second later, they seize the shard and pull it out, tossing it aside. They straighten up again. I can't even see the wound anymore—just a little smear of blood left on their clothes. It's like it already healed.

I've never seen anything like it.

I'd be lying if I said I wasn't intrigued.

"How—" I say.

They dive at me again. We land painfully in the pile of glass, and this time, they get the bag over my head and bonds around my wrists. They start to drag me off. I refuse to stand, so I squeak along the floor of the inner chamber defiantly. I felt the glass digging into my back as we were wrestling on the floor, but strangely, I'm not in any pain now.

My captor and I reach a set of stairs. They seem perfectly

willing to pull my limp body down each one, so I decide to retain a shred of dignity and get to my feet. The air around me is growing colder. I think we're entering the catacombs.

I wiggle desperately at my bonds. My captor seems to sense this, because they stop and yank them tighter. I decide to stop wiggling and focus on memorizing each turn we take, and the way they yank me down the halls is so quick and aggressive that it takes all my concentration.

At long last, I come to a stop, and the bag over my head is ripped off. I find the person in black standing right in front of me—uncomfortably close. I back up and run into someone else. I catch a whiff of a scent that makes my heart leap into my throat and look around to discover Verene is right behind me. We're in a tiny room with metal walls. The two of us are back-to-back, our hands bound, a black-robed captor on either side.

"So?" Verene whispers over her shoulder. "How did your brilliant plan to leave me behind turn out?"

"About as well as your brilliant plan to rule Iris forever," I say.

She vibrates with resentment. It makes me feel a lot better about our current situation.

The floor jolts suddenly. Verene and I tense, but our captors don't react. Somewhere nearby, metal squeals, and we start to move laboriously downward.

I try to look like I get dragged into the catacombs and put into a moving box every day. I study my captor, catching the faintest glint of their dark eyes through their mask. I can't be sure, but I just don't feel like I've looked into these eyes before. I don't know if that makes me feel better or worse.

"Who do you work for?" I say.

Nothing.

"What do you want with us?" I say.

Nothing.

"What's happened to our cities?" I say.

And still nothing.

I'm desperate for them to say something. I'm desperate for this to add up to anything other than the realization that's slowly taking shape in the back of my mind.

I know what happened to me when the veil burst in and covered me in darkness. I felt it. Only for a second. But I felt it. I don't doubt what I know about my own body. I never have. But right now, I want to. For the first time in my life, I desperately want to be wrong.

We come to an abrupt halt. One of our captors pushes a door open to reveal a hall with tall, arched ceilings. There are six people in black robes waiting for us, arranged in a semi-circle. Their hoods are pulled low, leaving their faces in shadow. Our two captors step out to join them. They don't let go of our ropes, tugging us forward until we're facing down all eight figures. For a long moment, everything is quiet. Beside me, Verene has stopped breathing, her eyes darting from hidden face to hidden face.

"Well," I say. "What is it?"

Silence.

"Oh, come on," I say. "You didn't bring me down here just to stare at me, although I wouldn't blame you if you had. Whatever you want to do to us, go ahead and try—"

One of the people in the middle steps forward. She takes down her hood, and the rest of my words dry up in my throat.

The watercrea of Occhia looks just the way I remember her. She has strikingly pale skin and dark hair and a tall, commanding presence. But the thing that always stuck out in my mind were her eyes—endless and black. She used to look at me with a sort of ancient emptiness to her gaze. When she arrested me at my wedding, I was just one of a million noble girls she'd locked in her tower. But then I broke out of her tower, and fought her, and pushed her over a balcony. And then she was dead. She was very much dead.

Now, she's here, and she's looking at me with loathing. That should delight me. It's quite an accomplishment to catch the attention of someone who was alive for a thousand years.

But in this moment, it doesn't feel like one.

"And here they are," the watercrea says, venom in her voice. "The girls who murdered every single person in the eight cities."

NINE

THE RULERS DRAG US THROUGH THE ENTRANCE HALL, AND we emerge into a round room with vaulted ceilings. In the center is a table carved from dark wood and shaped, auspiciously, like an eye. There are eight chairs around it. One chair is clearly the best—the back is taller than all the others, peaking in intricate spikes, like the roof of a cathedral. The watercrea sits down in the fancy chair, and Verene and I are made to stand across from her.

So the watercrea is the leader of this little group. And she was the first one I killed. This fact, at least, is extremely delightful. I cling to it.

The ruler holding me captive forces me into the nearest chair without bothering to undo the bonds around my wrists. Then, to my surprise, she leaves, disappearing through a side door. The ruler who was handling Verene has mirrored her actions, and she follows suit.

I want to ask why they're leaving before the show even

starts, but I suppose I shouldn't complain that there are only six women in here who hate me, instead of eight.

Verene is trying to keep her chin up defiantly, but her eyes, wide and terrified, are still darting between the shadowy faces. The watercrea is the only one of the rulers who's taken down her hood.

"So," the watercrea says.

Then, for a long moment, all she does is look at me. My veils got ripped off sometime during this little escapade into the catacombs, but I'm still wearing my red cloak—the exact same vivid shade the watercrea used to wear. This displeases her. I can tell.

"So," I say.

"Do you know where you are?" she says.

"In your ugly dining room?" I say.

"You're in the afterlife," the watercrea says. "And so is everyone else. Thanks to you."

I try to say something. I find that all of my words are stuck in my throat.

"Are you surprised?" she says. "This is what our people believed, isn't it? That when we die, we return to the veil and join everyone who came before? What did you think would happen when you brought the veil crashing down?"

I thought the afterlife was something my devout people told themselves for comfort as they died naked and alone in a tower. I was never supposed to find out if it was true.

"My companions told you over and over that there was no other way," the watercrea says. "They told you our magic protected the eight cities. They told you that you weren't enough to replace us. But you two…you thought you knew better. Well? Did you?"

I force myself to stare the watercrea down without a smidgeon of regret in my eyes. I have the horrible feeling she's seeing right through it.

"Maybe we did this on purpose," I say anyway. "Maybe we were just so desperate to see you again."

"Everything was fine for a thousand years," the watercrea says. "And then…" She looks at Verene. "One little girl decided to disrupt things. After the leader of Iris fell, it all began to wobble. Then it got worse. And worse. Until finally, the two of you combined your efforts to push the last piece over, and the entire thing collapsed. But that's just how you operate—isn't it, Emanuela?"

So the watercrea knows my name now. Good. Great.

"Oh yes," she continues. "I've heard the stories from my companions. I've heard about every single deed that you bragged about while you were holding them captive. I've heard how you decimated them and their cities. And you." She looks at Verene again. "In a way, you're even worse. Every single thing that's happened can be traced right back to your actions."

Verene looks very much like she wants to argue. She also looks very much like she's going to vomit if she tries.

"So are you going to lecture us for all of eternity, then?" I say. "Where's the prison? Just go ahead and throw us in. See how long it holds us."

The watercrea is quiet.

"If we're…not alive, then you can't kill us," I say. "You can't even hurt us. We heal right away. We know that."

At least, I think we know that. I'm waiting for her to confirm it.

And still, she remains quiet. The silence has now stretched on for an uncomfortably long time. The other rulers haven't moved a muscle, but even with their hoods pulled low, I can see their gazes are all attentively turned to their leader. The watercrea is making us all wait, because she can. I did that as the ruler of the six cities. Often.

At last, the watercrea gets to her feet. She walks around the table, slowly, until she's standing directly behind me. I would rather she not. I'd feel better if I could see what she was doing.

"You saw the red towers at the center of the eight cities, I presume?" she says.

"Yes," I say. "They were hard to miss."

"Those towers comprise the afterlife as it has existed for a thousand years—also known as the ninth city," the watercrea says. "And the ninth city has its own ruler. Her name is Marcella. Long ago, the eight of us...clashed with Marcella. As a result, we are forever at odds. Her magic is repelled by ours, and ours is repelled by hers. We can't set foot aboveground here—not without great consequence. We'd never be able to make it to the center of the ninth city. That's where she's currently residing, because that's where her power is the strongest."

I'm afraid to say anything. This is the closest the rulers have ever gotten to telling me something about who they were before they were ageless women in towers who took blood and made water.

"And?" I breathe carefully.

"The two of you, however, are perfectly able to enter the city center," the watercrea says.

"And?" I say.

"I can just imagine what would have happened if we hadn't

intercepted you," the watercrea says. "Marcella's guards would have taken you and brought you to her lair. You would have seen her incredible power. You would have said to each other, *Oh, we can defeat her. We'll just kill her, like we've killed every other ruler.* And then...she would have destroyed you."

"Well," I say. "We don't know that for sure—"

"Marcella's power is enormous," the watercrea says. "You may think yourself capable, but trust me, you will not last long in her city. Unless...you have the proper tools."

"What tools?" I say.

"We'll give them to you," the watercrea says. "In return, you will go to the center of the ninth city. You will find Marcella. You will capture her. And you will bring her back to us."

I'm very still, trying to process it.

"You're sending us..." I say. "To go capture...your enemy?"

"Don't you think you'd be good at such a thing?" the watercrea says.

Of course I do. I'm just surprised that instead of being locked up, I'm being handed an opportunity by the last person I ever expected to hand me one. But I'll never say no to an opportunity. Especially now.

"What are you going to do to her once you get her?" I say.

"Handle her," the watercrea says, as if that explains everything.

"Well, what's in it for us?" I say, pretending to be resistant. "Why would we ever just go up there and do your bidding?"

The watercrea leans over the back of my chair and puts her hands on my shoulders.

She's never touched me before. Maybe once, last year in her tower, when she put a needle in my neck to drain my blood.

But now, she's leaning down to speak into my ear, and she's so uncomfortably close that I can smell her sweat. I never thought of the watercrea as being someone who sweats.

"Why do you think we kept the eight cities the way they were, for as long as we did?" she says. "Why do you think we never faltered, locking up babies with omens and noble girls on their wedding days?"

"Because it kept you in power?" I whisper.

"We were protecting you from the veil," she says. "We were protecting all of you. It was never supposed to be like this, but it is. You're in here now, Emanuela. We all are. And Marcella isn't like the rest of us. The worst thing we could ever do to you is death. She can do so much more. So I want you to ask yourself... after what you did to the eight cities, do you think you're in any position to pretend you know what's best here? Perhaps, the only thing you're good for is doing our bidding."

Obviously, there's so many things wrong with what she's saying. I handled the eight cities rather well. Yes, everyone has become... not alive, but that was the rulers' fault, for not telling me about this whole thing where the veil collapses without them. Also, if she expects me to be afraid of someone doing something to me that's *worse than death*, she's sorely misguided. There's nothing worse than death. So really, I have nothing to fear now, and no reason to worry about anything. The worst has already happened.

I want to tell the watercrea all of that. But instead, I decide to stay quiet. I sense that will get me out of here faster. Also, I seem to have a lot of bile rising in my throat.

The watercrea claps me on the shoulders, and in spite of myself, I jump.

"So we have an agreement," she says. "Lucinde, take the girls to finish the preparations."

It's so strange to know that these women have names that, for a moment, I can't even comprehend that the watercrea is speaking to one of the other hooded rulers around the table. The ruler in question stands up. She grabs both of our ropes and leads us away by the wrists.

We pass through the side door into a narrow hall. This mysterious hideout of theirs appears to have been built into the catacombs, which I assume wind their way under the ninth city, the same way they do with the other eight. We pass by seven doors made of metal. All except one are shut, and when I peek inside, I catch a glimpse of the two rulers from earlier. They're sitting together in a sparsely decorated bedroom. One of them is vomiting blood, and the other is holding a bucket for her.

I remember what the watercrea said about the rulers not being able to go aboveground here without consequences. I think that means they've been stuck down here, in this dismal place, ever since they died. It's only what they deserve.

Lucinde stops outside the eighth door, still holding our ropes. She turns to face us.

"So, I heard something about us getting tools?" I say.

Lucinde takes down her hood. One look at her face is all I need to know which city she used to rule. She has pale skin and dark, curly hair that's pulled back severely. There's a haughty quality to her features that feels familiar, but it's the proud, graceful set of her chin that really strikes me. I've spent... quite a lot of time admiring that same feature on someone else.

I look over at Verene. Her whole body has gone rigid. She looks afraid to even blink.

Verene told me exactly how she killed her maman. Three years ago, the ruler of Iris brought her two children into her study. She told them that, contrary to what they'd believed all their lives, they weren't actually going to rule together. She wanted to select one heir—the better heir—and she was going to do it by keeping them locked in her study until one of them did the ritual on the other.

Then Verene broke a glass jar and used a big shard to stab her maman. Repeatedly. She told me, actually, that she was so overcome with the righteous passion of murder that she didn't even notice when her maman disappeared. She just kept stabbing the floor.

And there I was thinking no one could ever top what I did to my own papá.

"I'm going to cut your bonds," Lucinde says. She has a very quiet voice. None of the rulers have loud voices. They don't seem to need them.

Lucinde cuts mine first. I keep the rope—one never knows when one will need rope. Then Lucinde turns to slice Verene loose, her movements quick and matter-of-fact. When she's freed, Verene rubs at her wrists, still staring at her maman with large, wary eyes, but Lucinde is already preoccupied with reaching into her robe. She pulls out two necklaces. Each one has a small metal pendant shaped like an eye.

"These are disguises," she says. "They don't change your appearance—people will see and hear you as you are, but they won't be able to remember if they've encountered you before.

You'll be, for all intents and purposes, anonymous. Use this stealth wisely."

I narrow my eyes. "What is this magic? How did you get it?"

She drops the tokens into our hands. "We have one other tool prepared. A dagger. As you may have noticed, people in the afterlife cannot be injured in any lasting way. Except with this dagger. It has enough magic in it to inflict one permanent injury."

"Hmm," I say, trying not to look too gleeful.

"You will not be in charge of the dagger," Lucinde says. "We're giving it to your leader. He'll only use it if one of you gets . . . out of control."

"Wait, what?" I say. "Who's our leader?"

Lucinde knocks on the door at her side. It swings inward to reveal a tall, broad-shouldered boy dressed in all black. He steps out, shutting the door behind him, and stands with aggressively straight posture, his hands behind his back.

At the sight of her twin brother, Verene backs up against the far wall.

"What . . . is *he* . . . doing here?" She bites out the words, venom in each one.

Theo gives his sister an equally cold look. "Hello to you, too, Verene. In case you weren't aware, the veil also came down on Iris."

"I found your brother in our underground well," Lucinde says. "Even amongst all the chaos, tending to it was still his first concern."

The words are spoken without emotion, but there's something pointed about them that almost make me feel like the irresponsible daughter here. Almost. I haven't spent much time with Theo, but I'm not exactly surprised to find out he's the boring child who does all the duties expected of him. I didn't get the impression he had much of a life—it seemed to consist only of keeping things in Iris orderly while Verene cavorted around with her lavish fountains.

"So, where's our leader?" I say. "All I see a boy with a stick up his rear end."

Theo gives me a look of pure loathing. We really bonded last year during all the great happenings in Iris, like me burning down his cathedral home and beating him up with an iron pan. Also, I killed his sister in front of him and forced him to shove an eye down her throat to save her, which resulted in her hating him. That was a big one.

"Theodore kept a city alive, all by himself, for an entire year," Lucinde says, entirely ignoring my hilarious quip. "He's shown himself to be capable. Perhaps the others are still a bit sore about the stolen water…but he's going to make up for that now. Aren't you?"

"Yes, Maman," Theo says.

"Those are all the tools we have for you. Let's go." Lucinde puts a hand on Theo's arm and starts to usher us back the way we came.

"You're really not going to say anything about it?" Verene says.

Lucinde stops. She turns to look at her daughter, her expression flat. "About what, Verene?"

I can see the thoughts whirring behind Verene's eyes as a million words run through her head. Verene always has so much to say. I can't imagine her growing up with this brick wall of a mother—a woman who apparently doesn't want to acknowledge her own murder, or the fact that one of her children put the other in a prison, which she must know about by now.

After a moment of deliberate silence, Lucinde turns away dismissively and keeps walking.

"You deserved it," Verene says.

Lucinde stops. I wait, holding my breath, and so does Verene, braced like she's expecting the worst.

But Lucinde doesn't even turn her head. Instead, she tightens her grip on Theo's arm and pushes past me, heading down the narrow hall.

Verene is left standing there alone, visibly shaking. Her gaze goes to me and I feel, suddenly, like I'm intruding. I have the urge to apologize—something Verene and I have never done in the entire year we've known each other. But she turns and marches away before I can even open my mouth, which is a mercy. If there's one thing I know about Verene, it's that she doesn't want me interfering in her life. I don't know what I was thinking for a second there.

We return to the entrance hall. The watercrea and the other four rulers are waiting there by the open door to the metal box. The watercrea hands black cloaks to me and Verene.

"But I like mine," I say. "The red looks good on me, don't you think?"

"I'm sure Marcella and all her guards will think so, too," the watercrea says.

I change, but I'm very slow and annoying about it. As I tie on my new cloak, I notice that the other rulers are staring at Theo behind their masks. Lucinde seems aware of this, and she bristles, pulling Theo closer to her. One of the other rulers leans forward slightly.

"He has your eyes," she whispers.

Lucinde softens a little. "He does, doesn't he?"

In the context of this being a room full of women who ate eyes for power, that's the creepiest thing I've ever heard. I can tell from his barely concealed alarm that Theo thinks so, too. But when a moment passes, and nothing sinister happens, it occurs to me that maybe, against all odds, this other ruler wasn't sizing Theo up as yet another victim. She was looking with curiosity at her accomplice's child, because she never had any of her own. None of them did. I saw their lonesome lives at the top of their towers. They lived like women who had secrets—so many secrets that no mortal outsider could ever be allowed in.

I wonder if Lucinde got in trouble for going against the grain, and if she got in especially big trouble for trying to pass on her title. A quick glance at the watercrea's face tells me everything I need to know about that. She's not impressed. Perhaps she thinks that if Theo and Verene had never been told about the ritual, none of this would have happened. What she's forgetting is that, no matter what was going on in Iris, I would have always happened.

We're ushered into the metal box along with Lucinde, and the watercrea sweeps over to the doorway, blocking us in.

"Lucinde will take you through the catacombs to a strategic exit point," she says. "When you emerge, you'll be inside the ninth city. Be vigilant. And do not fail."

"You're forcing us to go kidnap your enemy for you, and that's all the advice you have to give?" I say.

The watercrea sneers at me. Without ceremony, she slams the door on us. That's fine. I don't need her advice. I'll just look forward to the moment she realizes that it was a mistake to ever try and get me to run her devious errands for her.

We have an extremely awkward ride in the metal box, followed by an equally awkward walk through the catacombs, shivering a bit in the cold. At last, Lucinde stops at the bottom of a long, steep staircase and points up ahead. There's a door at the top with glowing red light around the edges.

Verene and I put on our eye tokens. Lucinde does a double take, even though she knew it was coming. They must be working. We must look like strangers to her now, although we look the same to each other. That's unnerving. Verene doesn't seem to have noticed, though—she's already starting up the stairs without a single backward glance, like all she wants is to be out of the catacombs. I'm following her when I hear Lucinde speaking in a low voice.

"Theodore, wait," she says.

I glance stealthily over my shoulder to see that she's holding Theo back, preventing him from putting on his own token. She takes his face in her hands with the barest suggestion of motherly tenderness. I move excruciatingly slowly on the stairs, trying to look like I'm not eavesdropping. I want to know what extra information our so-called leader is being given.

"Everyone else may blame the girls for all of this," she says. "But we both know whose fault it really is. Don't we?"

"Yes, Maman," he says.

"I raised you to be someone special," she says. "Someone capable of handling your responsibilities. You were supposed to keep your sister in line. You were supposed to keep Iris in balance. But now..." She sighs. "Things have gone further than they ever should have. Understand this: Now that Marcella has everyone who ever lived under her domain, she will grow more powerful than she ever has before. There will soon come a time when she is impossible to stop."

Impossible to stop. That's an intriguing phrase.

"You must get to her before then," Lucinde says. "The girls will be useful to you, if you're clever enough to direct their energies where they should be directed. Don't let them delay you with any other antics. Don't let anything delay you."

"Yes, Maman," Theo says.

"And, Theodore?" she says. "If you fail at this, and Marcella gains all the power she's looking for . . . you won't like what happens to the cities. You won't like what happens to you. But you will deserve it."

Theo is very quiet.

"Yes, Maman," he whispers finally.

When I glance back, he's bending down obediently to let her put his eye token over his head. I quickly pretend like I was running up the stairs all along. Verene is almost at the door, and I'm not letting her into the ninth city without me.

I'm ready to hunt down this woman who thinks that she can make herself impossible to stop.

TEN

VERENE AND I ARE ABOUT TO LEAVE THE CATACOMBS WHEN our leader intervenes. Rather forcefully.

"And where, exactly—" Theo shoves past us both, almost sending me toppling down the narrow stairs. "—do you two think you're going?"

"Oh, you're still here," I say, as if I wasn't just spying on a somewhat personal conversation he had with his maman. A quick glance down tells me she's already disappeared back into the shadows of the catacombs, melting away like a ghost.

"Yes, I am." Theo plants himself in front of the door, staring us down imperiously. "And whatever you two think you're about to do...you're not. I'm in charge. I have a map of the ninth city, so you're going to stand here quietly while I look at it."

He fumbles in his shirt pocket and pulls out a folded piece of paper. He alternates between studying it and giving us a suspicious look every two seconds.

Verene glances back down the stairs, then drops her voice.

"So you're really just going to do exactly what Maman told you to do? You're not going to consider, I don't know...anything besides being her little evil minion?"

Theo looks up from the map. His dark eyes are cold.

"I just died, Verene," he says.

"Well, so did I," she says.

"Do you want to know where I was, when it happened?" he says. "Hiding in the ruins of our cathedral. That's where I've been this whole time."

That explains why he's so scruffy, his curly hair a bit rough around the edges. I remember him as being immaculate. I was assuming that he just gave up on grooming himself after I ruined his life on every level.

"I felt the rumbling and ran out to look, and people were all over the cathedral square," he continues. "And they—they swarmed me. They wanted to know what was happening. They wanted to know why we abandoned them. I saw the rest of our family, and they were trying to get me to hold the littlest children, like they thought I had some magic that could still protect them. That was the exact reason I'd been avoiding everyone. I knew they wanted me to give them answers, and I had none. None that they would want to hear."

Verene swallows hard, and I know she must be imagining it—the exact same scene that happened in Oga playing out in her home city.

For a split second, I start to imagine it playing out in my own home. I imagine the veil crashing down over the dark, empty manors of Occhia. And I don't let myself wonder if maybe there was one person standing alone in the streets, watching it happen.

"It's pretty simple," Verene says. "The answer is that I had a good system going. Then, we were attacked by an outside enemy, but instead of helping me fight her, you gave her all our secrets and betrayed me."

"I see you're still throwing around imaginary accusations," Theo says. "I didn't betray you. Your system was unsustainable. You were unsustainable."

"And you went behind my back instead of just telling me that," she says.

"Sometimes, when people tell you things you don't want to hear, they die," he says.

"If your concerns about Iris were so rational, you had nothing to worry about," Verene says. "I'm rational."

Theo scoffs. "That's actually the most ridiculous thing you've ever said."

"What about this—my brother is a lovely person who's definitely not an underhanded schemer, and he's also really fun at parties and has lots of friends?" Verene says. "There's something even more ridiculous."

"Good one," I say.

"Stay out of this, Emanuela," Verene snaps, despite the fact that I'm crammed into this stairwell with them.

"You had your chance to be in charge, and absolutely everyone died," Theo says. "I'm not saying that I agree with everything Maman has ever done. But I think, maybe, after being alive for a thousand years, there are some things she knows more about than you. Like how to not end up with absolutely everyone dead."

"It seems like you're harboring some negative feelings about this," I say.

"I wouldn't expect you to understand, on account of you being a literal demon with no feelings at all," Theo says.

"I wish I was a literal demon," I say. "Imagine the sort of powers I'd have in the afterlife."

He's right about my feelings, in a sense. I don't have feelings about this—none that are any of his business. I've already come to terms with the fact that I'm...not alive, and now I'm only worried about what's next.

"You're not in charge here, Theo," Verene insists. "And I don't care what Maman wants us to do. I'm going to see the city and decide for myself."

She reaches past him to grab the doorknob.

"Don't—" he says.

I kick him in the shin, which gives us enough time to slip out.

The only reason I don't try harder to stop him from following us is because I've figured out where he's hiding the magic dagger the rulers gave him. On his right side, there's a little ridge under his black shirt. If I'm walking into a city full of guards who want to capture me, and a ruler who's more powerful than any other, I think it's only wise that I figure out how to get my hands on the only weapon in the afterlife that truly works—and sooner rather than later.

I was expecting to emerge in an alley of the ninth city, but instead, I see a very red, very round room lined with lanterns. We seem to be passing through a hidden door, and when I cautiously creep forward, I discover that we're in the base of a spiral staircase that winds up the center of a tall, thin building.

We're in one of the enormous towers we spotted from a distance. I haven't been inside a tower in a year. This one doesn't smell like blood—the scent is almost sterile, like cold stone. But it feels horribly, sickeningly familiar, as if I was being dragged into it by the Occhian guards last night. It's hard to forget the place I almost died. Twice.

Verene and I exchange a glance, and somehow, I feel us coming to a wordless agreement. Before we do anything else, we need to see Marcella's prisoners for ourselves. We need to know exactly what we're dealing with.

"I'm aware that neither of you knows the meaning of the word I'm about to say," Theo whispers, barely sticking his head out of the door. "But we need to be *careful*—"

We're already starting up the stairs. There are a few turns of nothingness, and then, we come upon two rows of arched red doors sitting across from each other. I stop, holding my breath, and wait to hear something—the thumping footsteps of guards, or the muffled noises of trapped people. Then I realize that the doors closest to us are cracked open. Verene approaches one, and I follow her. We peek inside to find a small room that's unlit and completely empty.

Verene pushes the door wider and steps inside. She immediately shrieks. I do, too. The room has transformed into a very messy study, scattered with papers and books. Before I can see any of the details, Verene has flung herself back through the door, and the room is suddenly empty again.

"What just happened?" I say.

Verene is staring at the doorway like she's seen a ghost.

"I don't know," she says.

I glance at Theo, who's caught up with us. His eyes are wide. He's looking at the room like he recognized it.

"You try." Verene shoves me at the door.

I protest, but she was too quick—my foot goes over the edge, and I catch a glimpse of a dark room with a green canopy bed. The wardrobe is open, and there's the ruins of a frilly black dress all over the carpeted floor.

It's my childhood bedroom in Occhia. The last time I saw it, my nursemaid was frantically preparing me for my wedding and just about losing her mind with exasperation at my schemes. Everything looks perfectly preserved. It feels like I could waltz in and sit down at the dressing table, and in the mirror I'd see the girl I used to be—a girl with long, luscious hair and a hidden omen on her hip and a perfect vision of how her life in Occhia was going to play out.

I can't pull back fast enough.

"How is it doing that?" I whisper, my mouth dry. "That was..." I'm not going to tell Verene about my childhood home, especially not with the way her eyes are lingering on the room with obvious curiosity. "A place I've been before."

"Do you think Marcella keeps people...trapped in their memories?" Verene says. "Why?"

"Because she's dangerous," Theo says. "Maman told me some things about how her magic works, and they're not pleasant. That's why you need to hold still for two seconds and let me look at this map, because if we get caught..." He pulls it out of his shirt pocket again. "Tell me if you hear anyone coming."

The watercrea told us that this city was different. But maybe, possibly, I didn't fully comprehend what she meant.

But I won't be afraid. I'm not afraid of this city. I'm not afraid of the woman who rules it, and I'm not afraid of her powers. I'm the one who dragged the eight cities into the veil.

Whatever's happening to the people now, it's my job to free them from it.

It's my job, and my job alone.

And I think, actually, I might be able to use these rooms to my advantage. While Theo is preoccupied with his map, I turn my attention to Verene.

"I wonder if these rooms can conjure up any place you've ever been," I say. "You might end up in a place that would... *create a distraction.*"

I give her a significant look on the last few words. I point to Theo, then point to my own right side. Then I mime stabbing.

"Hmm," she says thoughtfully.

She steps back into the cell. It changes around her, morphing into a hexagonal space with white walls and marble floors. Everything about it is exceedingly neat.

"All right." Theo folds up the map and puts it away. "We need to get a look at the street and find out how many guards are roaming about. We might have to wait until we have the cover of darkness to—why are you in my bedroom?"

"Just testing," Verene says.

Theo narrows his eyes. "Testing strange magic that you know you shouldn't be messing with? Typical."

I've crept around to his right side. I can see the dagger faintly, but I won't be able to pluck it free until I get his shirt untucked. Untucking boys' shirts isn't my forte, but I'll manage.

"I'm testing to see how detailed my memories are." Verene walks over to Theo's dresser and opens the second drawer. "Oh, here they are. His precious cravats." She holds two of them up. "Do you notice how they look exactly the same, Emanuela? But wait…he stitched the days of the week on the underside, so that he could wear them in the *correct* order. I'm so glad he had enough energy left for such a vital task after working so hard on his plots to run our city without me."

She starts pulling out cravats and chucking them in every direction. Theo watches, his face stony.

"Are you done?" he says.

Verene shuts the drawer and opens another. "Goodness, look at all this cologne. Remind me again who you were trying to impress with this? I worked so hard to set you up with someone nice. I used all my connections to throw that great tea party. And then you were rude to everyone, and you told me that we weren't allowed to have parties and that you don't want to court anyone because it's a pointless nuisance. And then you moped in your room for three days."

A muscle in Theo's jaw twitches. I take the opportunity to delicately tug on his shirt.

"Do you really want to do this right now?" he says.

In answer, Verene opens one of his colognes and pours it all over the white marble floor.

Right as I'm about to make the final tug on Theo's shirt and dive for the dagger, he turns around. He goes through the door across the hall, and the moment he steps inside, it turns into Verene's old bedroom—a twin of his, but much untidier.

"What do you think you're doing?" Verene says.

"Traumatizing myself all over again." Theo gets on his hands and knees and pulls a small journal out from under the bed.

At the sight of it, Verene's face goes gray. "Theo—"

"Perhaps Emanuela would like to learn about your own charming habits," Theo says.

"Theo," Verene says, a deadly note in her voice.

I would indeed like to learn about her charming habits. And that means I'm stuck hovering between the two rooms, no closer to getting the dagger.

"After she became the Heart, Verene got so many adoring letters from our people," Theo says. "I think, perhaps, she became a bit addicted to them. So when she felt like she wasn't getting enough, she would write her own. She was especially fond of going on and on about her own beauty.... Let me see if I can find the one that's seared into my brain. Ah, yes. Here it is. *Dearest Verene, I'm just writing this to let you know that your skin radiates like that of an ethereal being, and your lips look like the most beautiful rose. I wish I could—*"

Verene is already running across the hall. I'm still trying to figure out what's so wrong with writing screeds about one's own beauty when she tackles Theo to the floor. She tears at his side and rips the dagger away from him. He struggles against her, and the dagger clatters to the floor as they fight.

Ah. I can work with this.

I swoop in and pick the dagger up. In an instant, I'm back out of the cell, and I slam the door on them.

Only then do I discover that these doors don't actually seem to have locks. In a panic, I pull out the rope I saved from my encounter with the rulers. I loop it around the lantern on one wall, then quickly pull it taut across the door and tie it to the next lantern. I'm sure Verene and Theo are trying to escape, but I can't hear them. The cells seem to be curiously, unnervingly soundproof.

That's good. Then I don't have to listen to Verene cursing

my name—or maybe, reminding me what happened the last time I trapped her somewhere.

But I'm not going to think about that. We're in the ninth city now, and things are different. When the veil was coming down on me, there was a moment when I thought it was all over. I thought I was never going to get to do what I really need to do—to save all of the cities, once and for all.

But this is my second chance. Marcella and this strange power of hers aren't going to last long against me. I'm going to find her, and I'm going to defeat her, and then, finally, people will understand that I deserve to be at the top. If everyone would just stop fighting me, or withholding information from me, or coercing me into doing their bidding, they would realize that for themselves. But they don't seem to *want* to realize that, so I'll just have to show them.

I pull the magic dagger out of its sheath and examine its small, jagged blade. I'll only be able to use it once, so I'll have to choose the perfect occasion. I tuck the dagger into my boot and creep carefully to the bottom of the tower. As I press my ear to the door, I hear a low, buzzing hum outside that I'm not sure I like.

Holding my breath, I push open the tower door to see what Marcella's city is like. But what I see isn't at all what I expected.

I see...life. Or, I suppose, afterlife.

There are people—so many people that I can barely comprehend it. They've filled every inch of the cobblestone street. I cautiously step outside, and I'm bombarded by a pleasing cascade of different languages, including ones I've never heard before. It smells, somehow, like freshly baked bread and garlic and chocolate all at once. When I take a closer look at the peo-ple, I can see that some of them are strolling along, but some are simply sitting. They've beautified this street, setting up little tables in the center, protected from the flow of the crowd by low hedges. Overhead, garlands of ivy are strung between some of the tower windows, along with lanterns that are probably lit when evening falls.

I don't know what to make of it. I touch my eye token to make sure my disguise is still in place, and I slowly start to move along the street.

The next thing I notice is the outfits. I've never seen outfits like this. Only a few feet away, there's a woman in an osten-tatious ball gown with fine silk gloves. The vividly dyed fabric and fussy embroidery speak of something only the wealthiest family in the city could afford—except that I see a dozen other people passing by who are dressed in similar riches. There's a woman with an absurdly tall diamond tiara and a man in a vel-vet coat that's inexplicably changing color as I watch—I squint at that one for a long time with open jealousy. At the man's side, deep in conversation with him, is another man in pajamas. No one seems to find any of it strange.

A boy in a striped jacket walks by, and I find myself reach-ing out for him.

"Excuse me," I say in my most polite Culaire.

He stops. "What is it, Madame?"

"The towers," I say. "Why aren't you in the towers?"

"Well, they're not really in fashion, are they?" he says. "Per-sonally, I was trapped in there for two hundred and three years, so even if they're not malicious anymore, I'd rather be out here."

"You were... trapped?" I say slowly.

"Ugh," he says. "You're so very new. Were there not guards at the edge of the ninth city for this very reason? I went to watch you all crossing over after the veil came down. For the most historic event of all time, it was a bit dreary. It was mostly just people getting delayed because they tried to bring sentimental items from the eight cities. The guards don't want you to bring anything here because you can just make it anew, see? Just go to the city center and ask for it."

"You've been freed," I say. "Who freed you?"

He sighs impatiently. "Before, we were all stuck in the towers. The veil kept us in those horrible cells, and it stole from us. It stole every feeling and thought and memory. But then the Eye was able to free us, and the veil doesn't steal from us anymore. It gives."

"The Eye," I echo slowly.

"You're very lucky, you know," he says. "Thanks to the veil, I don't remember half my life. But you'll always have yours. Now, if you'd like to find someone else to bother, I'm going to start planning my outfit for the wedding."

He walks away, melting into the crowd.

For a moment, I'm very still, watching the people meandering along the street. There are couples arm in arm, and bouncy children, and even babies—babies who will never grow older, I realize with an odd twist in my stomach. Everyone seems to be going wherever they like, doing whatever they like. They seem to be free, and immortal, and endlessly provided for. But I've seen too much to walk into a miraculous city and accept it at face value. There's only one person who can give me answers about what's really going on here. Marcella.

And then I'm walking. I stop a few times to ask directions to the city center, bewildered by the maze of streets. It's a long journey, but at last, I round a bend and find myself on a long street lined with towers. At the end of it, the towers abruptly clear out to form a circle. Sitting in the middle of the circle is a manor. Even though it's surrounded by towers that are much, much taller, it still manages to look grand—flanked on either side with a wing that's five stories high, the whole thing covered in ivy.

I recognize the manor right away. I stop in my tracks, uncomprehending.

No. I must be imagining it.

I move closer. Closer. When I reach the edge of the city center, I slow again, unable to deny my own eyes.

The House of Morandi used to sit at the end of the street where I grew up. Even though its dark walls have turned ghostly white, I would know it anywhere.

It shouldn't be here. It should be back in our empty city of Occhia. I wonder if, perhaps, this is like the mysterious rooms in the towers. Maybe I'm just seeing a memory. Maybe this is a trap.

But I'm already walking for the front doors in a daze. They're tall and grand, with ivy leaves carved around the frame. Without really thinking about what I'm doing, I push them open. It's how I always used to enter this house—like I owned it, because I thought that, one day, I would.

The foyer is empty, but elsewhere, I can hear footsteps and the muffled sounds of activity—doors opening and shutting, cups clinking, and chattering voices. It smells just the way I remember—like candles and old books and an indescribable scent I never encountered anywhere else. This isn't my home. But it smells like home in a way I haven't smelled in a year.

I hear soft footsteps from the top of the grand staircase—barely there, like a whisper. And when I look up, I see a tall, thin boy staring down at me.

My first thought is that he looks incredibly different. He's dressed in a dark red suit with white trim. There's a black eye-patch on his face, embroidered with a single white leaf. His dark hair has gotten longer—longer than his nursemaid would have ever allowed.

My second thought is that he looks exactly the same. Just like the house, I would know him anywhere.

"Hello," Ale says in polite Culaire. "Can I help you?"

I can't comprehend the fact that he's not speaking to me in Occhian, our native language. I can't comprehend the fact that after an entire year, we're meeting again in the middle of the afterlife, and the first thing he says to me is something so banal. Then I remember.

He doesn't recognize me.

"Oh," he says. "Are you here to assist with the wedding?"

I curtsy, and I say the first thing that comes to mind.

"Yes," I say. "I am. I'm a seamstress."

Ale smiles.

It's been so long since I've seen my best friend's face. It's been even longer since I've seen him smile.

"Join us upstairs, please," he says, beckoning me.

In spite of myself, I glance back at the front doors. They've swung shut of their own accord.

I came here for answers. And I'm going to get them.

So I follow Ale up the stairs.

Eleven

I'm very familiar with the House of Morandi. As a child, I spent hours and hours roaming around its intricate halls, wreaking havoc as Ale trailed behind me and wrung his hands. Now, he's the one leading me along the second-floor corridor. We pass by the sitting room where his aunts spent every morning drinking coffee and gossiping. I'm surprised to find it absolutely bursting with activity. There are a dozen people crammed in there, buried under red fabric and working busily.

"You have a lot of seamstresses already," I realize.

"Don't worry about being late," Ale says. "There's still plenty of time to help. Would you like some coffee first?"

"I...yes?" I say.

I seem to have forgotten how to form sentences. I've seen a lot of odd things, but this is all too much, even for me. I've never seen Ale so at ease with a stranger, which is what I've become to him. I've never seen him with a stranger at all. When we were growing up, he couldn't walk into a room if I wasn't by his side.

Maybe he's not real. Maybe none of this is real.

Ale leads me into a room that I also recognize, because it was a room I was very much not supposed to enter, and therefore had great interest in—his papá's study. The elder Signor Morandi was the head of Parliament when he was alive. He conducted business in here and often dragged Ale in to watch and observe. I spent a lot of time trying to spy on those meetings, knowing that they were wasted on Ale. He was always squirming miserably in the corner, wanting to go back to his romance novels.

The study is grand, with a whole sitting area and an elaborate wooden desk at the back. The large arched window behind the desk has a view of the red towers outside now, which is very distracting. It used to be a view of the Occhian street where my family's house sat.

When I turn my gaze away from the window, I jump out of my skin. Ale is right in front of me, holding a cup of steaming coffee out like an offering.

"I'm so sorry!" he says. "I didn't mean to startle you. Here."

Up close, I'm struck by sudden, subtle differences in his pale face. He's always had soft, graceful features, but now, there's a sharp, almost hollow quality to his cheeks. Above his upper lip, to my absolute astonishment, there's the tiniest smidgeon of dark hair. When we lived in Occhia, he would come over to my house for coffee every single afternoon. And every single time, he started by trying to convince me his mustache was finally coming in.

It never was. But now it is. I can't even really explain why, but I feel suddenly, desperately sad about it. I feel like something precious slipped right through my fingers as I watched, powerless to stop it. I should have been there for such an occasion.

I'm staring at him, I realize. I quickly take the coffee. He sits down on one striped red-and-white love seat. I sit down on another. I can't dump sugar into this coffee, like I normally would. I'm convinced that, somehow, that will be the thing that makes him realize who I am. I take a careful, polite sip. Even though it's far more bitter than I would like, it tastes just like the coffee we had every afternoon in Occhia. I thought I would never taste this coffee again.

"I didn't get your name," he says.

He might have already asked me when we were on the stairs. I'm so disoriented I might have completely missed it.

"Gisele," I say.

"Well, it's nice to meet you, Gisele," he says. "How long have you been—"

"A wedding," I blurt.

"Oh," Ale says. "Um . . . what about it?"

"A wedding is happening," I say.

Ale blushes all the way out to his ears. "Yes. Tonight."

Somehow, it's seeing him blush that does it. It makes me certain that this isn't an illusion. He's real. He's real, and he's here, living at the center of the afterlife.

But just because it's not an illusion doesn't mean it's not a trick. I already saw that Marcella's magic has a way of accessing my memories. And I'm certain that Marcella has heard of me by now, and that she considers me a threat. She's around here somewhere, and she must have lots of different ways of trying to find me. I have to tread very carefully, I remind myself.

"I'm very excited, of course," Ale continues. "This is about the whole ninth city. Not just me. I want you all to celebrate. Now that the eight cities are all here, we have so much to celebrate."

I find that I can't do anything but stare at him.

"It's you," I manage finally.

"Yes?" he says.

"*You're* the one getting married? But—"

I cut myself off at the uncertain look he's giving me. My voice came out rather sharp.

I can't do this. I'm going to make him suspicious. He's going to see right through this disguise and figure out it's me, and I can't talk to him as Emanuela. I'm the girl who killed his city and his family. The girl he put in a prison. The girl he wanted nothing to do with ever again.

"I'm very socially awkward," I say, hoping that will put an end to his polite curiosity.

"Oh, me too," he says, looking highly relieved. "Honestly, I'm the worst. I talk to people all day, and it still makes me so nervous. Like with you—I can't believe I could ever make you nervous, because you're making me nervous. You're very pretty. And you have a very nice way of holding yourself. You look so confident. I wish I could be like that—"

I stand up, so abruptly that I drop my coffee. The cup shatters on the rug.

"I didn't mean to," I say.

"Oh, it's all right," Ale says. "It's just a—"

"I didn't mean to!" I say.

He stops.

My voice is too loud. Everything is too loud. Especially the way he's looking at me, with a gentle concern on his face that I've seen so many times before.

"Gisele," he says softly. "It's all right."

It's not all right. He shouldn't be here. It doesn't make any sense. I should just rip off my disguise and demand to know what's happening. But then, I'll see what he really thinks of me.

So instead, I turn away. "I'm going to go start working. With the other seamstresses."

"If you need anything else—" he says.

But I've already made my way out the door. I bypass the room with all the seamstresses, and I duck into a back hallway. My entire body is shaking so hard I can barely stand.

When I left Ale last year—when he sent me away—he was alone in the catacombs, with nowhere to go and no one to go to. And he died. He must have died, because it seems like he's been here longer than I have. I was alive, ruling my six cities, and my best friend was dead. And I had no idea, because I never looked for him. I never even let myself think about him.

I need to know how long ago it happened. I need to know how he and his house ended up in the city center.

I need to know who he's marrying. And I need to know why.

Somebody walks past me in the hall, and I jump, but they completely ignore me. They slip into the nearest room, and I hear chattering and the clinking of teacups. I realize that I'm standing right next to a nursery—when I peek inside, I see children smashing up toys. At the very end of the hall, an older man and woman are strolling by. They pause to look out the window at the towers beyond.

I know some of these faces. They're Ale's family. I don't know why I'm surprised that they're here. This is their house.

And then, all at once, the reality of it all comes crashing over me.

Everyone who's ever lived is here, in the ninth city. That means I'm surrounded by all of the people I've killed. It's not just the watercrea and her accomplices. It's my prisoners from the six cities, whom I exploded without mercy. It's Verene and Theo's housekeeper, whom I stabbed in the gut and kicked out a window.

And it's the people of Occhia. They died in horrible, bloody terror because of me. Their last moments were nothing but fear and helplessness. And they think I did it on purpose. They didn't understand that I was trying to save them and lost control of my magic. I didn't give them any time to understand.

I knew this already. The watercrea told me I was in the afterlife with everyone who came before. I knew what that meant, and I knew it was why I was in disguise. But I didn't feel it. Not until I saw Ale.

I stumble down the hall, searching for somewhere to hide, and I find a linen closet. I step inside and pull the door shut behind me. My knees give out, and I collapse to the floor, where I curl up in a ball. I take deep, shuddering breaths and put all my energy into willing myself not to vomit. Even when the feeling passes, I just stay there. This is where I belong, because this is the only place I can't hurt anyone—in total darkness, alone.

I'm fine now. In fact, I'm so fine it's almost like I didn't just spend an hour lying on the floor of a linen closet. I'm out now, and I have a plan.

I don't care that this is my former best friend's house. I don't care that it's full of his family—whom I killed—and maybe some of our other people. I don't care about Ale's strange new clothes and his even stranger new ability to talk to people with something that almost resembles confidence. I'm in disguise. None of this has to affect me. I'm here for one reason—to find Marcella. And that's what I'm going to do.

I march into the room full of seamstresses. None of them even look up from their work, which is extremely rude. I sit down on a love seat, next to a young woman whose dark hair is twisted artfully at the nape of her neck. She's busy doing the very intricate work of embroidering a vest. She's rather talented. Not as talented as me, of course.

"Hello," I say, raising my voice over the chatter elsewhere in the room.

She doesn't look up.

I nudge her pointedly with my foot. She looks over.

"Do you need supplies?" she says. "They're in the wardrobe."

I recognize the accented way she speaks Culaire. She's Occhian. My stomach turns, instantly, but then I comprehend that I've never seen her before. I realize with a start that she might have lived and died in Occhia anytime in the last thousand years.

"Is that vest for Signor Morandi?" I say.

I switch to Occhian, which endears me to her. I see a bit of her stiff, distant facade melt away. I think about how overwhelming it must be to get to the afterlife and discover that it's full of everyone who lived in your city—and also, that there were seven other cities you didn't know about, and they're all here, too. Most Occhians lived in the same house their whole life, moving in the same small circle of people, and they're a bit tiresome about experiencing new things.

"Yes, it is," she says. "I'm actually Alessandro's great-great-

great-great-nonna. That's my mamma over there, and her mamma next to her."

She smiles at this, clearly proud. She has Ale's delicate nose and his sweet, innocent smile. For a moment, I'm overwhelmed by another realization—that the youngest in the family now have to contend with not just a couple generations of meddling aunts and uncles and grandparents, but every generation. My soul temporarily leaves my body at the thought.

"You must be looking forward to the wedding," I say.

"He's a lovely boy," she says. "We're so lucky that our family was chosen."

I narrow my eyes, slightly. "To marry someone so powerful is a great honor."

"Indeed," she says.

"I'm very new here, Signora," I say. "And I hope you'll indulge my curiosity—what was the ninth city like for you before? Say... last year?"

I'm speaking more formally now that I know she's hundreds of years old. I'm not usually one for respecting my elders, but I'll swallow my pride temporarily.

"Oh," she says, her eyes becoming distant. "We were in the towers. It's a bit of a blur. There's no need to dwell on it, really. Alessandro has a sway over the veil none of us have. Now that he's here, things are better."

Earlier, the boy on the street told me about a savior called the Eye—someone who freed them all from the veil and its towers. But he never explained how, exactly, the Eye accomplished that.

"I heard that when Alessandro was alive, he was betrothed to someone else," I hear myself saying.

I have no idea why those words chose to come out of my mouth. I wish, instantly, to take them back.

His great-great-great-great-nonna's face darkens. "We don't talk about that here. This is a new city—a better city. And that girl is gone."

"She's...gone?" I say.

"It was prophesied that the veil would come down, and everyone who was in the eight cities would join us here," she says. "Except for her. She and her accomplice went to an eternal punishment. They'll never torment us again."

"Have you seen it for yourself?" I say.

"What?" she says.

"Well, if you haven't seen it for yourself, then you'll never know for certain, right?" I say. "Those evil, murderous girls could be among us right now."

The woman hesitates, the tiniest bit of unease on her face. I laugh, and instantly relieved, she laughs, too.

"What's your name?" she says, with casual curiosity.

"Chiara," I say, and walk away before she can ask about my family, which is what she'll really want to ask questions about.

I approach the wardrobe to fetch some supplies, trying not to be too obvious that I'm scoping out the room. I think I've gotten about as far as I can get engaging with a fellow Occhian who'll know far too much about any family tree I could pretend to be from. I need to sit next to some gossiping girls and eavesdrop. I need to know more about—

I open the wardrobe, and hundreds of small, round objects come pouring out.

Eyes.

The other seamstresses scream as they roll all over the

floor, burying me up to my knees. I scramble, fighting the del-
uge, and slam the wardrobe shut, gasping for breath.

"Why did you do that?" a girl in the corner shrieks, climbing onto her armchair.

"I didn't—" I say.

"The wardrobe gives you whatever you're thinking about,"
another woman says. "It's magic. Didn't you know that?"

Magic. Just like the towers.

"We need to get this cleaned up," another woman says.
"Let's call—"

"No!" I yell.

They all stare at me.

Everyone in this room knows I was just walking around
thinking about eyeballs.

That's . . . not a very normal thing to think about.

"I made this mess," I say, more calmly. "I shall clean it up.
And my name is Chiara, by the way."

Thinking much more careful thoughts now, I open the
wardrobe and discover a large sack waiting for me. As the
women watch in rather disgusted silence, I herd all the eyeballs
into the sack. They're not actually real, although they look very
real, complete with blood smears. They feel more like glass. I
crawl around on the floor, digging under the love seats, until
every last one is accounted for. Then I drag the sack into the
hall. I think it's safe to say that my time in the sewing room
is over.

I spend a moment considering where to put this suspicious bag of eyes. As a child, there was a big trunk in the nursery that I loved to hide in, but the nursery is on the fifth floor,
right across from Ale's bedroom, and I'm not going all the way

up there. I decide instead to go down to the wine cellar and put them in the empty barrel in the corner. That was my hiding place for when I really wanted to win the hiding game. I stopped using it, actually, because Ale could never find me, and his hysterical crying got a bit sad.

The house is getting increasingly busy—we must be drawing closer to the wedding—but I walk with confidence, and no one in the kitchen bothers me as I march over to the wine cellar door and descend. A quick glance around tells me the room is devoid of people. Carved into the walls are tall nooks, arched like cathedral windows and filled with neat grids of absurdly old wine. Just as I hoped, my barrel is still in the corner. I open it and stuff the sack of eyes inside.

Then, up above, the cellar door opens, and I hear a familiar voice.

"I don't think I should drink too much before my wedding, Papá—"

It's Ale. I leap into the barrel, folding myself up. Fortunately, I haven't gained any height since I was twelve—just wider hips. Unfortunately, now that I'm crammed in with a bag of eyes, I can barely close the lid back over my head. I only have a few seconds to situate myself, frantically, before I hear heavy footsteps on the stairs.

I angle my head to look through the small round hole near the top of the barrel, just as Ale's papá comes into view. He's been dead for almost two years, and he looks just as I remember him—a huge, bearded man with a gregarious face. He seems to be already dressed for the wedding, in a sharp black suit with a dark red cravat.

"We're not getting you drunk, Sandro," he's saying, using the nickname he reserved for his son. "But I had been saving this…" He scans the wall of bottles. "For a special occasion. And I never got to open it."

Because he died in the tower, of course. The way Ale described it to me, his papá ran out of the house the second he got his first omen. There was no time to waste on things like goodbyes. He wanted to set an example for everyone else and show us the perfect way to die under the watercrea.

Ale's papá pulls out a bottle of white wine. He glances around, his eyes landing on my barrel, and my heart stops as he comes closer. He sets the bottle down on the lid with a thump that feels very loud to me, and I hear the corkscrew working. Ale comes into my view now as he shuffles over, his hands in his pockets. He looks a bit younger when he's standing with his papá. Ale still gazes at him with the same untainted adoration.

He used to look at me like that, too.

The elder Signor Morandi finishes opening the bottle and turns around. "Look at my son," he says proudly. "All grown up and getting married. And doing such good things for the city."

Ale turns scarlet. "I'm nervous," he whispers.

"Nervous?" his papá says. "About what?"

"It's just so many people," Ale says.

It's the most predictably Ale thing to say. It makes something in my chest twinge.

"So many people who adore you," his papá says. "You're a natural, like I always knew you would be."

Ale shrugs.

"It's not…it's not about the marriage itself, is it?" his papá says. "Because you know you have our blessing. We think you're a great match. You and Ma—"

"They haven't found Emanuela," Ale says.

Crunched up inside the barrel, I stop breathing.

His papá is quiet for a moment. "Still?"

"I mean, there's a lot of catacombs," Ale says. "And she's very good at things like this. Evading capture. And with the two of them together, they're…"

He trails off, and he shudders.

He looks a little bit helpless, and a little bit terrified. He looks exactly like the boy I remember. Every bit of confidence I saw before has been wiped away, just like that.

"The guards will find them," his papá says.

"But what if they don't?" Ale's voice has gotten thin and whispery. "What if—what if she comes here, and she—We should postpone."

"What?" his papá says.

"We should postpone the wedding," Ale says. "Until they've found her. We need to know for sure that she's not here. We need to know for sure that she's not going to—"

He cuts himself off, trembling. Abruptly, a couple tears roll down his face.

"Alessandro." His papá moves forward, putting a bracing hand on Ale's thin shoulder. "She's in the past. It's all in the past. You're here now, with all your family. With me. If she tries to hurt you anymore…she's going to regret it. All right?"

Ale nods, wordlessly. He wipes at his tears.

But he hasn't stopped shaking.

"Now, here." His papá hands him the wine bottle. "Forget

about that demon of a girl. You wanted to do this today as a celebration of the fact that all of the eight cities have joined us in the veil, remember? Think about that. Think about everything you have to look forward to."

Ale takes a little sip from the bottle. "Yes. We should...we should forget about her."

"She'll turn up," his papá says. "And when she does, it will be in chains. She's never going to lay a hand on you again."

He puts his arm around Ale and guides him back up the stairs. They disappear, and the cellar door clicks quietly shut.

And I lie there, my mind whirring.

So this is how it is, then. Ale has a sway over the veil that no one else has. Ale, who beat me here by several months, has found himself in a highly advantageous marriage to the ruler of the afterlife. It's wildly improbable to me that, out of everyone, he caught her eye, but then again, it does make a strange sort of sense. Ale was engaged to me for his entire life. Ale isn't particularly interested in women, but he knows all about being close to someone who's very powerful.

I can imagine just how he would do it. He's a perfect follower—an adviser. He has a steadfast way and a calming presence that would be valuable to anyone. Marcella must have freed everyone from the towers to humor him. There must be a greater plan at work that he doesn't understand.

I know the real reason why he would seek out someone so powerful, of course. He needs her help to stop me. And he thinks that he can just send his new guards out to track me down, and that will be enough.

He thinks it will be that simple to put me out of his mind.

But it's not. That much is obvious. I saw the look on his face when he talked about me. He went right back to being a scared little boy who can't do anything on his own.

Because that's what he is. That's all he'll ever be.

I wait for a few minutes, to be sure he and his papá are gone. Then I slide out of the barrel and creep back up the cellar stairs.

TWELVE

THE VEIL AROUND US HAS DARKENED TO THE DEEP RED OF
evening, and the crowd surrounding the House of Morandi is
starting to grow.

It's almost time for the wedding.

I've retreated to a nearby tower that overlooks the city center. I've been waiting on the stairwell, peering out a narrow slit
of a window, for hours. A lot of decorations were put up when
I was inside the house. There's now a long red carpet stretching from the city street to the front steps of the manor, serving
as an aisle, and an elaborate arch constructed out of ivy leaves
where the couple will stand. Plush chairs are set up in neat lines
for guests, although of course, that's not going to fit everybody
in the ninth city. Most of the chairs are already full of Ale's
family, stretching back generations and all dressed in dark red,
thanks to the seamstresses.

The nearby streets that feed into the city center—eight of
them in total—are packed. Almost everyone is avoiding the
towers, although as I can attest, they'd provide a very good

view. Just as the random man on the street told me earlier, nobody wants to revisit the places where they were imprisoned, even if those places are no longer malicious. All of the newcomers must have been told that my current hiding place is out of fashion. They seem to prefer trying to climb on one another's shoulders, falling over, and causing a ripple of chaos in the festive crowd.

Everybody is dressed, as is apparently typical for the afterlife, in wildly different attire. They mingle and chat and even sing as they pass around bottles of something that's almost certainly alcoholic. They don't seem to mind that arriving earlier to get the best spots also involves a lot of standing around waiting for the show to begin. They have infinite time, I suppose. And this is a big event—unprecedented, perhaps. Their ruler is getting married. This is the kind of thing people will talk about forever. And we really do have forever.

I glance at the window at the very top of the House of Morandi. I know it leads to Ale's bedroom. The curtains are closed, but there's light glowing behind them. I wonder what he's doing right now. Before his wedding to me, he was panicking so much he very nearly fainted. As usual, I had to calm him down. He wouldn't have made it to the altar without me.

As soon as I have the thought, the front doors of the House of Morandi open, and the crowd goes instantly silent—an impressive feat for so many people. Ale's papá steps out, his arm around Ale's shoulders. He kisses Ale on the cheek, then moves off the front steps, leaving Ale to wait underneath the arch alone.

I frown, wondering where Ale's mamma is. She was the most overbearing parent I had ever met. A few days before our wedding, I discovered that she still tucked Ale into bed at night, and expected to do the same once we were married. That was maybe the hardest I've ever laughed in my life. I almost passed out in my parlor, while Ale just sat there looking mortified. I wouldn't be surprised if she's run off with intentions to show up halfway through the wedding and object. I suppose if that happens, I'll just fight her again.

I turn my attention back to Ale. I would have picked a better outfit for him. Sure, the embroidering on his vest, from his great-great-great-great-nonna, will look good from up close. His dark red clothes are well cut, and I'm not too proud to admit that he looks a bit dashing now that he's forcing himself to stand up straight. I always told him he would be more handsome if he did that. But he needs something more dramatic. Like a cloak. He's about to marry the most powerful woman in this city. People should know that.

Then, the worst thing that could possibly have happened happens. The people gathered in the chairs start to sing an Occhian hymn. They're famously slow, and they repeat themselves approximately three hundred times. I recall this particular song as being one of the most tedious of the bunch, although for some reason, hearing it again makes my eyes feel a bit funny. Almost teary. I quickly blink the sensation away and reach for the dagger in my boot, idly checking to make sure that it's still there.

Only then do I hear the footsteps behind me. I try to turn around, but I'm not fast enough. The intruder gets their arm around my neck, dragging me down to the steps and enveloping me in a familiar, highly distracting scent.

"How long did you think that cell was going to hold me, Emanuela?" Verene says.

"I'm—" I struggle against her. "Pretty happy with how long it held you, actually—"

She flips us over, pinning my throat with her elbow. I feel her hand on one of my thighs. Then, abruptly, she moves to the other thigh, her touch searching and not particularly gentle.

She's looking for the dagger. Of course she is. I don't know what I thought she was doing, or why, for a moment, my heart was pounding ferociously.

"Have you looked out the window?" I say.

"I know there's something big going on, but I've been a little concerned with chasing you and fighting off Theo," she hisses. "I had to push him into a giant pool of olives—don't ask me why they had one of those sitting on the streets of the afterlife, but they do. We'll see how long it keeps him away, but until then—"

"You should probably look out the window," I say.

She draws back, giving me a suspicious look. When she gets halfway to her feet and glances outside, she goes very still. She won't recognize the House of Morandi, because she's never been to my city. But she definitely recognizes the boy standing on the front steps. After all, she's the one who cut out his eye.

"Is that...?" she says.

"Alessandro." I sit up, dusting myself off.

"I don't understand," she says. "Didn't he just get here? How is he already getting married? And... to whom?"

"To someone very advantageous," I say.

Verene gives me a wide-eyed look. "He's marrying Marcella? The ruler?"

"Your maman was married, wasn't she?" I say.

"It's just odd," she says. "Alessandro? Really?"

"I know," I say. "He's barely able to shake someone's hand without having a meltdown. But I've been thinking—out of all the people in the afterlife, he does know more about magic than he should, so he must have used that as a way in. Just the fact that he's missing an eye, that he clearly lost violently, would have drawn her attention—"

"I didn't get that vibe from him," she says.

"What vibe?" I say.

"A lady-fancy vibe," she says.

I stare at her.

"Someone who fancies ladies," she says. "Like me."

"Ah," I say.

Now I feel like she's the one staring at me. It feels like she expects me to say something else.

"Someone who courts ladies—" she says.

"Yes, fine," I say. "But it doesn't matter who Alessandro really fancies. As I said, this is an advantageous marriage for him. And a disadvantageous one for us." I give her a significant look. "He's already using her guards to try and hunt us down."

Verene's eyes go back to Ale. They narrow. "Oh."

The hymn finally winds to a halt.

"Oh, indeed," I say, and turn my full attention to the window.

Verene crouches down at my side, her eyes barely peeking over the sill. For a long moment, everything is silent, and the two of us just wait. Everyone in the crowd waits.

I can practically see Ale sweating from here. For a second, his eye darts among the towers that surround him, skimming over the windows. It almost feels like he's looking for me. It almost feels like, even now, he's thinking about me. I duck down a bit farther. I don't want to ruin the surprise.

The crowd at the end of the aisle starts to ripple and part. And then, someone appears. It's a tall, strapping boy dressed in black. There's a purple sash around his waist and gold embroidery on his jacket that all looks very traditionally Occhian. For a second, I can't make myself comprehend who he is. But I know that golden hair. He was renowned for his perfectly styled golden hair.

He starts to walk down the aisle.

A tentative smile spreads across Ale's face as he watches.

"Who is that?" Verene whispers. "A guard?"

"It's . . . Manfredo Campana," I say.

Verene pauses. "And who is that?"

"He's just some boy we grew up with," I say. "Ale was always infatuated with him."

"See, I knew it," Verene says. "About the lady-fancy vibe. And—wait. Are they the ones getting . . . ?"

Manfredo has reached the front steps of the manor. He reaches out and takes one of Ale's hands. He raises it to his mouth and kisses it gently. The two of them turn to face the priest who's emerging from the House of Morandi, and the priest starts to sing.

No one else appears.

Verene turns to me. "So you lied to me. What a surprise."

I just keep staring at the two boys.

"We don't have time for this, Emanuela," Verene says. "We need to find Marcella."

The priest pauses in his song to turn the page of his holy book. Ale and Manfredo sneak a quick glance at each other, then dutifully bow their heads again. In the first row of chairs,

INTO THE MIDNIGHT VOID

Ale's papá is beaming, holding hands with his little sister. His mamma is still nowhere to be seen.

"Are you sure you're not the one infatuated with Alessandro?" Verene says. "Are you making me watch this because you're jealous? Is that it?"

My head snaps over to her. Whatever she sees in my eyes clearly makes her nervous, but she quickly tries to hide it.

"Well?" she says. "Are you?"

"It doesn't make sense," I say. "That—that's his house, Verene. It's some magical replica of his old house in Occhia. And it has magical things inside it. Why would his house be in the city center if he wasn't connected to Marcella in some way?"

"Well," Verene says. "Maybe things in this city aren't the way they used to be. The rulers have been hiding underground. Is it so impossible that they don't have the full story? Change can happen overnight."

"What are you suggesting?" I say.

Verene shrugs. "We're looking for the leader of this place. He's the one dressed like a leader, standing right where a leader would stand."

"But this is Alessandro we're talking about," I say.

"The same Alessandro who helped you destroy Iris?" she says. "The same Alessandro who knows more about magic than any ordinary person should? You said that yourself."

"He could never do this on his own," I assure her. "You don't know him the way I do."

She shrugs again. "It looks to me like he's been dead for quite a while. You didn't know that about him. Anyway, were you going to dramatically interrupt the wedding or something?"

125

I look back out the window just as the priest finishes his song. Ale is already dabbing a little bit of holy water onto Manfredo's cheeks—the traditional Occhian gesture meant to bring about a long and happy marriage. Manfredo returns the deed, and the two take each other's hands again. They turn to face the city, and everyone bursts into raucous applause. All sorts of things spring up from the crowd, tossed wildly into the air—rice and paper confetti and rose petals.

And then, before my eyes, the city center starts to…change. The chairs that the guests are sitting in are all gently pushed to the sides, clearing a large space. Things start to pop up out of the cobblestone, inexplicably. First comes a large banquet table, overstuffed in a way that reminds me of every Occhian wedding I've ever been to. Then, on either side of the clearing, come tiered fountains gushing champagne. Finally, all around the edges, floating instruments appear in the air. They start to play a bouncy tune.

The people of the ninth city flood the clearing. At the center of it all are Ale and Manfredo, beaming at each other. As I watch, Manfredo takes Ale by the lapels of his jacket and pulls him in for a kiss. Then, they're swallowed up by the crowd, and I can't see them anymore.

I just saw about a dozen impossible things happen. But for some reason, the one I'm fixated on is the kiss.

I've never been kissed by anyone in my life. That was something Ale and I had in common. And I was certain that was going to change for me long before it ever changed for him.

Verene is on her feet now. "What just happened? Emanuela, I've never seen anything like that. And I pretended to be a miraculous water-making goddess for two years. How did…?"

She trails off. For her part, she's fixated on one of the

fountains, and how quickly and easily they appeared. Like there was no cost at all.

I stand up. I start walking down the stairs.

"Where are you going?" Verene says.

"To get to the bottom of this," I say.

Thirteen

I'VE SEEN A LOT OF PARTIES IN MY LIFE, BUT I'VE NEVER seen one like this.

No matter how many people approach the banquet table and load up their plates, it stays full. The guests are playing around in the fountains of sparkling wine, splashing it all over the place, and it never runs dry. And the dance floor looks highly treacherous. People are changing partners so quickly I can't keep up. After they dive into the fray, they're shuttled around for a few minutes and spit back out on the other side of the city center. This, I realize, is so all of the thousands and thousands of people crowding the surrounding streets can have a turn.

The surrounding streets, however, are having parties of their own. I keep glancing out the windows as I descend the tower, and from what I can tell, each of the avenues has been themed around one of the eight cities. This must have been what Ale was talking about when he said today is about everyone, not just him.

When Verene and I emerge, we're on the street that leads

directly to the front of the House of Morandi. This street has been decorated in honor of Occhia, and I feel like I've just walked into the biggest wedding reception of all time. It's positively frenetic, full of people who have already had too much to drink and chaotic groups having ten conversations at once. Even though nobody looks particularly withered, physically, I can tell who the oldest family members are. They're holding court, accepting cheek kisses and rapt attention from the others.

The noble houses spent a thousand years intermarrying in our little city. Even with the elaborate family trees the heads of household kept, it's hard for me to fathom how everyone is going to tease out how they're all related. But this is the sort of thing Occhians love. The chance to gather up the entire family is like a dream come true.

My family must be here somewhere. I wonder if the House of Rosa will be dressed in their traditional wedding attire, with matching black roses pinned to their chests.

I wonder if the House of Ragno can show their faces at all, or if I've disgraced the whole line. The last time I saw my papá, he was on the floor of the catacombs, blood pouring out of his empty eye sockets. I wonder if he found my mamma in this maze of a city. I wonder if he told her what I did to him. I wonder how much my little brothers know—they were far too young for everything that happened to them, but it happened nonetheless. Surely none of them were punished for what I did.

Verene pokes me in the arm. "So are you just going to stand here?"

"No," I say quickly. "We're going to ..."

We're going to walk into a party full of people I killed. My hand has drifted to my eye token, making sure it's still firmly around my neck. It doesn't feel like nearly enough.

"We need to find Alessandro," Verene says. "We need to get another look at all this so-called magic."

I glance at the city center. It's only a few steps away, but the way the street is choked with people makes it feel outrageously far.

"Yes," I say. "Yes. We need to—"

And then I see her. In the middle of the crowd, there's a small, stout woman with a touch of gray in her hair. She's alone, dressed in a plain gray dress. She's struggling to hold her own against the people, but she's moving determinedly away from the city center, her dark eyes swiveling around like she's looking for something.

I don't think. I just move. I dive into the throng, dodging elbows until I reach her. I take her by the arm and pull her, despite her protests, to the other side of the street. I push her into the nearest tower and slam the door on us.

"Excuse me," she's saying in fussy Occhian, trying to twist out of my grip. "Do I know you? You can't just—"

I turn to face her, and I take off my token. "Paola."

She goes completely still.

"Paola," I say again. "I…"

I move forward. She takes a step back, and something new creeps into her eyes. Fear.

The last time I saw my nursemaid, she was nothing but a bloody pile of clothes. She was the first person I killed with my magic. She raised me, and when my whole city had turned on me, she was the only one who didn't. And I murdered her with a single blink.

She's right to back away. She's right to be afraid. I don't know what I thought would happen when she saw me again, but I know what must be going through her head—that I've returned to do something even worse than what I already did. That's what everyone is going to think.

"Is it really you?" she whispers.

In a panic, I start to put my token back on. I'll tell her it was a trick. I'll convince her superstitious self that I'm just a demon, so then she won't tell anyone that she saw me.

Paola reaches out and grabs my wrist. "Emanuela."

It's been so long since I've heard anyone say my name like that—the way a native Occhian says it. But now that I've seen the expression on Paola's face, I don't want this. I don't want to hear her voice and look into her eyes and remember how much she suffered because of me. I can't tell what she's thinking as she studies me. I'm frozen there, waiting for her to mention the only thing the two of us could possibly talk about—what happened in that alley in Occhia.

She lets go of my wrist. "I don't like the hair."

"What?" I whisper.

"It's better than it was, of course." She reaches out and pushes it behind my ears. "But it used to be so long and beautiful. What is this supposed to be—some kind of modern fashion statement?"

I hesitate. "Well...I'm not surprised you don't understand, old woman. Look at the state of your hair."

The ghost of a smile flits across her face, and for a moment, it feels like nothing has changed.

"Paola," I say cautiously. "I didn't...what happened—"

"It's not important now," she says, which is such an

impossible thing for someone to say about their own death that I can't comprehend it. "I need to know if—"

Behind me, the handle of the tower door jiggles. I quickly clamp it down.

"It's just my accomplice," I say, because Paola is backing away. "What is it?"

"I need to know if you remember," Paola says.

"Remember what?" I say.

Paola touches something around her neck—her awful blend of protective herbs. She always said it warded off bad spirits and evil magic, and I always said it warded off any chance at having a gross tryst with another old person. Then, reliably, steam started coming out of her ears.

"Alessandro," she says. "He's..."

The doorknob vibrates furiously.

"He's what?" I say, struggling to hold it.

"He's a kind person," Paola says. "He always has been. That boy's heart is just a big, squishy tomato—and he's really stepped into his new role here. You'd be amazed. Everyone loves him."

I squint at her. "And...?"

She opens her mouth, but the doorknob is wrenched out of my hands by someone with a much stronger grip than Verene, and before I know it, a guard in a white coat is pushing his way inside. I just barely manage to get my disguise back over my head, but all of his attention is on Paola.

"There you are, Signora," he says. "We lost you."

Paola's eyes flicker to me, confused by my sudden change in appearance, but quickly putting it together. "I wanted to see my...cousin."

The guard inclines his head politely in my direction, but I

can feel the careful way he searches my face. Like he's trying to compare me to a drawing he's seen. I hold my breath, knowing the limits of my disguise are being tested.

"Would you both like to return to the house?" he says. "You can have a much better view of the party from one of the balconies. I'll fetch you some chairs and refreshments."

"She'll stay," Paola says.

The guard offers her his arm, and she takes it, and in an instant, he's leading her away. The look Paola gives me tells me, in no uncertain terms, not to follow her. I follow her anyway, bewildered. The guard steers Paola firmly back toward the city center, and within seconds, they've disappeared into the crowd.

Someone grabs my arm, and I jump. It's Verene.

"What was that?" she demands. "Who was that woman?"

I pull away from her. "No one."

"Is she going to tell the guards about us?" Verene says.

No. She had something she wanted to tell me. But she's being watched.

"You knew her," Verene insists. "Is she related to Alessandro? Is she—"

"She's my nursemaid, all right?" I say. "She's not going to say a word."

Verene draws back. "Oh."

"Why are you making that face?" I say.

"It's just…the idea of you having a nursemaid," she says. "It's so…"

This is why I don't tell Verene anything about myself. I don't want to hear all the comments about how horrible I must be to everyone who's close to me. I already know.

"Sweet?" she says.

I stare at her blankly. This is the first time in my entire life that someone has referred to anything about me as *sweet*.

Verene seems to realize what she's done. She opens and shuts her mouth like she's trying to figure out how to take it back, but then, she gets the look in her eyes that she always gets when we fight. "What? Are you offended? Good. I was trying to offend you."

"Offended?" I say. "How could I be offended when I already know that I'm the most adorable—"

"Let's go investigate this silly party," she says.

She holds out her hand.

I eye it. "What do you want me to do with that?"

"You're going to sneak away again if I don't—just—" She grabs my hand rather forcefully and drags me off.

We push our way through the crowd, heading toward the city center. It's too treacherous to try to walk through the dancing people, so we skirt around the edge, moving closer to the banquet table. As we push past a girl who's drinking with her friends, her eyes flicker over us, taking in our joined hands. I get a sudden thrill at the thought that she's noticing how pretty we are together. I hope it makes her feel woefully inadequate.

"Where is he?" Verene is peering around. "Shouldn't it be easy to spot him at his own wedding—"

A loud cheer goes up nearby. We turn to see that Ale and Manfredo are standing on top of one of the fountains of champagne. Manfredo is giggling and holding a crystal goblet to Ale's lips, and Ale is chugging for all he's worth.

I've never seen Ale engaged in such debauchery. Finding out I was in the afterlife was bad enough. Seeing this makes me feel like I've gotten stuck inside a dream—and not one of my own dreams.

I pull away from Verene and start walking.

"Where do you think you're going?" she says.

To find out why there are guards keeping my nursemaid under lock and key.

"To investigate the banquet table," I say. "We'll be faster if we split up. Unless you're worried that I'll figure out this mysterious magic before you do."

Verene presses her mouth into a thin, determined line. Then, just as I'd hoped, she whirls around and heads for the champagne fountain. She is, after all, something of an expert on fountains. She put them all over the city of Iris, each one topped with an elaborate statue of herself. I would never admit this to her face, but they were stunning.

I elbow my way through the throng. I bypass the banquet table and scurry around to the back of the house. It's still crowded over here, and I sidle along the ivy-covered wall, making for a door that leads to the servants' quarters.

I'm almost there when someone emerges from the crowd and blocks my way. I tense at my first glimpse of their tall, shadowy form in the dark, but it's not a guard. It's Theo. Verene said something about pushing him into a giant pool of olives earlier. I can see, and smell, the results. There's even a little bit of salt crusted onto his eyelashes.

"Where's Verene?" he says.

"Where indeed?" I say.

"Where's the dagger?" he says.

"Where indeed?" I try to duck around him.

He gets in my way. "What do you think you're doing? You can't just waltz into Marcella's house. Just because she's having some kind of party doesn't mean—"

I think it's safe to assume that Theo hasn't yet seen the front of the manor—nor has he spoken to a single one of its citizens, because charming his way into information doesn't seem like his style. I decide to use this to my advantage.

"I can, and I will," I say. "Unless you want to help me out by telling me everything you know about her—all those secrets your maman only told you."

He glowers at me. "Believe it or not, I don't."

I try to go around him again. He grabs my arm. I kick him strategically, and he makes a shrill noise that draws a bit of attention to us.

"I'm not getting in a fight with you," he says, bent double, through gritted teeth.

"A wise move, because the history suggests that you'll lose," I say.

"And because it will draw entirely too much attention to us, with the way you're lurking suspiciously around the door—"

I reach over and take both his hands. He goes very stiff, like I just put two dead bugs in his grip.

"Now we're not lurking suspiciously," I say. "We're just a pair of young lovers wondering where we can sneak off to."

He's absolutely radiating disgust. But he doesn't pull away, because he knows that I have a point.

"So what were you saying about Marcella?" I say.

"To you?" he says. "Nothing. Besides, it's too loud out here for a proper conversation—I can barely hear you—"

"Then let's go inside," I say.

"Wait—" he says.

But I'm already pulling him through the door. We emerge in the servants' quarters, just as I knew we would. We pass through a narrow hallway into the kitchen, and I feel Theo tense—it's full of people. Judging from the quiet atmosphere, and the way they're all sitting around casually nibbling on candied almonds, these are some of Ale's older relatives who can't handle the raucous nature of the party outside. A couple of them glance at us, but I just keep walking, like my only goal in life is to find a place to do scandalous things with a boy, and they turn away, unconcerned.

I lead us cautiously into the foyer, but there's no one around—not even guards. I decide my best bet will be to start at the very top of the manor and work my way down. Regardless of whatever cover story I have, it will be very hard to explain my presence on the fifth floor, which is a private space for the head of the household and his closest relatives, so I should search it while the party is still in full swing.

Theo rips his hand away from mine. He wipes it off on his pants.

"Oh, come on," I say. "You're wearing gloves. We weren't even properly touching."

"And yet, I still feel slimy," he says.

"Do you ever take those off, by the way?" I say.

"Do I want to explain to people why I have mysterious scars all over my palms?" he says. "No."

I used to have some of those scars, too. So did Verene. We all sliced our hands to feed the vide, but for some of us, doing the ritual healed all the evidence.

"You stopped sending food to Verene," I say. "When we were in prison."

"Well, don't act like you suddenly care about her well-being," Theo says.

"Why did you stop?" I hear myself say.

He gives me an icy look, and I become aware of how accusatory I sounded. Like I'm protective of her.

"I realized she was going to use the napkins to make a rope and climb out," he says deliberately.

"Well—I mean, I figured—" I stammer.

"I know exactly what's going on with you two," he says. "Don't think I don't."

My ears get very hot. The fact that I'm talking to Verene's sibling is suddenly uncomfortably clear.

"I don't concern myself with what you think," I say.

"She does this all the time," he says.

"Does what?" I say, making sure I sound bored.

"Picks up bad habits," he says. "She doesn't have a lot of restraint. She's a flawed person, but she's not a monster. And when it really comes down to it…" He gives me an extremely pointed look. "She's not compatible with one, either."

Without waiting for my response, he pushes past me. He glances around the foyer, then starts up the stairs to the second floor.

I hope he doesn't think he made some scathing declaration with that little speech. I was already well aware of his feelings toward me. And I'm well aware of the fact that Verene loves fighting me, and whenever the two of us start, we can't stop, and things tend to topple down around us. Of course we're not *compatible*. And I'm not going to wonder if he was suggesting any other kind of compatibility, either.

Fine. I am going to wonder. But I'm going to keep those thoughts to myself.

I follow Theo up to the second floor. He's peeking cautiously into the study, clearly wondering if he should venture inside to snoop. But I find myself hesitating in the doorway to the sewing room, looking at the magic wardrobe I discovered earlier. Verene was the one posing on top of Iris's fountains, but Theo designed them for her—including the giant structure in the cathedral that put on an amazing show for their citizens. If this magic is some kind of illusion, he'd be the perfect person to discover it.

I move closer to Theo and tap his shoulder to get his attention. "I found something."

Clearly expecting a trap, he follows me into the sewing room. I gesture at the wardrobe door.

"I don't think so," he says.

"You don't want me to open it," I say. "Trust me."

He stands back and inches the door open. I wait. Despite myself, I'm nosy, and I want to know what he's thinking about. We both stumble back as disgusting black sludge oozes out.

"What is that?" I say. "What were you thinking about?"

"Why is that any of your business?" he says.

"I have reason to believe it's a type of magic that gives you anything you think about," I say.

Theo narrows his eyes at the sludge on the floor. "If that's true...then I suppose this is a physical manifestation of how I feel about you."

"Oh," I say. "That's precious."

Theo shuts the wardrobe. He furrows his brow in concentration. When he opens the door again, a small golden pocket watch tumbles forward. He quickly bends down to catch it.

"I just told you that you could make anything, and you decided to make...a watch?" I say.

"My old one got ruined by olive juice." He's examining it

carefully. "And I like knowing what time it is. But that's neither here nor there, is it? The real question is...where, exactly, did this come from?"

"Is it so surprising?" I say. "Doesn't Marcella's magic do such things?"

"No." He eyes the wardrobe distrustfully. "The magic of the veil doesn't make things for us. It feeds on us. It consumes thoughts and memories to sustain itself. Marcella is... I don't know the details, but she's someone who isn't supposed to be alive anymore. Using magic to sustain herself has a cost. And that cost is, well, other people. That's what the rulers were doing in the eight cities—protecting us from the veil. Or trying to. They were never able to protect us completely."

I think about my omens, crawling mercilessly across my skin, and my gut churns with a sudden sick feeling.

"But Marcella is the only one who can control the magic of the veil, right?" I say. "So this is obviously her doing. She's here somewhere." I pause. "That is, of course, assuming that this magic is...real?"

Theo is quiet. He walks around to the back of the wardrobe. He pushes it away from the wall, slightly, and peeks into the gap. He gets down on his hands and knees and looks underneath. Then he returns to the front, pulling the already open door wider.

"Get inside," he says.

"Me?" I say.

"Do you see any other delinquent girls hanging around here that I could be talking to?" he says. "You're going to stand in there while I shut it and try to create something. And then you can tell me what happens."

"And what if that's...unsafe for me?" I say.

"We'll just have to take that risk," he says.

We stare each other down. Theo is approximately twice my size, but I'm considerably more delinquent. I'd very much like to see him try and get me into this wardrobe against my will.

"Oh, hello! What are you doing in here? The party's outside."

At the familiar voice, I jump out of my skin. When we turn, we find Ale standing in the doorway to the sewing room. His face is a brilliant shade of pink and his dark hair is wet and disheveled from playing around in the fountain. The glass of champagne in his hands is tilted precariously.

"The party's outside," he says again, helpfully.

"We were taking a break," I say slowly.

"Oh, me too," he says. "Do you want to sit down?"

I glance over his shoulder, but Ale's new husband is nowhere to be seen.

"We were just admiring this wardrobe," I say. "The magic inside is—"

Ale stumbles past me and wrenches open the wardrobe door. A dozen bottles of champagne fall out. Half of them break.

"Oops," he says. "Here—here you go—"

He hands me a bottle. He hands Theo a bottle. Then Ale staggers over to the love seat and flops down.

He's not just festively tipsy, I realize abruptly. He's drunk. Ale has always been rather shy around alcohol—far too shy to imbibe this much of it.

"What are your names?" Ale says.

I glance at Theo. He's gone rigid, staring at Ale like he's a ghost. This is, of course, more of a surprise for Theo than it is for me. They haven't seen each other since the day in Iris when Ale lost his eye. Also, they weren't particularly fond of each other. Theo must still have a scar on his side from that knife wound.

"Signor Morandi—" I say.

"Oh, no!" Ale says. "Don't call me that. Just call me Ale*sss*sandro."

He hisses his own name for no apparent reason.

"Ale*sss*sandro—" I say.

He laughs hysterically.

I'd be lying if I said it didn't feel good to make him laugh.

"How does this wardrobe work?" I say. "We're just curious—"

Ale interrupts me by vomiting into his own lap.

I didn't know we could still vomit in the afterlife. That's an unfortunate revelation.

"Ah," Ale says. "I feel much better now."

Then he just sort of sits there. His champagne glass starts to slip out of his hand and, more instinct than decision, I find myself moving forward to catch it.

"Alessandro," I hear myself saying. "Why don't we take you up to your bedroom? You seem like you might need to lie down."

Ale lifts his head, and for the first time, he really seems to look at my face. But there's no recognition in his eye. My disguise is working as intended. To him, I'm just some random girl who's very pretty and holds herself with confidence.

So I don't read too much into the fact that the way he's looking at me is so trusting that it hurts. With the state he's in, he'd probably look at a venomous spider just the same.

"We can go up there if you want," he says. "Then I can show you all my books."

"Sure," I say, setting the champagne glass aside.

I grab his hands and try to pull him up. He obliges me, but it still goes poorly. I feel like I'm trying to support a lanky pile of bones that has no control over itself.

"Look, you have to help me out here—" I say.

Then, to my surprise, Theo intervenes. He ducks in and grabs Ale, throwing Ale's arm around his shoulder with a swiftness that looks professional.

"What?" Theo says in response to the look I'm giving him. "I'm good at transporting drunk people."

"Hello." Ale is peering curiously at his new companion, his neck craned awkwardly due to Theo being on his blind side. "Has anyone ever told you that you smell like olives?"

"We're walking now," Theo says, forcing him toward the door.

"Oh." Ale's eye widens. "You have a very serious way about you. I can be serious, too. We can be serious together—"

He trips over his own feet and pitches toward the floor. Theo catches him with the sixth sense of someone who saw that coming, barely missing a step. I follow them out of the parlor, and we leave the mysterious wardrobe behind to head for a more private area of the house.

FOURTEEN

BY THE TIME WE MAKE IT UP TO THE FIFTH FLOOR, ALE IS singing. I don't recognize the song, and I suspect this is because he invented it. One very boisterous journey later, we finally reach Ale's bedroom, and I stop and turn back to the boys.

"I'll take him inside and make sure he doesn't crack his head open getting into bed," I say to Theo. "You wait out here and keep watch."

Theo gives me a stony look. "This is his house."

"Yes," I say.

"In the middle of the ninth city," he says.

"Yes," I say.

Theo is quiet, and I can see the calculations trying to happen behind his eyes. Despite the fact that Ale is still very preoccupied with his song, now tapping out an erratic beat on Theo's shoulder, there's a lot Theo is unwilling to ask out loud. And that's good, because then he won't realize that I don't have answers. Yet.

"I'll take him inside," I say again.

Theo's face is only getting stonier by the second. "Would he want you to help him?"

The question feels somehow weighted. Theo knows very little about my relationship with Ale, except that we were once accomplices. And I can feel what he's assuming—that I did something horrible to change that. After all, if Ale and I were still on the same side, I'd have no reason to stay in disguise.

"Alessandro." I reach out and grab his hand. "Come here."

I try to pull him away, but Theo won't let go. The look he's giving me is full of suspicion.

"Oh!" Ale says. "This is my room—thank you so much for bringing me here—"

He wiggles away from both of us and barges into his room. I duck through the door in an instant. I'm still not fast enough to stop Theo from following me, but it suddenly felt very important that I be first.

The last time I was in Ale's bedroom was the night I killed the watercrea. She threw him through his balcony door, smashing the whole thing to bits, and when she stepped out to finish him off, I dove at her. One little push over the railing was all it took. But here, the balcony door is smooth and untouched. The whole room is cozy and lived-in, like it's never been in a fight. The bedsheets are rumpled, and as always, there's a towering stack of books on the nightstand and a few scattered at the foot of the bed.

Ale is now lying facedown on that bed. He managed to get out of his pants in the two seconds I wasn't looking. It's probably for the best, because they're in a rancid, vomit-soaked pile on the floor, but nonetheless, this is more of Ale than I wanted to see today. Or ever. I grab a blanket off the nearby armchair and throw it over him.

"Turn onto your side, Alessandro," I say, nudging him.

By the time he manages it, Theo is on the other side of the bed. He neatly slips a pillow up against Ale's back to prevent him from rolling all over the place. Ale lies there like a very content slug.

I glance at the door to his room. My window of time to search the fifth floor is rapidly narrowing.

"It's my wedding night," Ale says.

My head whips back in his direction. He's speaking in Occhian. In his current state, his native language is undoubtedly more comfortable for him, but I can't help but wonder if it means something.

"That reminds me..." I switch to Occhian, too, cautiously. "Could you tell us the story?"

He looks up at me. "What story?"

"The story of how you came here and found your husband," I say. "I've heard it from others, of course. But I want to hear it from you."

"My husband," he murmurs, like he's trying out the words. "My husband is perfect. I've always thought so."

"Yes," I say.

"We knew each other when we were alive," he says. "We weren't together then."

That's an understatement. I'm not sure Ale ever managed to speak a single word to Manfredo. He preferred to stare at his rear end during worship and, occasionally, steal Manfredo's belongings and sniff them. I actually engineered a meeting once by strategically leaving Ale alone in a gazebo with the object of his desire. The second Ale realized that I was gone, he panicked so much that he forgot gazebos had exits. He climbed right over the railing and got stuck in a rosebush. I had to pull him out, laughing hysterically, while Manfredo kicked a ball around the gazebo, oblivious to the suffering going on in front of him.

"How did you come to be together?" I say.

"Well..." Ale says. "First, I died. That was almost a year ago."

My stomach turns. He didn't last long without me. But of course he didn't.

I should have known. I should have felt it somehow.

"How?" I whisper.

"I got sick," he says simply.

I'm about to ask what he means, but then I realize that I already know. Ale had his eye carved out of his head with a dirty knife, and because Occhia was out of water, the wound was never properly cleaned. And then he was all alone, with no one to help him try and salvage it.

"But really, that was a blessing," he says. "Because when I got here, I realized that I have a sway over the veil that no one else does. People wanted me to rule, so now I do. And I think I'm doing a pretty good job. I never imagined—I won't bore you with all the details, but when I was alive, I was a very different sort of person. I was afraid of everything."

"And you're not anymore?" I say.

His face becomes distant, and for a moment, he doesn't answer me. On the other side of the bed, Theo is looking rather agitated by this conversation he can't understand, but I've chosen to pretend I don't see him.

"Something terrible happened to our people," Ale says finally. "You must know that. I could have stopped it, but I was too afraid to do what needed to be done. So I promised myself that I would never again be so afraid that it kept me from acting." He pauses, and the distant look on his face vanishes abruptly, replaced by a little smile. "That includes not being afraid to talk to boys. It's not as hard as I thought, actually. It turns out boys are just people, even if they're so devastatingly handsome you can barely look at them."

He picks idly at a loose thread on his duvet.

What needed to be done. His voice was so cold when he said those words.

"When you say you have a sway over the veil that no one else does...what do you mean?" I say.

He looks surprised that I even have to ask. "I have magic."

"How does it work?" I say.

"It's magic," he says.

His eye flutters closed.

"I've never seen magic like this before," I say.

He doesn't respond. His breathing has turned soft and slow.

For a split second, it occurs to me that in another lifetime, where none of this had happened, I might have one day found myself in this exact same position. I imagine that Ale and I are the ones who are married, as we were always intended to be. I imagine that he got too drunk at one of my parties, and his cousin carted him upstairs, and now I'm hovering over our bed and taking care of him, because he belongs to me. Because he's always belonged to me, and he always will.

I don't want to be the one kissing him. I certainly don't want to be the one fumbling around with him in this bed and doing marriage things. I don't even want his house or his family anymore—not when I know there are much bigger things out there.

And yet, when I imagine the life we could have had, I'm struck with a sudden ache deep inside my chest. It feels disconcertingly like longing. Before I can stop myself, I'm leaning down and pulling the blanket up to cover his shoulders.

"All right," I say. "You don't have to answer any more of my questions. Get some sleep, Ale."

He opens his eye. He looks at me, his gaze glittering in the dim light.

"What did you say?" he says.

"I just..." I start.

But then I realize.

I'm the only one who's ever called him *Ale*. I've been using it since we were children, when my mouth was too small and clumsy to sound out his full name. I liked having my own nickname. I made sure no one else ever took it. Not even his family.

Ale sits up, so abruptly that Theo stumbles back.

"No." The blood is draining out of Ale's face. "No—you're not—you can't be—"

"Well," I say. "It was fun while it lasted."

I reach for my token.

"Don't—" Theo says.

But I've already pulled it off.

"You didn't think you could keep me away forever, did you?" I say.

Ale is trembling, his gaze locked on my face. I know this is his worst nightmare. I know he must be terrified. I know he must be fighting the urge to dissolve into tears, just like he did earlier, when I spied on him in the wine cellar.

"Hello, Emanuela." He manages to sound calm as he forces out the words, but I know it's an illusion.

I put my token safely in my pocket. "Congratulations on the wedding. I'll be honest—I never saw that one coming."

He doesn't say anything. He just watches me.

"You really should get better security," I say. "It wasn't very hard for me to get into your house. How hard do you think it will be for me to figure out what's really going on with your so-called magic? Or do you honestly think you have me fooled? In case you forgot, I already did this dance with Verene, and you certainly remember how that ended."

"This isn't going to be like last time," Ale says.

"And why is that?" I say.

I expect him to stand up. I expect him to run for the door, or call for his guards. But instead, he leans back on his pillows, relaxing into his bed like the drunken newlywed he is.

"Because I know you," he says. "And that means I'm prepared for you. And your..." He gives Theo a sideways look. "New accomplice."

"I'm not—" Theo says, looking highly offended.

"I've heard about Marcella," I say.

"Who?" Ale says.

"There's no need to play coy, Ale," I say. "There's another ruler of this city. A true ruler. And you can pretend all you want, but we both know that it's not you."

Ale says nothing. But then, one corner of his mouth turns up in something that almost looks like a bemused smile.

"Of course you would think that," he says. "But you're wrong. It's only me."

"But—" I say.

Somebody seizes me from behind. I'm dragged backward across the bedroom and thrown up against the wall.

I assume, of course, that Theo has lost his patience and decided to intervene. But as I look wildly around the room, I realize that Theo is still standing next to the bed. He's staring at me with bewilderment on his face.

I struggle, but I can't get free. There's some kind of invisible hand behind me, clutching my cloak so tightly that I'm in danger of choking. My heart thrums with something that I desperately try to tell myself isn't fear. This isn't real. This is all a sham, somehow, and I can fight it.

I fumble with the knots of my cloak and slip free. I whirl around, trying to see what grabbed me. There's nothing on the wall. When I try to turn back, my feet don't cooperate. I look down and discover that somehow, my feet have sunk into the hardwood floor like it's molasses.

"You're not going anywhere, Emanuela," Ale says.

I'm already unbuttoning my boots. I slither out of one, then the other. I grab the dagger as I go, shoving it gracelessly down the front of my shirt, but when I collapse onto my hands and knees to crawl free, the rest of me sinks into the floor, too.

It's the house, I realize all at once. I barely even understand what he's doing, but as long as I'm in his house, he can keep doing it.

So maybe he was a little bit prepared for me, after all. He's forgotten one thing, of course. I'm not some ordinary enemy who can be subdued with simple restraints. I was his best friend.

"If you're going to trap me, does it really have to be on your bedroom floor?" I say. "I don't want to be stuck in here watching you act out your favorite novels with yourself—I'm still scarred from that one time I saw you—"

Almost like a reflex, the floor lets me go. This time, I'm ready for some other part of the room to try and attack me. So I take full advantage of the fact that Ale is momentarily flustered, and I leap up and sprint for the balcony door, grabbing my boots as I go.

As I shove the door open, I feel something cold slip across my belly, and before I know it, the dagger has fallen out of my shirt. My tiny breasts are tragically unskilled at holding things, despite my constant efforts to persuade them into cleavage. I turn around to try and recover it, but Theo is right behind me, and he's gotten there first.

"Don't stop!" He shoves me toward the door. "Go, go—I don't like this one bit—"

Then he collapses, nearly taking me with him. The floor has grabbed him now. It's very clear that I have less than a breath to make my choice. I can risk going back to get the dagger. Or I can seize my chance to escape this magical house where everything bends to Ale's will.

I turn and run, and I throw myself over the balcony railing.

I fall the exact same distance the watercrea fell when I killed her. When I hit the cobblestone, everything goes white hot with pain. Even though I heal instantly, about a dozen of my bones have to snap back into place, and that's almost worse. But I drag myself to my feet, breathless.

I'm reaching for my pocket, intending to put my disguise back on, when I realize that it's too late. There's a couple of party guests standing right in front of me. They're frozen solid midway through bites of delicate spinach tarts, staring at me in confusion and terror.

Before I can say anything, I become aware of a strange

rustling noise behind me. When I turn around, I see that the ivy on the front of the House of Morandi is...moving. It's coming to life, reaching out for me like a dozen skinny arms.

Ale's not going to catch me this easily. Maybe he's the one with magic now. But I still have my own kind of power.

I turn back to the couple. "Move."

They turn and run into the crowd, dropping their plates in their haste. I hear one of them say my name, and in an instant, the temperature of the entire party has changed. I advance, and people scatter out of my way. The ivy snatches at my back, and I march faster, faster, but I refuse to run. I'm not going to let Ale see me run. I hit the banquet table, and it's too long to go around it, so I climb on top, kicking aside a steaming vat of soup. I try to leap down neatly, but the ivy grabs me around the shin, and I face-plant onto the ground, barely wrenching myself free.

Well, maybe I am going to run.

I barrel toward the nearest street, and the people can't flee fast enough. I'm steps away when the ivy seizes me around the ankles. I go down hard, the breath knocked out of me, and for a moment, I feel myself being dragged helplessly backward. I grab at the cobblestones, willing myself not to panic.

But I'm still sliding. And sliding.

And then, all at once, I'm not. For a second, I assume that I've saved myself through some brilliant accident, of course. Then I look up, and I see the girl clutching onto my hands.

I don't know who she is, but I know that she's the most beautiful girl I've ever seen. She's so beautiful that I'm certain she's not real. It doesn't seem right that she's saving me. I should be saving her. I should be sweeping her into my arms and carrying her away. I should be setting her gently on a bed of roses, and pushing her pretty curls out of her face, and touching the charming little freckle she has at the corner of her mouth—

"Are you even going to try and contribute here?" she says. "Come on, Emanuela—kick your feet or something—"

Oh. This isn't a strange girl. It must be Verene in disguise. And I'm lying here like a buffoon, staring at her with my mouth wide open.

I kick my feet, and once I'm actually helping her, she's able to wrestle me out of the ivy's grip. We're up and running, but the ivy grabs at us again. And again. We scramble, pulling each other free in a frantic back-and-forth, but we're barely making an inch of progress at a time.

Then, all at once, I heave Verene forward by the front of her shirt, and the ivy stops. For a moment, we're just lying there on the cobblestone, tangled up in each other and breathing hard. Then I sit up and look behind us.

The ivy is spilling out from the House of Morandi, but when it reaches the edge of our street, it abruptly withers away, like it's lost its will to live.

"The power is strongest in the city center," I realize aloud. "He can't touch us out here."

Verene lifts herself up on one hand. "So I'm guessing you got yourself caught?"

I glance at the window at the top of the House of Morandi— the window that I used to look at every night from my own childhood bedroom. Ale is standing there, looking like nothing but a tall shadow.

Our gazes meet, just for a moment. But then he turns away and disappears.

He doesn't look particularly distressed that I've escaped.

I get to my feet. "We need to run."

I reach down to pull Verene up, and only then do I notice that a necklace with the token of an eye on the end has somehow gotten wrapped around my wrist. At first, I think it's my own, but then I realize that it's hers. At some point during the struggle, I accidentally ripped it off.

For a brief moment, it felt like we were alone on the crowded street—like I'd scared everyone away. When I look up, I find that they're giving us a wide berth, but they're definitely still here. And now, they're not just looking at me. They're looking at the girl sitting on the ground beside me.

"Verene!"

Before I can make a single move, a boy I've never seen before emerges from the crowd. He's dressed elaborately for the party, his fine silk clothes covered in bows and ruffles, and he's visibly shaking.

"You lied to us," he says. "We trusted you, and you were on her side the whole time. You're selfish and evil. You're even worse than she is, you—"

"Be careful." A nearby girl grabs him back. "Don't provoke them, or they might—"

"Why should I worry about that now?" he says. "We're already dead. And based on what I've seen, the Eye is more powerful than they ever were. They were little girls with one magic trick." He gestures around. "Look at everything the Eye can do."

A murmur spreads through the crowd. The people hadn't considered that. But they're considering it now. In an instant, I can hear words darting back and forth in all sorts of languages—proof of how quickly the stories about us have spread between people of every city.

"She was just pretending to be a good person so that we would give her gifts and worship her—"

"It was just about getting attention—"

"In the end, she's no better than her mother, is she?"

The last one is spoken in Culaire, and it could only be coming from a citizen of Iris. It seems somehow louder than all the rest.

Verene hasn't moved from the ground. She's gone very still. She has the helpless look of someone who's watching one of her nightmares unfold in front of her eyes, with no idea how to stop it.

I step in front of her. I lift my chin, and I give the crowd the coldest look I possess.

"Move," I say.

Something flies out of nowhere and hits me in the head. For a second, everything goes black. When my vision returns, I find myself bent double, a shattered champagne glass at my feet. There's pain in my temple, and I reach up and find a trickle of warm blood.

I have no way of knowing who threw it. There are hundreds of people in front of me, and their faces are all blurring together.

"She's not using her magic," someone whispers. "Maybe it really is gone."

"Well, what are we waiting for?" the same boy from before yells. "They can't kill us again!"

He runs at us. And then, everyone is running at us.

The people of the eight cities are no longer cowering and

demure. They're ferocious. I have just enough time to turn back and reach for Verene when they hit me like a wall, and then their hands are everywhere, grabbing at every inch of me they can reach. Somehow, in the midst of all the screaming and shoving, I have enough time to wonder how many of these people I've personally killed. It feels like they've suddenly realized that they have the chance to give that pain back, and I'm suddenly one very small person with a fragile body. There's a gash on my arm and one on my cheek. There are fingers around my neck. There are injuries blossoming across my skin, healing, and then blossoming again, so quickly I can hardly breathe.

But I don't even care about that. All I can think about is Verene. I've got ahold of her, and if I let go, she's going to be swept away from me. I shove us both to the ground, covering her as best I can, and try to crawl. In the dark swarm of people, we're able to disappear, and soon, we find ourselves crawling into an alley. We don't even look back. We help each other to our feet and start to run.

"Wait!" Verene pulls me to a stop as I start to go in a random direction. "This way. I have a surprise for you."

"A...what?" I gasp out.

She tugs me across the street and into the nearest tower. We push into the foyer and slam the door behind us, then stop to catch our breath.

I hold out her token. I wait for her to say something about how I probably ripped it off on purpose, but she doesn't. She takes it without a word, and then she points to something in the middle of the foyer.

It takes a moment for my eyes to adjust, but when they do, I see a boy with golden hair squirming on the floor. His wrists and ankles and mouth are bound. His clothes are wet, like he was, perhaps, traipsing around in a champagne fountain. When he sees us, he goes stiff with fear.

"Well?" Verene says. "What do you think? Will this be helpful?"

I glance over at her. She's shaken by what just happened. I can tell. She's trying to hide it, but something in the way she's looking at me feels like she's seeking reassurance. We have so little at our disposal. We're in desperate need of something helpful.

"You kidnapped Alessandro's husband?" I say. "On their wedding day?"

"Yes," she says, a bit defensively.

I smile. "How very heartless of you."

Verene hesitates. Then, slowly, she smiles, too. The sight of it makes me feel like I've swallowed something delicious and warm.

"I knew you'd like it," she says. "Let's see if he has anything interesting to say."

FIFTEEN

BETWEEN THE TWO OF US, VERENE AND I MANAGE TO GET
Manfredo up the stairs of the tower. We push him into one of
the cells. Verene is the first to enter the room, so it transforms
according to her memory. An instant later, I find myself standing in a replica of the cathedral quarters I lived in when I ruled
the six cities. It's dark and cold, and having just come from
Ale's childhood bedroom, I'm struck by how bare it looks.

"This is the scariest room I can think of," Verene says. "It
never hurts to put your hostage on edge, right?"

I lock the door behind us. Verene pulls Manfredo over to a
far corner of the room. Then we move out of his earshot, so we
can plan our interrogation. She sits down on my desk, just like
she always used to do in the real version of this room. Escaping the mob has ruined her perfect hair and left dirt on her
cheeks. She looks thoroughly bedraggled and, I think, still a bit
trembly.

I want to go back and kill everyone who tried to lay a hand
on her. They have no right to accuse her of being just as bad as

her mother was. They have no idea how hard she worked for the cities. She bled for them, and she killed for them. No one else was willing to do it.

"What?" she says.

I'm staring at her, I realize abruptly.

"You have paper confetti in your hair," I say.

"Well, you're falling out of your shirt," she says.

I glance down. Sure enough, the mob ripped open my blouse. One of the buttons is missing.

"I hope you enjoyed the view while it lasted," I say as I redo the buttons that are left.

She opens her mouth to say something snide, and I wait patiently. She makes a little noise in her throat. Nothing else comes out.

It's very quiet in here. I don't know when it got so oppressively quiet.

"Your brother is—" I say.

"I didn't," she says.

More quiet. Too much quiet.

"I didn't enjoy the view," she says.

"Your brother is trapped in the house, by the way." I want to move on from whatever just happened as quickly as possible, because I'm already feeling unbalanced, and I need our usual rhythm back. "He found me and insisted on coming in with me. So I sacrificed him to save myself, naturally." I pause. "Also, he got the dagger back."

"Did you find out anything more about Marcella?" Verene says.

I don't answer her, but she reads the look on my face entirely too easily.

"Nothing?" she says. "See, I told you. Whatever's going on here, it's all Alessandro. He's found his own way of doing things. Just like I did in Iris—"

"But..." I say.

"But what?" she says.

"Nothing." I don't want to talk about this with her.

"Why is this so hard for you to believe?" she says. "You should know better than anyone that when you come into a strange city, you have to work with the evidence right in front of your face instead of some story the old rulers—"

"He doesn't have what it takes," I say.

Verene goes quiet for a moment, looking puzzled. "What do you mean?"

"He just doesn't," I say. "Is that not obvious? He's too..."

"Too what?" Verene says.

I fumble for the words. I don't even know what I'm trying to say. I don't even know what there is to explain.

Verene slides off the desk. "Whatever, Emanuela. It's obvious that Alessandro is the real threat here. He's clever, and he has magic, and everybody in this city loves him. And if he learned anything from watching me, he's left absolutely no trace of his secrets. But let's hope his husband has gotten close enough to catch a whiff of something."

She walks across the room toward our hostage. And I'm just stuck there, staring at her retreating form. I don't know how to comprehend her words, because I don't even feel like we're talking about the same person. If she had grown up with Ale, she would understand. If she had even seen him talking to his papá in the wine cellar, she would understand.

Verene drags Manfredo back in our direction. She props

him up using pillows from my love seat, so that he's in a slightly more dignified sitting position, then gives me a pointed look.

"So?" she says. "Are you ready to do a successful interrogation, for once?"

I shake myself and approach Manfredo. I walk in a slow circle around him, letting him sweat, and he follows me with his wide brown eyes. Then I crouch down and undo the gag around his mouth.

"You're not supposed to be here," he says in Occhian. "They said you went to eternal punishment."

"Let's speak so our friend here can understand," I say in Culaire. "We'd like to discuss—"

"This could be good, though," he says, switching languages obediently. "I think it might actually be helpful for me to talk to you."

I narrow my eyes. "Is that so?"

"Just...you promise you're not going to go hysterical and kill everyone in the city again, right?" he says. "You can't do that anymore...right?"

I studiously avoid looking over at Verene. That wasn't supposed to come up.

"That's for me to know and you to find out," I say.

"Then we should talk," he says. "About Alessandro."

"Oh, good," I say. "That's what we want to talk about, too."

"You were engaged to him for your whole life," he says.

That wasn't supposed to come up, either.

"One could say that," I say slowly.

"He said you weren't actually romantic," Manfredo says. "He said you were very close friends. Is that true?"

"Do you not believe him?" I say.

"It's just…" Manfredo says. "Every time I saw you two, you were together. He was right by your side at every party. And I always saw you sneaking off and holding hands and things. We didn't exactly run in the same circles when we were alive, did we? But Alessandro loved you. That was one of the only things I knew about him, before. I knew that he was rich, and I knew that he was the one who vomited in front of the whole cathedral during First Rites…and I knew that he loved you."

I try to speak, and I find that I can't. A painful lump, jagged as a bread knife, has taken up residence in my throat.

"Does he ever do magic in front of you?" Verene cuts in.

"Oh, sure," Manfredo says. "It's amazing. He can make anything. He has a sway over the veil that no one else does."

"Is that why you wanted to marry him?" Verene says. "Because he's just so amazing? And he makes you anything you ask for?"

"I mean…" Manfredo says. "He does make me anything I ask for. But that's not why we got together. It was more complicated than that."

"Tell us about it," I manage.

"He'd only been ruling for about a month when he threw this big dinner for a bunch of families from our city," Manfredo says. "He decorated the city center to look like a garden, and there was a hedge maze out back. I decided to wander through while everyone else was finishing up with dessert, and I found him. He was there, alone, sitting on a bench."

If it had been a party in Occhia, he would have been out there with me. Just like Manfredo said, we were always sneaking off together.

"I said hello to him," Manfredo says. "Then he looked at

me, and out of nowhere, he just...confessed. He told me he'd always thought I was the handsomest boy in Occhia, and he'd always wished we were in a city where we could get married. Honestly, I had no idea what to say. Things are different in the afterlife, of course. Getting married used to be about your family line—your heirs, I mean—and now it's something entirely different. I barely even knew him. But I did notice how good-looking he was, and then...well. Then we were together."

I'm at a loss for words. It sounds so unlike Ale. Ale yearns for things from afar. He doesn't take them by the collar and... actually get them.

"What does he spend his days doing?" Verene says. "Tell us about his schedule."

"Um..." Manfredo says. "I don't usually see him until the evening. We have dinner with both of our families. Before that, he's very busy. People come by all day to ask him for things. And he likes to meet them. Especially his favorite authors. You should see how excited he gets when one of them visits. Even if they had most of their memories stolen by the veil, he'll still talk to them for hours."

"And what about the nighttime?" Verene says.

"What about it?" Manfredo says.

"Well, you were engaged, weren't you?" Verene says. "Did you have a habit of spending...quality time together?"

Manfredo goes very quiet. I'm worried Verene is going to have to elaborate when he speaks up again. "That's actually what I wanted to ask you about."

"Me?" I say. "I'd rather you didn't."

"It's just..." he says. "You knew Alessandro very well. Better than anyone."

I wish he would stop saying things like that.

"And?" I say.

"I just want to know if it's true," Manfredo says.

"If what's true?" I say.

"That he's always liked me." Manfredo's voice has gotten small. "That he's always... wanted me."

I stare at him and the sudden, startling vulnerability on his face. I've always thought of Manfredo as a rather simple boy with simple needs. He likes playing sports and doing silly stunts with his friends, and it stands to reason that he wouldn't say no to living in a luxurious manor where he could get end-less sports equipment and endless magic. That, I assumed, was as deep as it went for him.

"You just got married," I say. "Doesn't that tell you what you need to know?"

Someone knocks on the door of our cell. My hands dart toward the gag around Manfredo's neck, and I shove it back over his mouth before he can call for help. Silently, Verene reaches down and slides open my desk drawer. She pulls out two knives.

At the second, more insistent knock, Verene tosses one of the knives to me. Manfredo tries to say something, and I press the blade to his throat.

"Will you just let me in?" A muffled voice comes from the other side of the door. "I'm not the one you have to worry about right now."

It's Theo. Verene makes a face of disgust that would be very unflattering on anyone else. Somehow, she still looks gorgeous.

"Don't talk to him," she whispers.

"Verene," Theo says. "I know you're in there."

"He has the dagger," I whisper.

"I don't care," Verene whispers back. "We're making progress with this interrogation. As soon as we let him in, he's going to ruin that. Don't talk to him."

"But you control this room. We can let him in and restrain him. Two hostages are always better than one."

"*Don't talk to him*," she insists.

"This isn't the subtle hiding place you think it is," Theo says. "The guards saw you. They have this tower surrounded."

"What?" Verene says. "Then how did you get in here?"

So much for not talking to him.

"I have a map of the ninth city and all the secret catacombs," Theo says impatiently.

"How did you get out of Alessandro's house?" I say.

"You caused a distraction by getting attacked by an angry mob," Theo says. "Thanks for that, I suppose. Can you just open the door now? Or is your plan to sit there and wait for the guards to swarm? Because they're about to."

"We happen to be in possession of a bit of leverage," I say. "It seems to me like our best option is to stay safe and let you get snatched up."

"So you don't want to know anything else about Alessandro's magic?" Theo says. "Because I've figured out where it's coming from."

Verene and I exchange a glance. I creep closer to the door and open it a crack. The first thing I look for is any sign of the dagger, and I find it, tucked carefully into Theo's waistband.

"Well?" I say. "The door is open. Tell us what you know."

"Strictly speaking, the magic we're talking about isn't actually Alessandro's," he says. "But you already knew that."

My pulse thrums. "Marcella. You saw her?"

"She's in the house," he says.

"Where?" I say.

"Moving about, as one tends to do in a house," he says, like this is a silly question. "I saw the two of them talking—just for a second. Then I ran for it."

Verene shoves in next to me. "What did she look like?"

"Like an ancient ruler," Theo says impatiently. "Do you see where I'm going with this?"

"Somewhere condescending?" I say.

"We know where she is," he says. "Now we're supposed to capture her."

"Ah," I say. "And you need us to do the dirty work."

"You do have such a talent for it," he says.

Verene has drawn back. "You can't possibly still want to stick to the plan the rulers gave us. This city is different than they said it would be. Alessandro is in charge. He is. And I don't know how Marcella factors into that, but—"

"Oh, that's why we should capture both of them," Theo says. "The rulers can sort that out. All I know is that this magic is too powerful for my comfort. It needs to be contained before something gets... out of control."

Verene doesn't look convinced. But I have to admit that Theo has a point. This magic does need to be contained. Whether it then ends up in the hands of the rulers, or in the hands of someone more deserving... well, that's where we might disagree.

"So what, exactly, are you proposing we do next?" I say. "You just told us this tower is surrounded by guards. And I think it's safe to assume the House of Morandi is, too."

Theo rubs his temples. "How many times do I have to say

this? I have a map of secret catacomb tunnels that can get us out of here and back into the house undetected. And..." He pauses, looking like he's in pain. "Once we're there, and we're sneaking up on them—and if you've behaved thus far—I might, possibly, allow you to have the dagger."

Well, that's a very generous offer. I'm sure it won't come back to bite him.

I turn to my accomplice. "Verene?"

For a moment, she just eyes me, and I know what she's thinking. She's well aware that I don't agree to anything unless I have a secret plan to turn it in my favor, and she's wondering if she's part of that secret plan, or if she's going to end up locked in a cell again.

I have no desire to lock her in a cell again. It's such a strange feeling that I don't even know how to communicate it, but before I can even try, she shrugs.

"Fine," she says. "But we're bringing our friend."

She strides over to Manfredo and tugs him to his feet. As our little trio steps out into the hallway, Theo takes in Manfredo's bindings and sighs.

"Is this hostage actually going to be helpful?" he says. "Because he'll slow us down."

"He's Alessandro's brand-new husband," Verene says. "So, yes. I think he'll be helpful."

"How precious," Theo says, looking unimpressed. "Let's go, then."

We follow him down the dark spiral staircase, listening anxiously for the sound of any guards below. Manfredo's presence does indeed slow us down, but we manage. He only falls and breaks his collarbone once, and it heals instantly, of course.

As we enter the foyer of the tower, our steps become quiet and careful. If I strain my ears, I can hear the buzz of people outside. Theo runs his hands along the red stone wall until he finds the barely perceptible outline of a door, pushing it open. Now that I know these doors are all over the place, I can probably find the next one without his help. He stands back and waits for Verene and I—who are holding Manfredo between us—to go first.

"Wait," Verene says.

I pause halfway through my next step. "What?"

Verene is eyeing her brother, a wary look on her face. "He's lying about something."

I raise my eyebrows. "Is he?"

"Look at the way he's fiddling with his gloves," she says. "He only does that when he's nervous and he thinks I'm not looking."

Theo immediately stops his fiddling. "I'm obviously nervous about having to do this with the two of you. Don't make this about your dramatics. We're so close to actually taking a productive step forward—"

"What's really in this tunnel?" Verene lets go of Manfredo and advances. "Is it the rulers? Did you go and find Maman and tell her—"

"How would I have even had time to do that?" Theo says. "If you're going to accuse me of something, at least make it logical—"

Manfredo chooses that moment to rip himself out of my grip and sprint for the front door of the tower. I realize, entirely too late, that all the stumbling and falling down the stairs has loosened the bonds around his wrists and ankles enough to make this a viable option. By the time I catch up to him, he's already got the door open. I grab the back of his shirt, and when that slips out of my grip, I wrap my arms around his legs. He trips and falls through the door, and I frantically try to subdue him.

As we struggle, I brace myself for the wave of guards surrounding the tower to descend on us. But it doesn't come. I look wildly around the street. It's a blur of noise and movement. The longer I look, the blurrier and noisier it gets.

I grab Manfredo by the hair, dragging him back into the tower, and manage to slam the door after us.

"Verene!" I yell. "Everyone is out looking for us—guards, ordinary people—but they don't know where we are. They don't have us surrounded. It was so frantic I don't even think anyone saw me."

"What?" Verene whirls around. "Then how did Theo find us so quickly?"

"We have our ways," Theo says. "And we decided it would be best to handle this quietly,"

I turn to him. "We?"

Theo knocks on the wall by the secret entrance. A moment later, four guards in white coats and red cravats come charging out of the darkness.

Verene and I put up a good fight. But all the damage we're able to do—and it's not an insignificant amount—heals so quickly that, in the end, we find ourselves on the floor with ropes around our wrists, men on all sides.

Verene shakes her mussed hair out of her face, glaring up at her brother. "I knew it. I knew it was something. Don't ever try and tell me I'm being illogical again, you piece of—"

Theo ignores her. He's busy pulling out his pocket watch. He flips it open and then, for some reason, he starts talking to the face of it.

"It went about as well as we thought it would," he says. "But they're here."

"And you're bringing them in now?" Ale's voice comes out of the watch, small and tinny but unmistakably him. Verene and I are both so startled by this that, for a second, we stop struggling.

"Indeed," Theo says.

"That was so quick," Ale says. "Nice work."

Theo looks a bit flustered. "Don't patronize me with unnecessary compliments. You already apologized for the stabbing thing."

"I wasn't trying to—" Ale says.

Theo shuts the watch.

"Oh," Verene says. "So you and Alessandro are working together now."

"We came to an agreement," Theo says. "We agree that you two need to be stopped."

"But what about his magic?" she says. "What about Marcella? Do you actually know what's going on in this city, or were you just lying to get us out of our cell? Because the things he can do...no one should be able to do things like that. Is he the one who made your watch magic? How? Come on, Theo. You're always the one whose worried about the cost—"

"Frankly," Theo says, "nothing he's doing worries me as much as...this." He gestures to us.

Verene's face turns mutinous. "So power is only a problem when I'm the one who has it."

"Something like that." Theo turns away dismissively.

While this was going on, I've been gnawing on the ropes around my wrists. And now, I've created just enough of a fraying that I'm able to slip one hand free. I have very sharp teeth.

I don't try to fight the guards again. Instead, I lunge up and snatch the dagger out of Theo's waistband.

"Wait!" Theo says as the guards come after me. "Wait—be careful with the dagger—"

I'm already diving behind Manfredo, who's still a bit hampered by the bindings around his wrists—apparently the guards were so busy with us they didn't think to address that. I reach around to press the dagger to Manfredo's neck.

"Tell Alessandro what I'm doing," I say. "Let's see what he thinks about having a little negotiation."

Looking irritated, Theo pulls out the watch again.

"They're making it difficult," he says.

He turns the watch around, and I'm surprised to discover that I can actually see Ale. He's in the study in the House of Morandi, sitting in the ornate desk chair carved with ivy leaves. It hasn't been that long since we left his house—not long enough for him to have sobered up all the way, I'm certain. But he looks like he's making a valiant effort. He's changed into a fresh crimson shirt that's not covered in champagne, and there's a cup of coffee in his hands. His hair is a dead giveaway, though. It looks like it was styled by a group of hyperactive children who also hate him.

Ale doesn't say anything. He looks at Manfredo. Then he looks at me.

"Did Theo tell you what this dagger does?" I say.

"Yes," Ale says evenly.

"Well, I assume you want your husband back unharmed," I say.

The placid expression on his face doesn't change. "I do."

"That puts us in an awkward position," I say. "Because I don't want to let him go."

"It doesn't have to be like this, Emanuela," Ale says.

"What else could it be like?" I say.

Ale takes a long sip of his coffee. Then he sets it down with a clink. He reaches for the watch and delicately turns it around to reveal that there's a man sitting across from him.

I tense before I even take in the man's face, knowing that Ale could have plucked out anyone and everyone who's ever lived. The newcomer is tall and thin, with dark skin and a perfectly groomed beard. He's dressed in a fine suit, but the collar is loose and his tie is around his neck, which is the way I suspect most of the wedding guests look by now.

I don't recognize this man. But something about the elegant lines of his face—and also, strangely, the annoyed look he's giving the watch—feels strikingly familiar.

"Theo?" he says. "Would you care to explain what's happening? Or are you going to slam the watch on us again like someone who was raised with no manners?"

Theo smiles, which makes me realize that I've never seen him truly smile. He and Verene have the exact same dazzling grin. "Sorry, Papa."

I become suddenly aware of how still Verene has gone from her position on the floor. She looks like she's stopped breathing, staring at the man with a blank sort of disbelief on her face.

"It's what we were afraid of, Monsieur Sauveterre," Ale says in the overly polite voice he uses when talking to his elders. "Our misunderstanding has really gotten out of hand. I'm sure we can clear it up once we're all together, but right now...well. This is just Emanuela doing what she does best."

The man hesitates, his dark eyes darting around what little he can see of the tower. "Verene? Are you there?"

I've been around plenty of people who adored Verene and adored screaming her name, but I've never heard anyone say it with quite that much tenderness.

On the floor, Verene doesn't move. The thought of seeing her papa again must have crossed her mind. We've already run into her other parent, after all. But then again, maybe it didn't. Maybe, after six years without him, it was one of those things she didn't even want to let herself imagine.

"Your papa wanted to come to you," Ale says. "Unfortunately, he can't leave the city center. Not yet. It's not safe for him. There's this thing going on, with my magic and the old rulers of the eight cities—we know they're still out there, and now, thanks to Theo we know even more. We're working on it—"

The rage that fills me is sudden and swift. Before I really know what I'm doing, I've let Manfredo go and lunged at Theo, grabbing the watch from his hand.

"You're lying," I say.

"What?" Ale sounds befuddled, which only makes me angrier.

"He can leave anytime he wants," I say. "It's just that if he does, he'll be out of range of your magic, and then you can't use him against us. Against Verene. Is this what you're doing with everyone we cared about? Keeping them trapped in your house?"

"I'm keeping them safe—" Ale says.

"I saw Paola," I say. "I saw her, and I know she's in there—" Theo is trying snatch the watch back from me, and I zigzag frantically around the room. "And you know what else? I saw her try to escape. She made it out of the city center just fine. But then, your guards dragged her back."

A little furrow appears between Ale's eyebrows. "Is that what you think happened?"

I sprint up the stairs, duck into a cell, and slam the door. I conjure up a lock and slide the deadbolt into place.

"I know it's what happened," I say. "You've sold us all out to Marcella. You're letting her hold the people in our lives hostage so she can use them as tools against us. And you know what it's like to lose your father, Ale. You knew how much it would overwhelm Verene to see him again. And now, you're going to just stand by and let her be manipulated like this—"

"Let me explain something to you, Emanuela." Ale is on his feet now, too. I hear Verene and Theo's papa say something in the background, but Ale has already left the study. "The people I'm supposedly holding hostage? The people the two of you supposedly cared about? They want to be here, in the city center, with me. Because they can't live normal lives. They can't go onto the streets and be among ordinary people and pretend they don't know the things they know. You murdered your nursemaid. She was trying to help you—she was always trying to help you—and you blew her head off. She has nowhere else to go. She has no one else who understands the kind of scars you leave on a person."

I open my mouth. I shut it.

"And this thing you keep saying, about someone called Marcella?" Ale says. "I don't know who that's supposed to be, but you need to let it go. This is my city, and it's being ruled by my magic. Do you understand?"

He's shut himself in a dimly lit room somewhere in the house—I can see the wooden panels of the door behind him. Somehow, just from the look on his face, I know exactly how hard he's clutching his watch. Almost as hard as I'm clutching mine.

"So you've really changed," I say. "You're practically a new person."

"Yes," he says. "I am."

"A new person who's terrified of his own husband," I say. "Manfredo told me how timid you are around him. And that's why you got drunk and snuck off during your own party, of course. You probably should have warned him that you'll never actually have a wedding night, because you'll never be able to work up the nerve."

Perhaps, for a second, Ale forgot how many soft, vulnerable parts he has, and how good I am at striking them, but he's remembered now. For a moment, he's just frozen there, mouth half-open, and I let us both hang in that silence. Returning to his house and seeing his face and drinking Occhian coffee all felt familiar. But nothing feels more familiar than this.

"Anyway," I say. "We can keep doing this dance, if you insist. But you must know that I'm going to find out the truth. So you might as well—"

"Do you feel better about yourself now?" Ale says.

"What?" I'm so taken aback that the word comes out of my mouth before I've fully processed what he said.

"Great," he says. "I'm so glad I could help. See you soon, Emanuela."

He shuts his watch, leaving me alone to stare at an ordinary clock face. Only then do I look up and realize that the cell around me has transformed into one of my memories. I'm standing in a small, narrow room with red carpet. At the far side is an altar covered in flickering candles. Against one wall is a gold screen with tiny holes in it, revealing the suggestion of an identical room on the other side. It even smells just as I remember it, heavy and full of incense.

This is the prayer room in the Occhian cathedral where Ale and I gathered before our wedding. That was the last time our lives were the way they'd always been.

That was the moment I was supposed to tell him about my hidden omen. That was my final chance before we were officially joined for life. And I didn't take it.

There's an ominous scraping noise behind me, as I turn around just as the door falls completely off its hinges with a loud crash. Four guards are standing there, tools in their hands. It looks like they were rather prepared for the possibility of me locking myself in a cell. One of them tosses a loop of rope over my head and yanks so hard that I lose my balance. I struggle on the stairs as they drag me out, clawing at the doorway, but the men's hands are rougher than before. They've clearly lost their patience with me.

The dagger falls out of my hands as they drag me to my feet. As I struggle to grab it back, I feel something else slip out of my pocket. My eye token.

It hits the floor with a soft ping. And it bursts into black flames.

Not just a little flicker of them. A whole column shoots up to the ceiling, and I barely manage to leap out of the way. The flames catch in an instant, spreading out to engulf the whole hallway. And the guards. Just like that, they're all scattering, trying to put out the fire that's viciously eating up their fine white jackets.

Well, my little trinket is even more useful than I thought. I hope Ale isn't too disappointed when his guards come crawling back, traumatized and empty-handed. If there's one thing he should know about me by now, it's that I always find a way to get what I want.

I scoop up the dagger, which is already hot from being so close to the fire. Then I turn and run down the stairs.

SIXTEEN

WHEN I REACH THE FOYER OF THE TOWER, VERENE IS ON her feet.

"What did you do?" she demands.

But she doesn't sound angry. She sounds almost like she's proud of me.

I tear at the bindings around her wrists, undoing the knots in record time. "Let's go."

We turn to the secret door that will lead us into the catacombs, and we find Theo blocking our way.

"Move," Verene says.

"Verene, wait," Theo says. "Just wait. Before you do anything else, just listen—"

"I don't want to listen to you," Verene says. "First, you were on Maman's side—not that that's surprising. But now you're trying to turn Papa against me? Before I even get the chance to talk to him again?"

Something almost like hurt flashes across Theo's face. "You don't really think I was *on Maman's side*, do you? After what

she did to us? She had useful information, didn't she? And...
look, you wouldn't understand, because she was always so
lenient with you—"

"Lenient?" Verene says. "What are you talking about? She
was always with you, giving you all the special information and
special lessons, and she left me locked in my room. She won't
even look at me anymore—"

"Because you killed her!" Theo says.

"So you would have rather I fought you, like she told us to?"
Verene says. "We can still do that. We have a dagger that will
get the job done. Is that what you want?"

The pocket watch warms unexpectedly in my hand. When
I realize what must be happening—I'm being contacted—my
first instinct is not to answer. But then I decide that I want Ale
to hear the fire upstairs roaring and the guards screaming, so I
back away and open the watch.

It's not Ale. It's Verene and Theo's papa. He looks harried,
and something tells me he might have snuck this watch away
from Ale. I don't think Ale would have given it up easily.

"Oh, hello," I say.

He fixes me with a stern look. "I've heard a lot about you."

"All good things, I'm sure," I say, ignoring the sudden flutter
of nervousness in my stomach. I have no reason to be nervous
about meeting the man who raised Verene—and no reason to
care that he already has an opinion of me. Everyone does.

"Let me talk to my children," he says.

He tries to make it into a command, but on the last word,
his voice slips into something that sounds much closer to desperation. And instead of shutting the watch and carrying on,
which is what I should do, I find myself turning toward Verene.

"I want you to think," Theo is saying now. "Think about what you really want here, Verene. Because I want to do what's best for the cities. I don't want to chase some impossible solution that will never be real, or burn everything down just so that I, personally, can be in charge."

"You're such a martyr," Verene says mockingly. "It must be so hard for you, having to make the *practical* decision to sacrifice me all the time."

"Verene—" I move closer to her, holding the watch out.

"If I don't do something, you're going to take things too far," Theo says. "You always do. If you could just…if you could just stop long enough to see things from someone else's perspective, and think for two seconds instead of trampling over everything—"

"I killed Maman for you." Verene's voice is loud. "For us. I would have done anything for us, no matter the cost. You've never cared about me the way I care about you."

Theo goes quiet. Verene does, too. I don't think she meant to say that quite so bluntly. In the watch face, her papa has gone deathly quiet.

"Fine," Theo says finally. "If that's what you want to believe."

"It's true," she says.

"Yes," Theo says. "Fine. It was all just me biding my time until I could turn on you and do everything my way. That's why I cleaned Maman's blood off the floor of her study, because you couldn't look at what you'd done. That's why I carried your drunken self to bed every night and stayed with you so you wouldn't have nightmares. That's why I spent months building your fountains—"

"Stop trying to make me feel guilty!" Verene screams.

"That's not what I'm doing!" he says. "I'm telling you that you make it so hard to care about you! Everything you do ends up a mess, and I always have to clean it up. Don't blame me for the fact that everyone in this city wants you locked up. You're just mad because they've finally seen your real self, and they've realized how impossible you are to love."

Verene draws back. She looks stricken.

Theo hesitates, taking in the look on her face. He opens his mouth, like he's about to take it back, but then he shuts it. I watch him determinedly swallow down any hint of regret.

When I glance down at the watch in my hand, it's clear that their papa has heard every word. He's perfectly still, his face uncertain, like he's waiting for one of them to say something else—like he can't possibly comprehend that being the end of the conversation.

But Verene doesn't say another word. She marches for the secret door, shoving her way past Theo. He doesn't try to stop her.

I drop the watch on the floor, because for all I know, Ale has a way to track it, and I race after Verene.

Verene grabs a lantern off the wall, and we walk. And walk. Just as I'm about to ask her where, exactly, she thinks we're going, she stops, and I realize we're at a familiar staircase. It's where her maman first led us when we entered the ninth city.

Verene sits down on the bottom step, and I sit next to her, leaving a very careful amount of space between us. Despite the fact that I'm in the afterlife, and I don't seem to need food or sleep, I'm exhausted. But we don't have time to rest. We have to figure out what to do now that we have no more information and no hostage. The only thing we have is the dagger I've now put in my boot.

I must admit, it's nice not to be alone. I'm getting a bit too comfortable with Verene's presence at my side. I'm probably going to regret it the next time she turns on me, but for right now, I decide not to care.

"Really, Theo changing sides isn't much of a loss," I say. "Seeing as he wasn't properly on our side to begin with—"

Verene makes a very unattractive sniffing sound. When I look over, I discover that there are tears streaming down her face. Verene has cried in front of me once before. But we were in our dark prison cell. I didn't have to see it.

I inch away and consider standing up, pretending I don't see this. Maybe we've allied for long enough to get out of a few scrapes together, and maybe I've even met both of her parents now, but I'm certain she doesn't want me around for something this unflattering and private.

"He doesn't understand," she whispers.

I hesitate.

"He acts like…" She wipes at her eyes. "He acts like I have no reasons for anything I do. Like I'm an irrational monster who ruins things just to ruin them. But I was always trying to help people. I was trying to help Iris, or one of the other cities— and no, it was never neat and orderly, but it was the best way I knew how. And yes, maybe I liked helping them when I, personally, got to be in charge. Maybe I like being the center of attention. Is that so wrong?"

"I don't think so," I say quietly.

"He's right, though," she says. "I am impossible to love. Because I'm not perfect, and that's what people want me to be. They want a girl who looks perfect, and acts perfect, and—"

"He's not right," I say.

Verene glances up at me. Her eyes are hesitant and glittering with tears and excruciatingly vulnerable.

I wonder if I should tell her about what Theo said to me when the two of us were alone in the House of Morandi. He made it very clear that he doesn't think his sister is a monster. But I've never seen Verene quite this miserable, and something about it is…comforting.

"Why do you even want everyone to love you?" I say. "Why is that the most important thing you think you could ever achieve?"

"Because if everyone loves me, that means I've done things right," she says. "That means I've made a difference. And then…then I'll…"

She trails off. She looks like her thoughts are too big and tangled for her to explain.

"Then you'll live in their heads forever," I say. "And that's what you need. Because it doesn't take much to erase one girl. So you have to be bigger than just one girl."

For a long moment, Verene is quiet. I think I've made a mistake. I think I've said too much.

"Yes," she says.

Our eyes meet, and my heart flutters up into my throat. She's looking at me like I've just put into words something that she's always felt but never been able to say out loud—something she would never dare to say out loud anyway, because no one else would ever understand.

Then she looks away, so abruptly that I worry I did something wrong. She sniffs again, wiping her nose.

"That fire back there," she says. "How did you start it? It looked almost magical."

"Oh, that little trick?" I say. "It came from my eye token. It fell on the floor, and that was all it took. Do you think it has something to do with what the rulers said about their magic? How their magic repels Marcella's, and vice versa?"

Verene pulls her own token out of her pocket and spends a long moment examining it. When she speaks, her voice has gotten much quieter. "What do you think this token is made out of?"

"Metal," I say.

"What sort of metal?" she says.

She holds out the token like she wants me to sniff it. So I do, cautiously.

I would know the smell of iron anywhere. Verene and I spent a month in a cell that smelled like nothing but iron.

And then we're both on our feet.

"What does it mean?" Verene says, her voice hushed.

I think about something the watercrea said when they first captured us. She looked right at Verene and told her that everything that's happening can be traced directly back to her actions.

"It means we don't have the full story," I say. "But we're going to get it."

And then we're walking. After several very wrong, very confusing turns, we find the door that leads to the tiny metal box the rulers use to access their hideout. We step inside and quickly realize what makes this a hideout—the box can only be operated from down below.

So we start banging on the floor. Obnoxiously.

"We're back!" I yell. "We captured Marcella!"

We wait. Nothing happens. So we keep banging.

Eventually, there's a loud squeal, and the box starts to descend. Verene and I brace ourselves, vibrating with tension. The moment the entrance hall comes into view, we slither free, moving quickly.

The watercrea is there waiting for us, but she looks...odd.

Her dark hair is loose and disheveled, and her black robe is askew. She's frantically trying to straighten it even as we walk toward her. It takes me a moment to realize that, of course, we surprised her. The only reason the watercrea looks odd to me is because she looks less like a pristine, untouchable being and more like a normal human. I don't like seeing her like this. It's unnerving.

But it doesn't stop me from pulling the dagger out and putting the point of it to her throat.

"I lied," I say. "We're just here to ask you a few more questions."

The watercrea eyes the dagger hovering in front of her neck. "That's not the weapon we gave you. It's a fake."

I hesitate. "What—"

She grabs it from me and immediately tosses it onto the floor, like it burned her. "Marcella's handiwork, I see."

So the real one must still be somewhere in the House of Morandi. Something ugly and resentful stews in my belly. I can't believe Ale thought of that, too.

One of the other rulers scurries out from the adjoining room. She uses a gloved hand to scoop up the fake dagger and drops it into a bucket. An iron bucket.

"So?" the watercrea says. "Why are you back here? Why haven't you done what we asked?"

I narrow my eyes at her. "What…is…Marcella, exactly?"

"She's a person," the watercrea says.

"Is she?" I say.

The watercrea gives me an enigmatic look that I don't particularly like. "She was. Once."

"And you weren't going to…tell us that?" I say. "Don't you think that would have been helpful to know?"

The watercrea turns and walks back into the meeting room. Verene and I exchange a glance and follow her. Spread out on the large table shaped like an eye is some sort of card game that's clearly in progress. Two of the rulers seem to have abandoned their hands, scattering when we arrived. But Lucinde is still sitting there, her back straight and her face tense. Her dark curly hair is still tied artfully back and perfect, but she's dressed in a very plain gray gown. I could walk past her on the street and think she was just an ordinary noblewoman.

I don't like seeing the rulers like this. They spent a thousand years locking people up and taking their blood, and they've never shown a hint of remorse for making us follow their nonsensical rules. I don't like knowing that they've been sitting around playing cards. I understand, of course, because I was also immortal and isolated, and it leaves one with not much to do. But it makes me very uncomfortable *how much* I understand.

The watercrea sits down in her fancy chair. She deals out a few cards, and Lucinde observes quietly. She sets down a few cards of her own.

I lean over the table and aggressively mess up their game. They both look at me like I'm a mild annoyance.

"We know what Marcella is," I say. "She's the...she's the *thing*. The thing that was imprisoned at the bottom of the catacombs. The thing that Verene let out by accident."

Lucinde's eyes flicker to her daughter, who's still hovering in the doorway, but she says nothing.

"We called it the vide," I say. "We thought it was just... I don't know. A ghost. But it's Marcella. And Marcella hasn't been in the afterlife the whole time. She only came back last year, and that's why things are so different for everyone up there. Because she's returned, and she's working with—did you know?"

"Know what?" the watercrea says.

I stare her down. "Did you know that I was going to walk into the afterlife and find the boy who used to be my betrothed ruling it? He has magic. Or he says he does. But it's coming from the vide, isn't it? When I left him last year, he was in the catacombs, and he must have…he must have captured it, somehow, and he's getting it to do magic for him. Did you know any of that?"

The watercrea is silent. But her mouth twitches upward, the tiniest bit. Like she thinks this is funny.

"What do you really want from us?" I say. "What do you want from any of us? What has this all been for?"

The watercrea sets down her cards. "Lucinde, show them out."

"What?" I demand. "No. You're going to tell us—"

Then, all the rulers have reappeared in a sudden mass of black robes. They push us through the entrance hall and toward the metal box. We fight, but we're surrounded. They shove us in, and I cling to the doorframe, struggling. Lucinde squeezes in with us and pries my hands off. And then it's just me and Verene, alone with her, as the box starts to move up. Lucinde stands as far away from us as she can get, her hands folded over her gray skirts.

I fume quietly. I expect Verene to say nothing, because she already tried talking with her maman, and she didn't get very far, but after a few moments, she speaks up.

"Aren't you going to ask where Theo is?" she says.

Lucinde doesn't look up. "I know you two weren't getting along."

"Papa is up there," Verene says. "Looking for us."

Lucinde's gaze snaps to her daughter. I watch a dozen questions fly across her face, but all she says is a single, very quiet word. "Good."

"It's not good," Verene says. "He's not even going to recognize me. Not after everything that's happened."

Lucinde says nothing. She sinks back into being unreadable, and the rest of the ride is extremely silent. Lucinde walks us all the way back to the bottom of the staircase. The moment we reach it, Verene doesn't linger. I'm hovering there, shivering in the cold air and desperate to get something else out of the one ruler we have at our disposal, but Verene immediately turns to go.

"Verene," her maman says.

Verene stops with her foot on the first stair. I can tell that she's already braced for the same thing she got before—nothing. But she just can't stop herself from turning back.

Lucinde glances down the dark hallway. Then she turns back to us, her hands still folded over her skirts. "We lied to you. But I'm going to tell you the truth now."

I don't speak. I don't even breathe. I'm convinced that the slightest shift in my expression is going to make this ancient woman change her mind.

"Long ago, the cities were a very different sort of place," Lucinde says. "We didn't have a veil at all. But we had magic. Everyone had magic."

"Everyone?" Verene breathes.

"Not much," Lucinde says. "But a little. It was just a part of who we were, like the air we breathed. But then someone discovered a ritual that allowed her to take the magic from another and grow her own power. Can you guess what that ritual was?"

My stomach churns.

"Marcella was always like that," Lucinde says. "She was never satisfied with what she had—she always needed more. The nine of us were already rulers back then, in a sense. We used our magic to distribute water to our cities, but things were quite different. Peaceful. And we were young. Most of us had only recently inherited our positions from our mothers. It took us...too long to realize what Marcella was doing—and what it was doing to all of us."

"What do you mean?" Verene says.

"It started with her," Lucinde says. "But it spread. People found out they could get more magic for themselves, and all they had to do was take it from someone else. We were naive. We thought the violence would remain isolated. We thought there would never be enough people willing to do such a cruel thing for their own gain—not enough people to truly threaten our way of life. But there were. So we tried to make it stop by going after their leader. We killed Marcella—or we tried to. And that was when it happened."

"The veil?" I whisper.

"Marcella tried to use her magic to make herself unkillable," Lucinde says. "And her magic responded by creating this—a city forever suspended in the afterlife. We managed to get Marcella into a prison, but as long as she exists, so will the veil. There's nothing but her magic here, all around us, and she's the only one who can control it. And it's always feeding. Because it always wants more."

I'm frozen, half-convinced this is all an elaborate lie. It seems truly inconceivable that after spending my entire life wondering where my city came from and why it was the way it was, one of the rulers, of all people, would tell me the truth. This is exactly what I was looking for when I took the other six captive—an explanation.

And I'm terrified to know what the catch is.

"So?" I say. "What did you lie to us about?"

Lucinde sighs. "We told you that we want you to capture Marcella. But that wasn't true. We want you to destroy her. That's why we had no hesitations about setting you loose on the ninth city. You've destroyed everything else. We thought you would destroy this, too."

"Well...I suppose I see your reasoning for that," I say.

And I suppose Theo, who is allegedly her favorite child, was saddled with the doomed mission of following us around and trying to keep us in check. That seems about right for the rulers, though. We're all nothing but the means to an end.

"But how would we even destroy Marcella?" Verene says. "Is it possible?"

"The dagger," Lucinde says. "We told you it's a powerful weapon that can injure someone of your choice, but that was also a lie. The only person the dagger can injure is Marcella. It's infused with all of the magic the eight of us had left. If it so much as touches Marcella, it will destroy her. And that will destroy the veil itself."

Silence.

"And...then what?" I say.

"We don't know," Lucinde says.

"What do you mean?" Verene says in a low voice.

"Technically, we're not alive, but we're also not dead," Lucinde says. "This isn't death. We're trapped in an unnatural afterlife created by Marcella to sustain herself. So if it's destroyed…"

"Then we're all going to die?" Verene says.

Lucinde shrugs.

"But you know what it would be like if we truly died," I say slowly. "Don't you? You know what would come after?"

"No," Lucinde says. "Do you see now why we kept the eight cities the way they were for a thousand years? We were trying to keep Marcella from getting all of us under her domain. We intended to leave her in that prison, letting the iron weaken her, until she wasted away entirely. We needed to keep our people alive so that when it all disappeared… there would still be something left."

A slow, cold knot forms in my chest.

"When we released the vide…" Verene says. "She wanted our blood. Why did she want our blood?"

"For the same reason someone would drink small doses of poison to become immune," Lucinde says. "When you freed her, she was probably so weak she could barely sustain herself in the domain of the living. Did she, perhaps, allow you to access some temporary magic in exchange for your blood? She was always smart enough to manipulate other people while making them think they were in control."

"We made her stronger," I say. "And Ale…he must have brought her back here. To her domain. And in return, she's doing magic for him."

"And she's getting even stronger," Lucinde says.

"What will happen when she gets so strong that he can't contain her?" Verene says.

"She will consume until there's nothing left," Lucinde says. "At this point, to speak of her as a human is…probably inaccurate. We've reduced her to her most basic instinct—the one we all share."

"She wants to survive," I say without hesitation.

"Yes," Lucinde says. "That's who she is. That's all she is."

"So if we destroy Marcella, we're all going to die," I say. "And if Marcella takes over, we're all going to die. So what do you really want to tell us? The other way?"

Lucinde looks at me, and I know, in an instant, what she's going to say.

"There is no other way," she says.

"No," I say. "You must have another plan. Your only plan can't be to destroy her and let us all die."

"We have no choice," Lucinde says. "I just wish…"

Her eyes fall on Verene, and for a moment, she's silent.

I can feel Verene holding her breath.

"I just wish you had been able to control yourself," Lucinde says.

She turns on her heel, and a moment later, she's disappeared back into the shadows of the catacombs.

SEVENTEEN

FOR A LONG MOMENT, WE STAND AT THE BOTTOM OF THE catacomb steps in complete silence.

Then Verene clears her throat. "Just another warm and fuzzy conversation with my maman. Can you tell where Theo gets it?"

I look at her warily, wondering if she's trying to hold back more tears, but her face is dry. She looks completely fine. She looks more fine than I feel.

"So," she says. "Now that we know—"

"What are we going to do?" I hear myself blurt.

Verene goes quiet.

"I mean—" I say. "Obviously, I'm not too worried about all of this business with the veil and Marcella. We'll figure something out. But if—if we can't, then—then we're all going to—"

I cut myself off. I don't want her to know that I'm panicking. I mean, I'm not panicking. But my thoughts are coming very quickly, and most of them are the same five words, over and over:

There is no other way.

Verene sweeps forward, and in a moment, both her hands

are on my shoulders. She leans down, bringing her face close to mine, and I go stiff with bewilderment.

"We are not going to die," she says.

She says it with the same conviction she once used to give her righteous speeches against me—the conviction that makes it impossible for people not to believe her. And in this moment, it's impossible for me not to believe her, too, and I find myself nodding.

"I know what we're going to do," she says.

"You do?" I say, breathless.

"We're going to go back to Alessandro," she says. "We're going to find where he's keeping the vide, and then we're going to win it over to our side. And then, we're going to control it."

"Control it?" I say. "But—"

"Maman said she'll keep gaining power until she's too strong to be contained," Verene says. "But maybe not if we're the ones controlling her. Think about how easy it was for me to control my magic, when we were alive. I think Maman is underestimating me. I think I can do it." She pauses, and her jaw tightens. "I know I can do it."

"But I couldn't control my magic," I whisper.

Verene's eyes flicker over my face. "I can teach you."

"What?" I say.

"If you let me..." she says. "I can help you. And we can do it. Together."

I pull away, overwhelmed by her presence.

"But you don't want to rule with me," I say. "Everyone will be terrified of you. It will be like it was at the front of the House of Morandi, when they all attacked us. All of the time."

Verene is already heading up the stairs. She turns back to stare me down, so intently that I feel myself start to shiver.

"I don't care about that anymore," she says. "We both know there will come a time when Alessandro can't handle this power. But that time will never come for us. We're going to rule this city. They can hate us all they want, but we're the only ones who really have what it takes."

Hearing those words come out of her mouth does unspeakable things to my body. I didn't realize how much I wanted her to say that until she said it. Even though I'm, technically, in the afterlife, I've never felt so alive.

"Then let's go," I say. "But not this way." I reach over and take her hand to pull her elsewhere in the catacombs. "I have an idea."

By the time we sneak back into the ninth city, dressed in new black cloaks with our supplies in hand, night has fallen. The streets are as crowded as ever, but there's a very different feel to the way people are moving. They don't seem like they're frantically searching for the dangerous girls who've invaded their paradise. They seem much more like they did when I first set foot in this place—festive and bustling, moving about with the cheerful, unbothered energy of souls who have an eternity to do all the things they want to do.

It doesn't take long for us to realize why. A group of friends who clearly overindulged at the wedding are lying in the street, staring peacefully up at the dark veil overhead, and as we skirt around them, I hear one of the girls speak.

"I can't believe the Eye caught them so quickly. After a year of her terrorizing our city, he ended it just like that."

"Of course he did," the boy sprawled out next to her says. "He's so powerful it's almost scary. Almost. He's too handsome to be scary."

"He literally just got married! Stop pretending you have a chance!" His friend shrieks with laughter that quickly fades into the buzz of the crowd as we pass them by.

Verene and I exchange a glance.

"So this is Theo and Alessandro's idea of *handling things quietly*," I mutter. "How embarrassing it will be when the truth comes out."

Verene gives me a smile that's so devilish I very nearly pass out.

Around the next corner, we find ourselves on a very colorful street. There are stalls set up all along the way, each one being visited by a flock of people. A nearby vendor hands me a rose, and when I sniff it, I realize it's made of sugar. I wait for him to ask for payment—some trade in return—but he doesn't.

I suppose people don't need payment. They have everything they could ever need. This is all for fun. I drop the rose on the street, because I'm not going to eat it. I haven't eaten in almost a year.

"Hello, hello!" A second later, a woman in a purple gown lunges over to stop us in our tracks. "Would you like me to read the secrets of your love?"

"And what does that mean?" I say as I pull the hood of my cloak a bit lower.

"One of my associates will jump off the top of the tower," the woman says, pointing at the nearest building. "I can read their blood splatters and divulge something to you about your truest love. Be warned—some people who have been married for hundreds of years don't like what they hear. But when we have eternity, you should go after the person you really want! We should all strive to be like the Eye."

A little knot of anger forms in my chest. Now Ale is getting credit for inventing romance, too. These people have no idea who he really is or what he's really like. If they did, they wouldn't respect him.

"Read mine, please," Verene says, right as I'm about to tell this woman to get out of our way and never speak to us again.

A girl falls out of nowhere and hits the ground in front of us with a sickening crack. She rolls away delicately as her body heals, leaving behind smears of blood that are barely visible in the dark.

"Ah," the woman in the purple gown says, inspecting them with her lantern. "Your truest love has dark eyes."

Verene blinks. "Is that all?"

"I can't read everything, dear," the woman says.

Verene walks away, looking irritated.

The woman turns to me. "Would you like me to read yours?"

". . . Yes," I whisper.

I wait anxiously as a young man comes falling out of the air, and the woman examines the blood he leaves behind. I mean, I'm not that anxious. This is obviously a waste of time. I only wish the woman would move a bit faster, so that Verene won't look back and see me encouraging such waste.

"Your truest love is taller than you," she declares.

"Everyone is taller than me," I say.

"Not everyone," she says, like I'm being unreasonable. "Would you like to consult further with my colleague?" She gestures to an alley, where a curtain is sitting half-open to reveal a woman sitting in a high-backed chair. "We assist anyone who wishes to move away from their life-spouse and find someone new. I know it may sound scandalous, but think about it—here, you have millions of options and all the time you could ever—"

I march away. I don't need assistance with that. There's no one out there who deserves the power to make my knees go weak. And if I do ever feel that when someone is around... well. I keep that to myself.

I catch up with Verene. I have to stick close to her in the bustling crowd, against my will, and our shoulders brush. It's nothing— or that's what it should be. But after hearing that woman talk about love and romance, it feels uncomfortably like something.

"What did she tell you?" Verene says.

Apparently, I wasn't as subtle as I'd intended to be.

"I didn't even bother listening," I say. "I already know I'm never going to find a girl who's worthy of me."

I'm not entirely sure what makes me say the words. I don't talk about this sort of thing, especially not with Verene. I'm a mystery. No one knows what sort of people I think about when I'm alone at night, and I prefer to keep it that way. But when Verene whips her head around to look at me so fast it nearly comes off her neck, I realize that was the exact reaction I hoped she would have.

She starts to say something, clears her throat, and tries again. But then, abruptly, we run into a crowd that's blocking the way. Everyone is jostling and yelling, focused on some spectacle up ahead.

I stop short. "What is it? Should we go around?"

Verene cranes her neck to peer over the heads of the spectators, cautiously lifting the hood of her cloak. Then she goes completely rigid.

"Verene?" I say.

She says nothing. But before I can prod her more aggressively, a girl steps up onto a stage. She's dressed in a rather low-cut blouse, and her dark hair is cut unusually short. There's a crown of thorns on her head that's interlaced with spiderwebs.

It takes me a long moment to realize that she's dressed up as me. She's not as attractive, of course, but that's not her fault. And she's holding herself much more sloppily than I ever would. She looks drunk.

The people scream their disapproval, and the girl waves mockingly. Then, she goes perfectly still, her arms poised like a dancer preparing for the opening notes of a song.

"Is that all she's going to—" I say.

An enormous blade falls out of nowhere, suspended on two columns on either side of the girl. It slices her entire body in half, perfectly. Like an art form.

The crowd roars as the girl splits and falls away. Moments later, impossibly, the two mutilated halves of her body crawl back together and stitch themselves into one piece, guts and all. When she gets to her feet, she looks entirely unaffected. In fact, she looks rather proud of her neat trick.

Well. People are certainly getting creative with the things they'd like to do to me.

I wonder if Ale knows about this. Maybe he does. And maybe he doesn't care. Maybe he thinks I deserve it.

I feel my lower lip tremble, just a little bit, which is utterly ridiculous. I'm not hurt by this. The energy of this crowd—this raw feeling, all focused on me—is the sort of thing I live for. In fact, the more people who put on shows like this, the better.

Then, when I'm in charge, I'll get to punish them all. That will be the perfect way to remind everyone how powerful I am.

A quick movement at my side draws my attention. Verene has pulled an iron fire poker out of her boot. We had a quick diversion to the first of the eight cities we could reach from the catacombs—Auge—where we raided a manor and picked up all of the iron we could find.

"Wait," I say. "We're saving them for the House of Morandi—"

She presses the fire poker against the cobblestone right in front of her.

A huge column of black flame bursts into the night air, catching several of the people in the crowd. They scatter, screaming, as their clothes alight. Verene is already moving forward, lighting up people and cobblestone alike. Within seconds, she's at the stage, and she lights that up, too. The street has devolved into a mess of fear and shrieking.

Verene glances back at me, and over the furious licking of the black flames, her smile is bright against the night. She no longer looks stiff and angry. She looks like she's having fun. So I pull out my fire poker, too. And then we're off.

We race down the cobblestone, scraping the iron pokers behind us as we go and leaving a trail of devastation. As we cross between two towers, I draw a long line across one of the walls, like I'm slashing a throat. When I glance back, the flames are crawling up the walls. We dart from street to street, setting fire to all the things people have gotten from Ale to set up their little lives—hammocks and benches and tables piled with rich food. Only a few minutes later, the streets are blazing and thick with smoke.

When we spot guards in white coats at the end of one street, Verene and I escape into one of the towers. We run up a few floors until we pass a narrow window, and we stop, entranced by the view outside. The burning city looks spectacular. Even with magic that can make unlimited water, it's going to take Ale hours to put it all out. And that feels spectacular, too.

I turn to Verene, laughter on my lips, and I find her staring at me.

She's not smiling anymore. Her dark eyes are searching my face, and she's standing much closer to me than I realized—too close, almost, overwhelming me with the faint scent of her sweat. She tied her hair up before we returned to the ninth city, and there are a couple loose curls framing her face. Her expression is so intent that it takes my breath away, and I find myself hesitating. Maybe she's changed her mind about what she wants. Maybe she doesn't want to do this—to be this. Especially not with me at her side.

Verene grabs my face. Before I can even figure out what's happening, she's kissing me, and somehow, it feels like both the most impossible and the most inevitable thing that's ever happened to me.

It's just like fighting her. It's not thinking—not really. It's a dance we've both always known the steps to, and finally, we've found someone else who can keep up. I push her back into the wall, and she wraps one leg around me and kisses me until I can't breathe. Our mouths are messy and greedy against each other, just like I always imagined they would be. We nearly lose our balance on the steps, and then we're stumbling our way into one of the cells. We topple to the floor and fumble with our newfound freedom, touching places we've never dared to touch and absolutely shameless about it. There's something incredibly desperate about the way I pull her clothes off. Every move I make is betraying how badly I want her, but I don't care. I don't care that she might think it's too much—that I'm too much—because I know she won't. She never has before.

It's like nothing else I've ever experienced. She's soft and beautiful and perfect under my hands. But she's also sweaty and squirmy and real—a girl who's full of wants and needs and things that aren't always pretty. I don't know which part I like best. I like it all.

I don't have a single other thought until it's all over. Then, I find myself lying on the floor in a pile of clothes, staring at the ceiling. All of our iron tools are next to me, carefully placed on my cloak. I don't even remember which one of us had the presence of mind to do that. Verene is curled up on my other side, her face pressed into my shoulder, her breathing slow and shivery.

"I'd never done that before," she whispers into my skin.

"Neither had I," I whisper back. "Can you believe how good I was? Much better than you."

She lifts her head. "Oh? Because I'm pretty sure you said *please* at one point. I've never heard you say *please*."

"I don't recall that," I say.

"You don't have to. I'll never forget." She glances around, like she's noticing our surroundings for the first time. "Why are we in here?"

I glance around, too. Our cell has turned into a greenhouse, filled with rows of lush grapevines. Beyond the glass walls, everything looks fuzzy and vaguely like the way I recall the city of Iris, betraying the fact that this is just a memory. My memory.

"Because I was thinking about all the wonderful fights we've had," I say.

"That one wasn't a fight," she says. "I captured you in three seconds."

"Well, I was looking down your shirt the whole time, so there," I say.

She leans over to press her mouth to mine. The way she kisses me is so hungry. It feels a little bit like she's trying to eat me alive, and I like it. I like knowing that even after what we just did to each other, she hasn't gotten enough. I like this version of her that wants things and goes after them without worrying about what other people will think. Especially if that thing is me.

"Mmm," I say into her mouth. "Verene?"

"What?" she says.

"Should we check to see if the whole city has burned down yet?"

"Oh," she says. "Yes. Probably."

We quickly pull together our clothes. Only once we're dressed do I realize we've switched shirts. I decide that I prefer it this way. We return to the window in the hall and look out.

The ninth city is a smoldering wreck. Some of the towers have completely collapsed. Others are still ablaze, the black flames pouring into every window. The people on the streets are frantic. It's all such a mess they don't even know where to start.

Verene reaches over and quietly slips her hand into mine. Together, we leave the tower. On the way out, we pull our iron pokers out of our boots again and send the stairs up into flames.

It's much easier to get through the streets now. Despite the fact that they're full of terrified people, no one really notices us creeping by, not even the guards. Soon, we reach the street that leads to the city center, and we stop short.

Ale and Theo are standing in front of the House of Morandi. They look very much like they're waiting for us.

"Hmm," Verene says. "Something tells me we're not going to be able to sneak in now."

"I suppose we'll just have to go through them," I say.

As we draw closer, moving easily through the scrambling crowd, Ale says nothing. He does nothing. He just watches us. I realize that my hand is still in Verene's, and I don't pull away. All of a sudden, Verene and I are together, and I want everyone to know it, including him.

When we're right at the border of the city center, we stop.

Ale's hands are in his pockets, his clothes rumpled and his dark hair still a mess. He looks like he hasn't had a moment's rest since our hostage negotiation ended in a flaming tower. Theo, on the other hand, appears to have taken advantage of having a new accomplice with the magic to make anything, and he's changed into a very crisp new set of clothes, complete with black gloves. He's holding a glass of wine. He looks at Verene. He looks at our joined hands. Then he leans over and whispers something in Ale's ear. For the flash of a second, it almost looks like Ale smiles. He whispers something back.

I really, really want to know what the two of them are suddenly whispering about together. But I don't let that show on my face.

"So," Ale says, glancing at the iron poker in my hand. "You seem to have made a discovery."

I glance around. There are guards running to and from the House of Morandi with buckets of water, and clusters of terrified citizens watching us from the edge of the city center. Ale doesn't seem concerned about anyone overhearing.

"Why are you just standing here?" I say. "Why aren't you out helping your people?"

"I think this is a problem that needs to be addressed at the source," Ale says.

"And how do you intend to address us?" I say.

He looks, pointedly, at the border of the city center between us.

"So you want us to fight," I say.

Ale pulls his hands out of his pockets. He rolls up his sleeves, carefully. Deliberately. When he looks at me, there's something on his face that almost seems like pity.

"I don't know what else to do with you," he says.

My fingers tighten around the handle of my fire poker. I look at Verene, and I see the same thing burning in her eyes that's burning in my chest. They put us in a prison. They tried to contain us over and over. They said we were unreasonable, and that we wanted too much, and now they think they can treat us like monsters who are destroying their perfect city—a city that wouldn't even exist if it weren't for us. None of this would exist if it weren't for us.

If they want monsters so badly, then that's what they'll get.

Together, Verene and I run into the city center.

Eighteen

THE MOMENT I CROSS THE BORDER, THE MAGIC RISES UP TO meet me. A shadowy hand springs up out of the cobblestone, materializing out of nowhere. It seizes me around the neck and lifts me high off my feet. I slash at it with my fire poker, and it recoils, letting me go. I fall to the ground, landing painfully on my ankle, and I'm instantly smothered by more shadowy hands. They pick me up and shake my hand, jostling it until the fire poker falls out of my grip. I hear Ale hiss with pain as it hits the ground and flames spring up.

I scramble back from the flames, but they're already being put out by a cluster of guards, who were waiting nearby with water. Ale has obviously prepared them for this.

Well, I'm prepared, too. I reach into my pocket.

Next to me, Verene is on the ground, struggling. Ale seems to be able to attack both of us at the same time, but I can tell that in this moment, most of his concentration is being spent on getting Verene to drop her fire poker. While he's busy with that, I pull out a handful of iron window latches that Verene and I lovingly dismantled from a manor in Auge. I throw them onto the cobblestone between us.

Ale yelps in pain as they hit the ground, sending out spurts of flame that the guards struggle to contain. I can barely see Ale over the mess, but I can tell he's turned all his attention to me.

Good. If I can distract him, then Verene can get Theo out of the way, and our path into the house will be clearer. The moment the fighting started, Theo retreated to the front steps. He's still sipping his wine, very casually, but his eyes are intent on his sister, like he's waiting for her to try something.

I approach Ale from the side, and then I run directly at him, knowing I'm probably going to regret it. Sure enough, two shadowy hands grab me around the ankles. They turn me upside down and shake me until all my little pieces of iron fall out, and then they toss me aside like I'm a doll. I hit the cobblestone face-first. I hear frantic footsteps, and when I look up, Ale is standing directly over me.

My nose is bleeding. He looks a bit shocked by it, and I realize that he's run closer to see the damage. I think, perhaps, he underestimated the force of his little magic hands.

This is the first time one of us has ever truly hit the other. I definitely thought it would be the other way around when it happened.

I scramble to my feet, wiping the blood off my nose. "Well? Is that all?"

Ale hasn't moved. He's just staring at me.

"What?" I say. "Come on, Ale. Surely you knew you'd need more than that to subdue me."

For a second, I think that maybe he's going to say this was all a mistake. Maybe he's going to back down and say that he was wrong, and I'm the one who deserves to be in charge, like I've always been. And he wants to go back to the way things used to be, because he can't handle this, and he knows that.

But he doesn't say any of that. Instead, he holds out his hands, and he looks at me expectantly.

I stare at him. "Are you asking me to...fight? Without magic?"

"Is that what it's going to take?" he says.

In my periphery, I can see Verene crawling toward the house, still wrestling with a shadowy hand. Theo is watching her struggle, unmoved. I turn my attention back to Ale. There's a strange desperation to the way he's looking at me, like everything in his life hinges on what happens next. He's looked at me like this so many times—when he had no idea what to do next, and he needed his best friend to tell him.

He keeps acting like he doesn't want things to come to this. But I think, maybe, he needs them to. He needs to be the one to take me down. Because whether he likes it or not, his life still revolves around me. It always has, and it always will.

I smile, and I dive at him.

I'm unprepared for the strength with which he meets me. I've spent a lot of my life pushing Ale around, literally and figuratively, and despite him being much taller than me, it was always like having a very large, very docile puppet at my side. It doesn't feel like that now, though. In an instant, he has me on the ground, and the two of us are struggling wildly against each other. He pins down my arms, and only when I manage to kick him between the legs does he let go.

Then, I do the thing I know he'll hate the most. I jab the heel of my hand into his one remaining eye. It's been a year since Ale had his eye cut out, but that's not the sort of trauma that goes away. Just as I hoped, he panics as he's blinded, and I'm able to get free, throwing myself on top of him instead.

I was the one who was there for Ale when he lost his eye. I was the one who dragged him back to our city. I was the one who turned myself in so that the watercrea's guards would find us and get him help. But he's clearly forgotten about all of that. He forgot about it almost as soon as it happened, actually. Because when I went back to the watercrea's tower, he left me there to die.

Once I'm thinking about that, I'm uncontrollable. I punch wildly at Ale's chest and face. Every single thing that's been festering inside me this whole year, while I was alone in my cathedrals, and then here, while I watched him cavort around with his little husband and his perfect magic, comes pouring out until I'm so frantic that I'm certain I'm unstoppable.

But somehow, Ale manages to throw me off. I roll and come to a stop a few feet away. He sits up. His bottom lip is bloodied, but other than that, he doesn't even look injured.

I want him to look injured.

"You don't deserve this," I say.

"What?" he gasps out.

"You don't deserve any of this," I say. "I'm the one who had to hide an omen on my skin for ten years. I'm the one who questioned the watercrea and got her out of the way. I'm the one who figured out how we could use the vide. I did everything, and you blamed me for it. You said I should be locked up forever. So why are you allowed to swoop in now, and benefit from all the dirty work I did, and rule the afterlife—and be *loved for it*? Why do you get to have everything that should belong to me?"

For a long moment, Ale says nothing. When he speaks, his

voice is very quiet. "I do deserve this. You saw how the city was, with me. Look how it is as soon as you get involved."

He gestures around at the smoldering towers.

"That's because of you," I say. "Because you won't get out of my way."

"It's because of you, Emanuela," he says. "This is who you are. You destroy everything you touch—"

"Just get out of my way!" I scream. "Don't make me do this to you!"

Ale gives me a strange look that I can't comprehend. "Do what? I'm the one who's winning."

I become aware of a noise behind me and turn around. Verene hasn't made it any closer to the House of Morandi. She's trapped in a tangle of shadowy hands, looking helpless.

At the sight of her, I'm on my feet. I look between her and Ale. All of my iron is gone, burned up on the cobblestone. So I do the only thing I can do. I run at Ale again, furiously. The shadowy hands grab my ankles, dragging me to the ground. Ale stands up, dusting off his shirt, which has a little dribble of blood on it. I think it's my blood.

"Please just stop, Emanuela," he says. "You're embarrassing yourself."

The shadowy hands drag me toward the house. As I go, I look wildly around the city center for anything I can grab to help myself, and I become aware that the crowd in the streets has grown. They must have been watching the whole thing.

Yes. This is something I can use. Ale's people will have seen how viciously he fought me, grabbing at me with his powers and scrabbling wildly in the dirt. They'll truly be scared of him now. He won't just be able to go back to the way he was before.

The shadowy hands drag me up the front steps of the House of Morandi and past Theo, who's holding open the door and looking extremely satisfied. Ale turns away from me. He turns to face his people instead, and a few of them creep into the scorched city center. The last thing I see is a woman reaching out and taking Ale's shoulder. She's beaming, and I see her lips form the words *Thank you*.

Verene and I are locked in the wine cellar.

Somebody has installed silver bars across the middle of the room, boxing us in on the side without the door. Naturally, we've decided to smash all the wine bottles we can reach. We're hoping that, somehow, Ale can feel this, and it's bothering him.

We've done an entire wall when the door up above cracks open. As soft footsteps descend toward us, I continue to smash the bottles, undeterred. Verene does, too. But when the man on the stairs comes abruptly into view, she stops.

It's her papa, his hands in the pockets of his fine suit. He stops on the other side of the bars. He doesn't say a word. He just looks at Verene, who's standing frozen in the middle of the wreckage we've created. Her face is uncertain, a wine bottle still poised in her hand. For a second, everything is utterly still, and I can practically feel the six years after his death hanging between them. He must look exactly the way Verene remembers him. She, of course, looks entirely different.

Her papa smiles. He pulls his hands out of his pockets and reaches through the bars. "Come here, Vee."

That's all it takes. She's already dropped the wine bottle, and she's running over to him. They hug as best they can through the bars, clumsily. To me, it looks entirely unsatisfactory, but then again, it's more than they ever thought they were going to get.

I catch myself glancing at the cell stairs. If Verene is being allowed a visitor, maybe I am, too. But the stairs remain empty.

"I—" Verene pulls back, breathless. "I just—I can't believe you're really—Papa, I have *so much* to tell you."

He beams. "Of course you do."

"You're getting us out, aren't you?" she says.

Her papa looks down at his shoes. A little piece of glass from one of the wine bottles has escaped from between the bars, and he delicately nudges it back into our cell. "I've heard the stories about you. Some of them were horrible, and I don't say that to attack you, or blame you. You're a child. You're my child. Everything you've done—everything you've had to do—is my responsibility. And I want us to find a way forward. We need to find a way forward. But…" He pauses, looking pained. "I won't choose sides, Verene. Not between you and your brother."

"Well, you have to, Papa," Verene says. "Otherwise, Theo's going to leave me locked in here forever. And if you let Alessandro keep ruling the way he is now, he's going to lose control of his magic, and—"

"I won't choose sides," he says again, sharper.

Verene hesitates. She looks wounded, and I'm pretty sure I know why. She's made a point of telling me, more than once, that she was never her maman's favorite. Perhaps she liked to think of herself as someone else's unconditional first choice.

Her papa takes in the look on her face and sighs. "This isn't what I wanted for either of you. One day, you were going to rule our city, and I was going to be there. We were going to change things, together. But first...first, you were supposed to have plenty of time to grow up. We have a chance to start over here, but I can't figure out how. Not unless you're both willing to work with me."

"You don't understand," she says. "It's not like it was when we were younger. Things have gone...too far."

He's quiet. His hands have returned to his pockets.

"What do you remember about the night I died?" he says.

Verene draws back, her face instantly shuttering. "Why?"

"Just tell me," he says.

"I remember that we were at the dinner table," she says in a slow, flat voice. "Maman and Theo were talking about something boring. And you kept waiting until they looked away to try to throw peas in my mouth. The table was covered in peas by the time they noticed. Right as I started laughing about it, you got an omen on your face. Maman didn't even hesitate. She stood up, and she told you to come with her, and you were gone."

His face is distant. "Ah yes, the peas. You were awful at that game."

"Why do you want to talk about this?" Verene says, her voice wavering. "There's nothing to say. She took you into the tower and killed you, just like she killed everyone else."

"Your maman did take me into the tower," he says. "As I followed her up the stairs, I didn't know what she was going to do. Sometimes, I almost forgot that she was immortal, but in that moment, I remembered, and I wondered...I wondered if it had all been nothing but a blink to her. But then she turned around. She told me the secret of the ritual. And she asked me to do it and stay with her. With you."

"And what did you say?" Verene whispers.

"All I could think about was you and your brother," he says. "I realized that one day, she was going to ask this same thing of you. And from there, it devolved. We fought. And she used her magic on me. She'd never done that before. I thought she was going to force an eye down my throat, but then . . . I was dead."

"So she did kill you," Verene says, her face cold.

"By accident," he says. "She lost control."

Silence.

"She couldn't have." I jump in, unable to help myself. "She'd had that magic for a thousand years."

"Yes," he says. "As I bled out on the tower steps, she knelt over me, and she said the exact same thing."

"So why did it happen?" I demand.

He shrugs. Without another word of explanation, he turns and walks back up the steps. The cellar door quietly shuts.

I have no idea what he's trying to suggest. The rulers had complete control over their magic. I could have controlled my magic, if I'd had enough time. With time and knowledge, I can control anything. I have to believe that.

Because otherwise, this has all been for nothing.

Nineteen

SILENCE FALLS ON OUR LITTLE PRISON, AND IT STAYS THAT way for hours. Verene and I sit next to each other in a wet mess of wine and glass, our backs against the wall. Eventually, Verene shifts, swinging herself around to sit directly in front of me. Her beautiful hair is still pulled up, a few curls escaping to rest on her neck. There are delicate tear tracks on her face. I didn't even realize she was crying.

She looks at me like she wants something. Before I can even ask what it is, she unceremoniously pushes apart my knees and scoots between them to kiss me. She tastes a bit salty.

"Verene—" I say.

"What?" She pulls away. "What do you want to talk about? That my papa isn't trying to get me out of here? It's not like I'm surprised, after the things I've done. I knew they were all going to turn away from me. Even him."

But I hear the way her voice wobbles a little bit.

"Verene," I say.

"What?" she says impatiently.

"What if we're wrong?" I say. "What if they can control the power of the veil forever? What if we try to stop them, and all we do is ruin everything? Again?"

She's quiet. I need her to say something. I need to know I'm not the only one thinking these thoughts. I've been thinking them ever since I caught a glimpse of Ale, fresh off a fight with me, surrounded by his adoring citizens. Everyone looked...so much better off without us.

Abruptly, Verene laughs. She has a pretty, tinkling laugh, like a bell.

"Emanuela, come on," she says. "I mean, you're obviously not being serious, because I don't think you're even capable of saying something like that seriously—but if you were...we don't doubt ourselves. That's not who we are. We'll learn from the mistakes we made last time."

She kisses me again.

"I heard what Manfredo said," she murmurs into my mouth. "You killed everyone in your home city—and you were never going to tell me, I suppose? And then, after you did that, we killed everyone in the six cities. We have to show them that we can do better this time. Otherwise..."

She tugs my collar aside to kiss me on the neck.

Otherwise, this has all been for nothing.

I forgot that she knew about what happened to Occhia. I was hoping that, maybe, that part of the interrogation had conveniently gotten past her ears. But of course she knows. This is the afterlife, where all of the eight cities are mixed together. Everyone knows everything I've done.

And she's right. I know she's right. Last time, Verene and I failed because we weren't working together. If we can work as a team, we can do anything. We have to.

The cellar door opens. Verene scrambles away from me.

"Button your shirt—" she hisses, like this is my fault and not hers. "No, you have them in the wrong holes—"

Fortunately, it's not her papa who comes down the stairs and sees me clumsily attempting to make myself presentable. Actually, it's someone I've never seen before—a young woman in a crisp, dark red dress.

"The Eye asks that you come with me," she says. "He also asks that you...behave wisely."

Two of the bars on our cell vanish, allowing us to slide out. Verene and I exchange a glance. We decide to go along with this. For now.

We follow the woman all the way up to the fifth floor of the house. Everything seems a lot quieter and emptier than it did when we first arrived. Maybe it's just because the wedding is over. A quick glance out a window tells me that the city is a bit smoky, but the fires are mostly out.

We're taken into a washroom. There are two tubs, separated by a privacy screen. I've never been in a tub—I didn't have one in Occhia, although I know the Morandis did when they were alive. Using so much water was a great luxury. I undress and lower myself in, tentatively. The moment my rear end touches the porcelain, the water instantly turns soapy and starts bubbling.

It's magic. But I only realize that after I've tried to fling myself out and nearly cracked my head open. Once I realize that I'm not being boiled alive, and I relax into the water, it's actually quite luxurious. I'm wiped clean without having to lift a finger—even my hair, I discover as I duck underneath. And yet, somehow, when I emerge, I'm dry in an instant.

Next, the woman wraps us in robes and shuffles us to a dressing room with a wardrobe. I assume it's another one of the magical wardrobes that gives us whatever we want.

"Why are we getting new clothes?" I say to the woman. "What's going on?"

"You'll be taken to see the Eye," she says. "He says you can wear whatever you'd like."

"Ah," I say. "Is this going to be some sort of public trial?" I turn to Verene. "What shall we wear for the show?"

She's fluffing out her newly cleaned hair. "You pick."

"What?" I say.

She sits down at the nearby dressing table. She crosses her legs, and her robe falls aside to reveal an indecent amount of skin. "Pick something for me."

My face is extremely hot. I know I have excellent taste, but this is a lot of responsibility. And I'm highly distracted by the sight of her thighs. Now I know how it feels to press my face into the soft skin there, and that makes it hard to think about anything else. Verene leans back against the dressing table, giving me a smug look, and I realize that she knows exactly what she's doing. This is very obnoxious of her. I adore it.

"Hmm." I reach into the wardrobe and pull out a black blouse that would look excellent on her.

"No," she says.

"Fine." I toss it aside and try another.

"No," she says.

I keep going, and she keeps refusing my offerings. I have

no idea what she wants. I have no idea what sort of test this is. But three blouses later, I have the sudden impulse to break the pattern. The next time I open the wardrobe, I conjure up a shirt that has a flattering neckline and frilly sleeves. It's not black—it's purple, which is a color I've never seen her in.

When I hold it up, Verene is quiet. Without a word, she holds out her hands, and I toss it to her.

"Why didn't you just tell me you wanted purple?" I say.

"I didn't know," she says.

She looks pleased with me. If I'm being honest, I'm pleased with myself. I think I could sit here for days on end, indulging her with pretty clothes, which is very unlike me. I don't indulge anyone.

Next, I make us each a pair of tight black pants. My own blouse is made of spiderwebbed lace. I tuck a red rose behind one ear, then give Verene a black one. When our escort clears her throat, I realize that Verene and I have been standing in front of the mirror admiring each other, and ourselves, for a solid five minutes.

As we follow the woman out of the room, Verene slips her hand into mine. She squeezes, and I squeeze back, suddenly not caring if she notices that my grip is a little too tight and anxious.

To my surprise, we don't even leave the fifth floor of the house. The woman takes us around the corner and opens the door onto a small parlor. I remember this as a relatively private space—certainly not one the family used for big gatherings. Ale and I would sit in here with his little sister, sometimes. Ale would play dolls with her, and I would ignore them and scheme against whoever had last slighted me at a party.

There are two white love seats with a coffee table in between. The table is laden with all sorts of food and drink, but there's no one partaking. The only people in the room are Ale and Theo, who are standing by the window with their heads together, whispering suspiciously. At the sound of the door, Ale quickly turns around. For a split second, I think I see him smile as he takes in my outfit. I hope he's not mocking me.

The door behind me shuts. Without a word, Ale and Theo move to sit down on one love seat. They look at us expectantly.

"What is this?" I say.

"We have food," Ale says. "If you want it."

Theo leans forward to reach for a bottle and pours himself a glass of red wine.

Verene and I exchange a glance. We decide to humor this. For now.

We sit down on the opposite love seat. Verene pours herself a glass of wine from the same bottle Theo used. She waits for him to take a sip before she follows suit.

"It's not poisoned," Theo says, rolling his eyes.

"Here." Ale reaches out and selects a plate, handing it to me. I immediately recognize the mushrooms, cheese, and olives— something both of our families often ate as the start of a meal. A quick glance around the table tells me that Ale has every- thing a traditional Occhian dinner needs right here, laid out and ready to go. That's not how it ever works. The main dishes won't be hot or properly timed. But then again, he is magic. I suppose he can make it happen.

I select a fork and take some for myself. Because I'm humoring him. But as I sit back with the plate, I hesitate. I haven't eaten—properly eaten—since the very first time I did the ritual. But if I'm being honest, this plate makes me want to try. It reminds me of the life I used to have, with all the lengthy dinners in my family's dining room and garden parties full of gossip. It's not that I want that life back, exactly. But I've felt so distant from it for so long. I think, maybe, it'd be nice to remember that part of myself. Just for a moment.

I eye a wedge of soft cheese on my plate. I cut off the smallest piece imaginable and put it in my mouth.

My very first impulse is to retch. My body got so used to eating eyes that it can't eat anything else. But I force the cheese down, and I sit there for a moment, waiting for the consequence. Only then do I discover that I'm ravenously hungry. I didn't think we got hungry in the afterlife. But then again, if we didn't, there would be no joy in eating, and the afterlife would be no good at all if we couldn't enjoy food.

I devour my plate, quicker than I should. I turn to examine what Verene is eating, and she cuts me off a little piece of onion tart, and I devour that, too.

Once we've finished the first course, we assume Ale and Theo are going to say something about what's to come, so we just wait. Ale has a glass of wine in his hands now, too. He takes a long drink, then sets it down. He looks at me, and I brace myself.

"Do you remember Chiara Bianchi's eleventh birthday party?" he says.

"When I snuck up behind her and cut off half her hair while she was opening presents?" I say. "Of course. What about it?"

Ale smiles. "Yes. That."

"What about it?" I press.

"Who's Chiara Bianchi?" Verene says.

"No one," I say.

"Emanuela was…" Ale coughs delicately. "Rather fond of her when we were growing up."

"She was my nemesis," I say hotly.

Verene has now leaned closer to me with obvious interest. "Nemesis? What sort of things did you do to this…" She looks me up and down in a way that feels extremely loud in this tiny room. "Nemesis?"

I have no idea why we're talking about this. I have no idea what Ale thinks he's doing. But now, for some reason, everyone is looking at me, waiting for a story.

"Hmm," I say. "Well, once, I was wearing a green dress, and she told me she didn't like the color. So I acquired a bunch of dye in that exact shade, snuck into her bedroom, and dyed all her clothes. And her bedsheets."

There's a breath of silence.

"That was horrible of you," Ale says softly.

I lift my chin. "Yes, it was."

Then, Ale smiles. I glance to my side and notice that Verene is smiling, too.

I falter. I don't know why everyone is smiling—well, everyone except Theo. It's very disarming to have both Ale and Verene looking at me like this at the same time. They should know better than to laugh at me.

"What else did you do?" Verene says eagerly.

I don't know why that's the question that unlocks something inside me, but it is. Slowly, Ale and I start trading off, trying to remember all of the horrendous, embarrassing things I did to someone at a party. Then we're talking about the letters we used to write each other every day, and telling Theo and Verene about the strange shorthand we used. It will make no sense to someone who doesn't speak our language. There's nothing important to say about it. But it feels somehow crucial to talk about it.

As we eat our main courses, Verene starts telling us about growing up in Iris. Not about being the daughter of a ruler. Just about the silly things she did to entertain herself in her cathedral home. And then Theo, who's been very quiet, is talking, too. Moments later, the two of them are tripping over each other to try and tell the same story from their childhoods—strangely, they always seem to remember the events in ways that make themselves look very good and their sibling look very incorrect. We get distracted for what feels like a full hour when we discover that Verene once tricked Theo into eating a candle—not just a bite, but a whole candle. We're all so certain that it should have been the other way around, and Verene is obviously the one who would eat a candle, and we have to dissect exactly how it got to that point.

Before I know it, we've eaten most of the food, and the others have drunk most of the wine. I find myself slowly working my way through a piece of deeply rich chocolate cake. Verene sets down her own plate with a clink. Then, she scoots closer to me, bending down to put her head on my shoulder. The gesture is so quiet and unexpected that I don't really know what to do with it. So I just stay very still, hoping she won't pull away, but also a bit self-conscious, because I can feel Ale looking at us.

"Are the two of you officially . . . ?" Ale says.

"Yes," Verene says.

I flush with pleasure. Ale, who's slumped back into his love seat and looking a bit tipsy, scrapes his fork along his dessert plate for a long moment. I find, inexplicably, that I'm very concerned about what he's going to say.

"I couldn't see Emanuela with anyone else," he says softly. Then he turns to look at Theo, who's slumped back alongside him. "They are cute together, aren't they?"

"Cute?" Theo says, wrinkling his nose. "I've never used that word in my life."

"Oh, come on," Ale says. "Look at their little matching roses."

"It's insufferable," Theo insists, taking another drink of his wine.

"Their wedding would be outrageous." Ale is giggling now. "Imagine the gowns."

"Imagine all the nonsense the rest of us would have to put up with," Theo says.

"Imagine the decorations," Ale says. "And the—"

He cuts himself off abruptly, and after a second, I realize it's because Theo is no longer paying attention to the conversation. Instead, he's looking at Verene, and tears have welled up in his eyes. Slowly but surely, they break loose and start to roll down his cheeks.

For a moment, we all just stare, uncomprehending. Then, Ale springs to his feet.

"Um..." He pulls Theo's wineglass out of his hand, setting it on the table. "I think...I think maybe you had too much to drink. Do you want to...?" His hands hover over Theo, like he's not sure if he's allowed to touch him. Theo tries to stand up, but abruptly, he sits back down and puts his face in his hands. He starts weeping.

There's absolutely nothing comfortable about watching

someone cry like this. Especially not someone I have such an intense mutual dislike for. It makes me remember, suddenly, whose house we're in and what we're doing here—something I don't know how I was ever able to forget.

Ale's face is all panic. He shoots me a look, and then, without a word, he takes Theo's shoulders and pulls him, rather firmly, onto his feet. He ushers him out of the room, shutting the door behind them.

Verene has now lifted her head off my shoulder. When she meets my gaze, I see the unease in her dark eyes.

"I've never seen him cry like that," she whispers.

And then we're on our feet. We scurry over to the door and press our ears to it. I can tell that Ale and Theo have moved around the corner, but they're not far away enough to escape our earshot.

"You don't have to stay," Ale is saying. "I can do it on my own."

"No," Theo says, then sniffs loudly. "We agreed. I should be there."

"Do you want my handkerchief—" Ale says.

"I'm fine," Theo snaps.

Silence.

"Thank you," Theo says, very grudgingly. There's another brief pause, which I assume is him wiping his face.

"It's like I told you," Ale says. "It's gotten…hungrier. But we can keep it sated and under control, if we work together. I know we can."

"And they won't be in pain?" Theo says.

"No," Ale says.

"Are you sure?" Theo says.

"Yes." The way Ale says the word is almost vicious.

"Maybe there's another way," Theo whispers.

The floorboards creak, like one of them is either stepping closer or stepping back.

"Someone has to put a stop to them, Theo," Ale says. "And we're the only ones who can."

Verene and I pull away from the door. Her eyes meet mine, wide with horror, as the realization sets in for us both. This little gathering wasn't the beginning of a trial—or even, against all odds, an offering of peace.

It was our last meal.

TWENTY

I DON'T KNOW WHAT I EXPECTED. I DON'T KNOW WHY I'M
surprised. There was only one way this was ever going to end. I
back toward the table and pick up the knife we used to cut the
cake. Verene grabs one of the wine bottles, prepared to swing it,
and we wait.

Only a moment later, there are decisive footsteps outside,
and Ale pushes the door open, Theo right behind him. Ale
steps inside and looks between us, holding our sad little weap-
ons. His face is unnervingly expressionless.

"So," I say. "You've figured out a way to get rid of us. What
are you going to do? Or rather—what is the vide going to do?"

Ale says nothing. He just reaches up and starts to pull off
his eyepatch.

I know what happened to Ale's eye. I saw the whole thing.
And Verene knows better than anyone, because she's the one
who did it. She carved it out of his head, cruelly and messily. All
that was left behind was a bloody wound.

That wound is gone. There's nothing there. Nothing except a

horrible, deep emptiness. The moment Ale unveils it, the whole room gets a little bit colder. I can feel the vide's presence—a familiar specter that I first met in the catacombs under Iris. The thing that's taken up residence on his face is, in its own way, alive.

And it's hungry. There's a faint hissing whisper floating in the air, and it seems to be getting louder.

Verene and I scramble back.

"Alessandro? There you are—"

The voice comes from the hall, and when I glance back, I see Manfredo running toward our parlor. Ale doesn't even react to the familiar voice. He's folding up his eyepatch and putting it in his shirt pocket. He doesn't seem at all concerned that we're going to run.

"Alessandro," Manfredo says again. "Can you please just talk to me—"

Theo turns around, reaching out to block the doorway. "Don't come in here."

Manfredo stops. I'm on top of one of the love seats by now, so I can see the suspicious look Manfredo gives the boy in front of him.

"You know what?" Manfredo says. "I've had it with this." He raises his voice. "I wasn't born yesterday, all right, Alessandro? You never want to be alone with me. You barely even let me kiss you. You're obviously fooling around with someone—or maybe more than one someone—and you're not doing a very good job of hiding it. Why did you even want to get married? Because I had other prospects, too, you know. But I like you. I care about you—*Alessandro!*"

Ale turns around.

Theo drops to the floor. But Manfredo isn't fast enough.

A shadowy hand with a long arm extends out of the hole in Ale's face. It grabs Manfredo by the neck, lifting him up with impossible strength. Manfredo has time to get out half a scream before he's dragged over and devoured, somehow plunged into a space entirely too small for him. And then he's gone.

Ale turns away. He just stands there, breathing hard like he exerted himself. He seems to be waiting for something to happen—listening for a signal I don't know.

"Maybe..." Theo whispers, still crouched on his hands and knees. "Maybe it will be happy with—"

More.

The disembodied hiss of a voice suddenly fills the room. Ale bends double, grimacing like he's in pain.

"I just gave you more," he whispers.

Everything you have is because of me. I can take it away.

There's a sudden noise from the table, and I turn to see the remains of our food crumbling into dust. The chandelier above the table breaks loose and falls.

"I know!" Ale yells. He straightens up laboriously, and he looks at me. "What about her? Will that be enough?"

No. He's not really going to do this. Not to me.

I stumble off the love seat. I move so that the table is in between us, although I know it's not going to help.

"Ale," I whisper. "If you keep feeding her, she'll get too powerful. She won't stop."

"I can control it," Ale says. "I've been controlling it the whole time."

There's not an ounce of doubt on his face. He looks utterly determined in a way I've never seen him look before.

I know where he got this confidence. I did this to him. I

killed his family and left him without a home. I told him he was nothing and that he always would be. I pushed him down, over and over, because it was always so easy, and he did the one thing I thought he would never do. He learned how to fight back—and how to win at any cost. And I don't know how to stop him now.

The whispering of the vide grows louder. Instinctively, I reach for Verene's hand. I can't die this way—helpless and unable to fight back. I'm not supposed to ever die, and especially not like this.

But I've already died like this once before, as the veil came crashing down around the eight cities. I thought I was special then. I thought I was the exception. And I wasn't.

The shadowy hand lunges out of the hole in Ale's face.

Behind him, Theo pulls out a small token shaped like an eye. He tosses it at Ale's feet.

A column of flame explodes up from the floor. Ale screams in pain and crumples to the floor as it engulfs him. Theo is already running around him, reaching for his sister.

"The window," he says. "He won't be down for long—"

As Verene yanks the window open, shadowy hands try to slam it shut, but they're weaker than usual, their incorporeal fingers feeble. Verene throws herself out, disappearing into the night, and Theo is right behind her.

But I'm not leaving this house. Not yet.

Ale is still writhing on the floor, trying to put himself out. He's sobbing, and something about the sound grabs on to my insides and won't let go. But I force myself to ignore it, and I leap around him and dart into the hall, slamming the parlor door shut behind me. My heart is pounding in my ears as I survey the empty hall, which suddenly looks dizzying and foreign.

The fifth floor is where Ale's closest family sleeps. If he's hiding people from me, he might have put them up here. So then I'm barreling down the hallway, opening door after door and finding nothing but empty rooms.

"Paola?" I hear myself whispering as I turn a corner. "Paola? Are you here?"

Behind me, the parlor door cracks open, and I duck into the closest room. It's the nursery where Ale and I used to play as children. I throw myself to the floor and paw through the dolls and blocks, determined to find something that can serve as a weapon.

Then I hear a soft *thump*.

I jump, dropping the doll in my hands, and look at the door, but it's still shut.

Thump.

It's not coming from the door. It's coming from the far side of the room. My eyes glance over the love seat and the crib. Then they land on the big wooden trunk.

Thump.

I used to hide in that trunk all the time—mostly to irritate my nursemaid. The lid was so heavy that once I was inside, I didn't have a hope of freeing myself, but that never worried me. Ale always knew where I was, and he was very worried about my antics. He would never have let me suffocate.

I stand up, clutching a wooden block in my hand, because it's the only thing I have. I approach the trunk slowly.

Thump.

I grit my teeth, then grab the lid and fling it open.

First, I smell the blood. Then, I see something wriggling and alive. I leap back as it flies out at me.

It's a foot. A foot attached to an ankle, viciously kicking at the air.

There's a disembodied pair of legs in the trunk. They're covered by a long purple skirt that's shredded at the top, and they're writhing around in a pool of blood like they're trying to escape.

I stagger back, unable to make sense of it, right as the nursery door opens behind me.

"No!" I hear Ale's voice, high with panic. "No—don't let her out—"

I turn around. Ale stops short. His eyepatch is back on, and as he takes in my expression, his face turns white with horror. And all I can do is stare at him.

"I tried to save her," he says.

"Who?" I whisper.

"It wanted to take her." He's speaking so quickly I can barely comprehend it. "She was—she was asking too many questions—and she snuck up on me when I had it uncovered—I tried to save her. She was halfway in. But I pulled her back out."

Behind me, the legs in the trunk kick frantically.

"It's your mamma," I hear myself saying. "Isn't it?"

"Do you remember?" he whispers.

"Remember what?" I say.

"Do you remember her face?" he says, and there's desperation in his voice. "It took...it took so much....I tried to stop it—and my papá. He knows something isn't right, but he can't put his finger on it, and I—"

A slow, cold horror has started to crawl up my spine, and I back away from him as my mind races with the realization.

In the parlor, I saw the vide eat someone. I know I did. But when I try to dwell on the specifics of the victim, I can't remember who they were. I can't remember anything about them. The vide isn't just consuming bodies. It's consuming everything about people—every memory and impression they've ever left in our heads.

"Ale," I whisper. "You…"

Our eyes meet, and I can see that he knows exactly what I'm thinking. I can see the pain of it filling his face.

He's done something that can't be undone.

The disembodied pair of legs flings itself out of the trunk, and something about it must draw the vide's attention. I can tell, because Ale falls to the floor, clutching at his face.

"No!" he says. "No—"

I run past him. In the hall, I find the nearest window, and I don't even stop to consider any other options. I throw myself out, hitting the dark cobblestone below with a crunch. I scramble to my feet and run desperately for the nearest city street, where I can see the shadowy figures of Theo and Verene. I've only taken a few steps when I hear a creak, and I look behind me to see that the front door of the House of Morandi is cracked open.

No. Ale can't have possibly gotten down here so quickly.

But it's not Ale's face that emerges in the shadowy gap of the door. It's my nursemaid, her dark eyes wide and frightened.

"Paola." I stop, moving back toward her. "Come on—I'll get you out of there—you have to get out of there before he—"

She reaches into the pocket of her apron and holds up a small, sheathed dagger. "We found this. The boy is very afraid of it. Is it yours?"

"Yes," I say.

"Will it put an end to this?" she says.

"Yes," I say hesitantly. "But—"

She tosses the dagger to me. I catch it, and I start to explain the rest—that she still has to come with me, until we figure out how to stop this. But then she's gone. A shadowy hand yanks her back into the foyer, and a moment later, Ale appears on the front steps. He's trembling and breathing hard. His gaze goes right to the dagger in my hand.

I turn and run. Behind me, I hear a rustling noise. When I glance back, the ivy that blankets the front of the House of Morandi is peeling itself off the walls, coming for me. I leap for the city street, and Verene lunges forward to catch me, pulling me to safety. I look back to see a swathe of vines reaching toward us, like a streak of paint, but they wither away right at the border.

"He can't get to us now," Verene says breathlessly. "His magic isn't strong enough to—"

From the front door, Ale closes his eye, like he's concentrating. Then the vines that were lying dormant on the cobblestone explode over the edge of the city center, heading right for us.

And we're running. The other people on the street scatter in confusion, but the vines swerve around them anyway, grabbing at us instead. We duck between two towers to get to the next street, and the vines follow us. In what seems like only seconds, they're coming at us from all sides, careening over all the burned furniture and rubble. We back up and find ourselves pressed against a tower door.

We can't go in here. We'll be trapped.

But we don't have a choice. We run up the charred steps, and we keep spiraling our way up until, abruptly, the tower ends. The walls crumble away in midair, leaving only a curl of winding staircase, suspended above it all. A quick glance around tells me that this tower's neighbor has burned and fallen away almost entirely—it must have taken some of our tower with it.

At a loud rustling sound from below, I turn back just in time to see the vines approaching. But then, only a few steps away, they stop.

I look down at the street below, a bit dizzily. It's ivy for as far as I can see—ivy and very confused people.

"Why…" Verene is trying to catch her breath. "Why did he stop?"

In the distance, there's a dull boom. I whirl around, trying to find the source of the noise. In the maze of tall, thin buildings, I can faintly see that one of the towers near the edge of the city is crumbling into dust. It melts down, like a candle burning impossibly fast, and below, the people scream. For a building so enormous, it crumbles surprisingly quickly.

"Is that one of the ones we set on fire?" I say, a bit nervously.

"He's overextending himself," Theo says. "He needs to… feed."

"Just so we're all clear about what's happening…" Verene says. "When we left you there after the wedding, you figured out that Alessandro had put the vide *in his face*, and he's consuming people for power, and you thought that was…fine? And you agreed to let him do it to us?"

Theo crosses his arms. "Well, I changed my mind, didn't I?"

"Or this is another trick," she says. "And you're still on Alessandro's side—"

"For the last time, Verene, this isn't all about me changing sides just to spite you," Theo says. "I admit, I got some enjoyment out of watching him thrash you both in that fight—but can you blame me?"

"You did seem pretty happy to help him," she says.

"It was the least I could do," Theo snaps. "I'm the whole reason the vide is part of him now."

I give him a slow, sideways look. "What do you mean?"

"I—just that—" Theo stammers for a moment. "Nothing. Never mind."

I advance on him, forcing him right up to the point where the building drops off. "What do you mean?"

"These stairs aren't doing you any favors," he says, referring to the fact that I'm a step below him and, consequently, even shorter than usual.

I pretend like I'm about to push him. He flinches and nearly goes over, barely regaining his balance. His instinct, unsurprisingly, was to grab my shoulder, like he was trying to pull me with him.

"Are you going to make me ask you a third time?" I say, throwing his hand off.

"Look," he says. "It was last year. I went to your city. I wanted to know what had happened—I wanted to know if I had to worry about you coming back. And I found…"

I know exactly what he found. An empty cathedral, full of the bloody remains of our people. And the one boy who survived.

"He was lying at the bottom of the cathedral steps," Theo says. "He was sick. Very sick. His eye socket was infected."

My stomach turns.

"It was obvious he needed a real doctor," Theo says. "I got him up and brought him into the catacombs, to go back to Iris. He was pretty delirious, but when he realized what was happening, he…resisted."

"He fought you?" I say.

"Oh, yes," Theo says. "He kept saying, *I can do this on my own*. Despite the fact that he obviously couldn't. I summoned the vide to try and transport us quickly, and that was when it all went wrong. The vide didn't act the way it normally did. It... attacked us. I felt those shadowy hands on me, and there was this whispering in my ear..." He shudders. "I didn't know what it wanted. But it clearly wanted something, and it wasn't going to stop until it got it."

"And what did you do?" I say.

Theo is very quiet.

"Look," he says. "I wasn't there for Alessandro. I was there to protect Iris, and I needed to get back, and he was making a fuss and slowing me down."

"You left him," I say. "You left him knowing that he was weaker than you."

Theo's mouth trembles, just a little bit. "It was the rational decision. But now, everything that's happened since—every person it's taken—it's my fault. What that thing is putting him through—it's my fault."

"It's not," Verene says quietly.

We both turn to her. Her arms are tightly crossed, her eyes on her feet.

"I'm the one who took his eye in the first place," she says.

And I'm the one who couldn't protect him from that. But I don't say that out loud. I don't trust myself to say it out loud.

"It's not your fault," Theo says.

"Oh, don't even," Verene says. "I know you blame me for everything—"

"I don't," he says loudly. "I...look. I know I may have behaved that way some of the time. Most of the time. But..."

Verene gives him a highly skeptical look, waiting for more.

He sighs. "I don't know what happened with us, Vee. I mean, you've always driven me up the wall, because you're an unbearable human being. But we used to be a team."

"We had to be," she says, a bit reluctantly.

"I know that I'm not very good at..." He makes a face that suggests the word he's trying to say is giving him indigestion. "Feelings. But I think we're all about to get consumed by the depraved ghost that we unleashed, so I just want you to know that I do love you, all right? At this point, it's pretty safe to say that there's nothing you could do that would change that."

I can see Verene wrestling with her pride. I can also see her wrestling with the fact that we probably are about to get consumed by the depraved ghost that we unleashed.

"Maybe..." she says. "Maybe, sometimes, I should do a better job of listening to you. Maybe we wouldn't be in this situation if we had worked together. And...I love you, too."

There's a brief, uncomfortable silence.

"Do we have to be nice to each other now?" Verene says.

"Let's not," Theo says.

It takes me a moment to realize that, just like that, the two of them have made a fragile peace. I'm not really sure how it happened. I feel a little bit like I just witnessed magic, and I'm a little bit unsettled by the way I'm suddenly out of the loop.

"If you two aren't fighting for my entertainment, then let's move on," I say. "We have to stop the vide. How are we going to do that?"

"I don't know," Theo says. "Like I said, it needs to eat."

In the distance, there's another boom. Another tower is falling down.

"If we get more iron, we can try fighting Alessandro again," Verene says.

Theo grimaces. "But that hurts him."

"Fine," Verene says. "We can try holding his hand and telling him how much we care about him."

"You go right ahead," Theo says. "I don't even think he's that good-looking."

"What?" Verene says.

"What?" Theo says.

I'm trying very hard to ignore the dagger I've tucked into my boot. But the cold metal seems to be digging into my skin more and more insistently.

No. There must be another way.

"We could trap him," Verene says. "Like the rulers did to Marcella before. We could put him in the prison at the bottom of the catacombs and let him get weaker, and then..."

"Then the afterlife would go back to the way it was before," I say, my voice hollow. "Without Ale's magic—the magic that Marcella is lending him in exchange for being fed, that is— we'd all be trapped in the towers."

"Then what are we supposed to do?" Verene says, desperation in her voice.

On the steps below us, the ivy rustles. We turn around, bracing ourselves, but the ivy isn't getting closer. It's parting, drawing to either side of the steps like it's making an aisle. And then, we hear soft footsteps just around the bend.

It seems the Eye has decided to come to us.

TWENTY-ONE

ALE COMES TO A STOP ON THE STAIRS BENEATH US. HE'S
draped in a black cloak, which I assume he was using to hide
his identity from his adoring citizens. He lowers the hood and
gives us a flat look.

"Where's the dagger?" That's all he says.

I glance at his eyepatch. "You don't even know what the
vide really is, do you? She never explained herself while she was
making demands?"

"It doesn't matter," he says in a careful way that lets me
know the question has been writhing around in his head for a
year. "I'm the one with the magic. I'm the one in control."

Out of nowhere, that horrible hissing voice fills the air
again, so cold I feel my skin prickle.

More.

Ale has fallen to his knees. Behind him, another tower
collapses—this one much closer to the city center.

"I can't!" he says to the invisible voice. "Not until I know which one of them has the dagger—it might hurt us. Just give me a second, please—"

I glance at Verene, breathless. We've bought ourselves a bit of time.

"Alessandro," she says. "The vide—she's just using you to get stronger."

"No," he says.

"Yes," she says. "If you give her too much, she'll overwhelm you—"

"No!" he says. "I won't let it happen! This is a good city. People are finally safe. They have everything they could ever want. I just... I just have to..."

He trails off, gasping for breath. Whatever the vide is doing to him, it's hurting him. The whispers are still swirling around in the air, and they sound faint to me, but I think they're much louder to him.

And for a moment, all I see is the boy I first met, years ago, when we were both far too small to have any idea that we were betrothed—the boy who was thrust into my life against his will, but who trusted me without hesitation. He doesn't have to explain himself to me. I know he wanted the best for everyone around him. He always has. But now he's trapped.

I have to help him. And once I realize that, I have an idea. It leaps to the front of my mind like it's been here all along.

"It's too much for you, Ale," I say.

"It isn't," he says.

"It's too much for any one person," I say. "But we could share it."

He's silent. He glances up, his face skeptical.

"We don't even know if that's possible, Emanuela," Verene says.

"But what if we agreed to figure it out?" I say. "What if we promise—really promise—not to fight until we've divided the vide's power into controllable amounts? And then we devote all our energy to keeping things from falling apart in the meantime?"

Verene raises her eyebrows. "You want...*us*...to promise... not to fight?"

I turn to her. "We did it. We realized we were better together. You trust me now, don't you?"

Verene is quiet for a long moment. So long that I feel sweat drip down my side. I've seen her in ways that no one else has, but I remember, with a sudden jolt, that I still can't see what's in her head.

"Yes," she says.

"Yes," I breathe. I knew I was right. "And Theo—"

"I don't trust you," he says.

"I know," I say. "But you trust Verene."

Theo's eyes flicker to his sister. "To a certain degree."

Verene kicks him in the shin. "You said that you would always love me no matter what I did."

"I can't believe you're already using this against me," he mutters.

"Ale." I turn to him now. "You can trust Theo, can't you? You two have so much in common. You've both given up a lot to try and do what you think is right. You're both very concerned with this mysterious *greater good*."

"And you're both dull," Verene says. "What did you do

when you weren't actively fighting us? Sit around organizing a bunch of books?"

Ale and Theo look at each other. They quickly look away.

"We can do this," I say. "We have to do this, or the vide is going to consume us all. But if we can get its power under control—truly under control—then...then the cities will be saved. And everyone can live forever."

"Is that what you want?" Ale says. "For the cities to be saved?"

"Yes," I say.

"Even if you're not the only one with the power to save them?" Ale says.

And I feel myself hesitating. "Yes," I say finally.

And it's true.

I think it's true.

Everyone else is silent. But they're going to agree. I know they are. This is the only way—and I, personally, think I made a very compelling argument for it. I knew I could find a way out. I always find a way out.

Finally, Theo speaks up. "I think it's a good plan."

"You do?" I say.

"Just with one small change," he says.

"What?" I say.

"I think we should feed Emanuela to the vide and then do all of it without her," he says.

"Well, that's about what I expected from you," I say.

Then I become aware that neither Ale nor Verene is saying anything. I look between them, trying to figure out the expressions on their faces. And I can't.

Ale turns his attention to Verene. "What do you think?"

As if he's seriously considering this. As if they're actually going to decide this together. As if they've both suddenly forgotten that she's the one who cut out his eye, and that they've never been on the same side of any fight in their lives.

"What—Verene is just as bad as I am," I say. "You can't punish me for what I did and then let her—"

"Remember what I said earlier?" Theo says. "That Verene and I used to be a team, and I didn't know what happened to change that? Well, I've remembered. So are you going to tell any of us why we should trust you?"

"Verene." I move closer to her on the stairs. "You trust me. You said you trusted me."

Her arms are crossed, carefully avoiding my eyes.

"Verene," I say sharply.

She finally lifts her gaze. Her eyes flicker over my face, and I can feel her searching and searching, and I have no idea what she's looking for. I thought it was all so clear. It's so clear to me.

"I would forget all about her, right?" she says.

I can't believe what I'm hearing. I can't believe that after all this, she thinks she can just wipe me from her mind.

I grab her arm. "Verene. You need me. What would you even do without me? No one else—" I stumble over my words, very aware that we're being watched. "No one else will ever make you feel like I do. No one understands you like I do. You're different from other people. We're different. You know that. What are you going to do—just go back to kissing ordinary girls who'll never appreciate what you're capable of?"

"Is that why we're together?" Verene says. "Because no one else is enough for us?"

"Yes," I say. "Obviously."

She reaches out and takes my face in her delicate hands.

"You're so beautiful," she says softly. "From the first moment you attacked me in Iris, you got into my head and refused to leave. I don't even know what it is about you, exactly, but it feels like I have to keep coming back. I have to try and figure out what you're thinking. I have to try and figure out what you're going to do next. No matter how much I get, I always want more. You're like the worst obsession I've ever had."

Those are all good things. She's changed her mind. She must have.

She leans down and kisses me. She definitely kisses me like she's changed her mind—long and deep, her fingers sliding around to the back of my neck to tangle in my hair. There's an intimacy to her touch that makes me completely forget that we're not alone. When she pulls away, I'm unbalanced.

I'm so unbalanced that she's able to lean down and yank the dagger out of my boot. Before I can even try to grab it back, she pushes me down the stairs.

"Do it," she says.

The first thing I feel is the sharp prick of the betrayal. It opens the door for a dozen other feelings that start to flood in. But then I look up, and I see Ale standing over me. I've tumbled right into his legs.

The only thing on his face is resignation. He starts to take off his eyepatch.

All of my feelings disappear. They're replaced by one thing, and one thing only.

The desire to survive.

I shove Ale in the knees, and he tumbles down the stairs. I get up and lunge for Verene, but Theo gets in my way. He gets both his arms around my neck, and I struggle like I've never struggled before.

"Theo, you have to let her go!" Ale says. "It will take both of you—it—augh—"

Ale crumples in pain again, and I hear Marcella's voice. *More.*

"Let me hold her," Ale says, and I feel his cold hands on me.

They try to pass me between them, and I make sure they regret it. I thrash with everything I have, and Theo loses his balance and tips backward. He lands precariously close to the end of the stairs, and as Ale tries to pull me back, I pour all my energy into throwing our little group off balance. Verene shrieks, and before I know it, we're all falling off the tower.

Good.

When we hit the ground, I barely even feel the pain. I'm already on my hands and knees, even as my neck pops painfully back into place. I scrabble around, ankle-deep in ivy, and find Verene lying only a few feet away, the dagger in her limp hand. I snatch it away from her.

"No!" Verene yells, struggling to get to her feet. "She's got the dagger—"

I've already found Ale, who's just getting to his feet. I point the dagger at his face. I advance, and he backs up until he hits the wall of the nearest tower.

I move closer. Closer. Until it's only an inch away from him, so that nobody else will dare to try and yank me away.

"Emanuela," Ale says, his voice ragged. "Please. I know you're scared, but it will be quick. And it's better this way."

"I'm not scared—" I say.

"Of course you are!" he says. "You're the most scared person

I've ever known. You're scared of walking into a room and not having anyone notice you. You're scared of anything you can't control, especially your own feelings. You're scared that you're not enough the way you are. That's why you did all this. That's why you think you need to live forever and have all this power. Because you don't know who you are without it." His eye flickers over my face. "But I do. I always did. You were my best friend."

"Then why do you have to destroy me?" I whisper.

"Because you're never going to stop," he says. "Being my best friend wasn't enough for you. Being the ruler of the six cities wasn't enough for you. Being in an eternal afterlife wouldn't be enough for you. You say that you want us to work together, but you would never truly be able to let it happen—not if it meant you weren't the only one on top. It's true, isn't it?"

I want to deny it. I want to make him understand. What I feel for him is so real. I love him. I want to help him. But I also want...more.

This is who I am. This is who I'll always be. I don't know how to not be that way. I don't think I can.

Ale lifts one hand, and I can see that he's shaking. Carefully avoiding the dagger, he pushes a few loose strands of hair out of my face.

"It will be all right," he says.

I think again about the moment when the veil came down on the six cities. I haven't let myself go back to that memory, because of what I felt. I died. And it was worse than I had ever imagined it could be, because I didn't feel anything. I just...was.

But maybe there's something after this. Maybe it's even better than here. Maybe I'll be all right, and this is the way things were meant to be all along. But I just don't know. I'll never know until it happens.

And I can't do that alone.

When it comes down to it, that's who I am. I'm a girl who's afraid to die alone. Maybe that's all I am.

I think it's all I am. Because whether I really want to or not—whether it's really the right thing to do or not—I've already plunged the dagger right through Ale's eyepatch.

I stumble back when I realize what I've done. Ale falls to his knees, and for a moment, everything is completely silent. Maybe, I think dimly, the dagger isn't really what it seems. Maybe he'll get to his feet, magically healed, and we'll go on fighting each other in this afterlife forever and ever.

Then, from somewhere—from everywhere—someone screams.

Marcella. The scream is raw and furious. But it's also, somehow, afraid.

All around us, the ivy shrivels up. The towers—all of them— start to crumble into dust. Among it all, the red haze of the veil swirls frantically, like it's trying to find somewhere to go.

Ale pitches forward. Right before he hits the cobblestone, Theo dives to catch him. He pulls Ale into his lap, and I see that Ale is sobbing in pain, helplessly. Theo looks up at me. His eyes are so full of hatred that I back away. I look around for Verene and find her standing in the middle of the street, far out of my reach. She doesn't look angry. She just looks terrified.

I move, instinctively, for her.

But I only manage to take a single step before everything around me disappears. And I go with it.

TWENTY-TWO

I WAKE UP ON THE COLD STEPS OF A BLACK CATHEDRAL.

The moment I realize where I am—the moment I realize that I still exist—I jump to my feet. I run up to the doors of the Occhian cathedral, which are sitting half-open, and push my way inside. I haven't been back to Occhia in so long that I'm not thinking clearly. I'm certain, somehow, that the whole place is going to be full—that I'll have caught my people in the middle of a sermon, or better yet, someone else's wedding that I can dramatically interrupt.

But there's no one inside. The inner chamber is just as I left it—soaked with dark, dried blood and the remnants of my people's clothes. I turn away, slowly. I survey the black manors laid out in front of me and find them empty and silent, their windows dark.

No one is here. No one has been here for a long time.

My next thought is of the veil, and I look up.

It's gone. I don't know what to call the thing over my head now. It's a huge expanse of white nothing. At least, it looks like nothing at first. But after a moment, I see little swirls and wisps of...something. Life. It all stretches wide, as far as I can see. In the distance, the spindly, endless towers of the ninth city are gone. It's just the eight of us again, sitting in a little ring. I return my gaze to the ground and look, again, around the cathedral steps. Just to make sure there's no one here with me.

There isn't.

I sit down. After a moment, I lie down. I curl up on my side with my head pressed against the cold stone. And I stay there. Alone.

I have no idea how long it's been when I hear footsteps—the graceful, barely there footsteps of someone with dainty feet. I open my eyes and see a girl standing in front of me. She seems a bit blurry, but as I sit up, she slowly comes into focus.

Verene is still dressed in the same clothes she was wearing at the House of Morandi, but there's a black jacket draped around her shoulders, which makes sense—it's colder here than it was in the afterlife, I realize suddenly. That explains why my body is so numb.

Verene is looking at me with dark, flat eyes. She doesn't seem particularly happy to see me.

"Everyone who was alive before the veil came down is alive again," she says.

And everyone who was dead is gone forever. The quiet, cold truth of it sinks slowly into my chest.

"We went to our family's house," she says. "Me and Theo. He stayed there. But I...I can't spend all my time sitting in the parlor with everyone else and acting like I'm a normal girl. Not with the way they look at me."

So she came to me. The only person she has left. Because, after all, we're too good for everyone else.

"Well?" Verene says.

"Well, what?" I say.

She glances around. "I want to see your city. Show me."

My first instinct is to turn her away. The two of us obviously weren't meant to be together. All we do is destroy things. All we do is make each other worse.

I only get up and join her because I know that she'll just annoy me until I give in.

We walk around the empty streets. At first, I say nothing. When I try to form the words—to tell her who used to live in what manor, or what sort of things they used to sell at a certain market—I think about all those people in the afterlife, and how they were happy until I showed up, and my throat clogs up. But slowly, slowly, I find the words trickling out of my mouth. We visit the greenhouses and the sad, dried-up public gardens. We visit everything except the cathedral and the House of Morandi.

When we've walked every other street, I take her to my family's home. After the watercrea died, my family was forced out by an angry mob. The door is hanging off its hinges and the front windows are broken, but when we go up into my childhood bedroom, we find it untouched. It looks exactly the way it did when my memory conjured it up in the afterlife's tower. I lose my breath at the familiarity of it.

Verene walks around, unabashedly touching all my things. She sifts through my sewing projects. She looks at my calendar, which was already full of social appointments I'd planned for after Ale and I were married. Then, without ceremony, she lies down on my bed.

It's an impossibly strange thing, seeing her on my bed. I was never supposed to meet this incredibly frustrating girl from another city. I was never even supposed to know she existed. Now, because of a few wrong turns I took in the catacombs, she's growing all over every part of my life like the most persistent rosebush in existence.

I approach the bed, a bit hesitantly. "I always sleep on that side," I say, indicating her position.

"So do I," she says. "I suppose you'll have to fight me for it."

I consider. "I suppose I will."

And I climb on top of her.

Night still descends onto the nothingness above our heads, melting into blackness with a comforting familiarity. I fall asleep, and it's the first time I've properly slept in months. When I wake up, it's still dark outside. Verene is no longer next to me. She's wrapped in one of my silk robes, sitting in the armchair by the bed and scribbling in one of my old sketchbooks.

"That better be a drawing of me in the throes of passion," I say.

"Hmm." She raises her eyebrows, still scratching away with the pencil. "You do make some interesting faces."

I sink farther under the covers, so that maybe she won't be able to tell that my entire body is blushing. "Let me see it."

She hesitates. Then she turns the sketchbook around and places it in front of me.

It's a drawing of me as I must have just been—sound asleep. And also, nude. This is the first time someone has ever drawn my breasts, and I must say, it's a very positive experience.

I'm focusing on the breasts so I don't have to look at the rest.

My hair is a mess, and my face is soft and unguarded. I look tiny and unremarkable. I look completely unlike the way I want everyone else to see me—the way I want her to see me.

For some reason, looking at this drawing is the catalyst. It brings my last memories of the ninth city and throws them into clear relief—the feeling of her mouth on mine, and her hands on the back of my neck, and then, the cold look on her face as she pushed me down the stairs toward the vide.

"Why would you draw this?" I say. "Why are you here at all?"

I wanted to sound angry. But instead, I sound hurt. And there's nothing I can do to stop it.

Verene withdraws, pulling the drawing into her lap in a way that looks almost protective. She stares at it, delicately tracing one of the lines.

"There's no water left," she says. "Anywhere."

I don't respond. It feels, somehow, like I already knew this.

"They're trying to find more," she continues. "Theo's helping with that, since people actually want his help. But I don't think they're going to find any. I don't think it exists."

I watch the gentle movement of her finger as it runs across the curve of my penciled-in cheek over and over.

"So we're going to die soon," I say.

"Yes," she says.

"And you want to die with me," I say.

She stops tracing the drawing. She looks up. "It's not about what I want. It's about what sort of person I really am, deep down. It's about what I deserve."

I frown as she closes the book and sets it aside, but before

I can get a word out, she's already climbed into my bed and silenced me with a kiss.

Somebody's knocking on the door of my family's manor. The sound is pointed and demanding in this otherwise quiet city, and it jerks me out of my sleep. For a second, I'm sure I imagined it. Then it happens again—three precise raps in a row.

I sit up. Verene is stirring, too, withdrawing the arm she had draped over my waist.

"Did you hear that?" she says. "It almost sounded like—"

I'm already up and moving. I grab some clothes off the floor and shove them on, and then I'm bursting into the hall. I scurry down our grand staircase, fling open the front door, and see someone waiting there. Someone tall, dressed in crisp dark clothes, who—

"Oh," I say.

"Oh," Theo says.

The two of us stare at each other. He has a very familiar look of distaste on his face, but I can't help but notice how tired he looks. There are dark bags under his eyes, like he hasn't slept at all since we returned to the land of the living.

Soft footsteps behind me interrupt the silence, and I turn around to see Verene. She's wrapped in my silk bathrobe again, and she's clutching one of my shoes, looking very much like she scavenged around for the first weapon she could find. When she realizes it's just her brother, she stops halfway down the grand staircase.

"What is it?" she says, a little bit of defensiveness in her voice.

"I told them everything," Theo says.

"Told who?" she says.

"Iris," he says. "All of them. I told them the truth about Maman, and what she did to us, and what you did to her. I told them how you found the vide, and how you fought Emanuela until it all went entirely too far. I told them every single thing you've done—and I made sure they got the full story. With all the gory details."

Verene's mouth trembles, the betrayal on her face clear. "Why would you do that?"

"Get dressed and come with me," Theo says. "And I'll show you."

We return to my room. Verene puts on my pants, which are charmingly short on her, because I accidentally put on hers in my haste. I linger in the doorway and watch her button up her shirt and take down her hair, quietly soaking in each delicate movement she makes. It's pretty clear to me that I'm not invited on this expedition, but on her way out, she grabs my hand and pulls me along, so I go.

It's a surprisingly short walk over to Iris. We're all so much closer than it always felt. It's very gray outside—a color I haven't seen up above before. The nothing over our heads seems to produce a slightly different hue every day, which is bewildering, but also fascinating. All too soon, we're approaching the familiar white manors of Iris. Theo leads us down an empty street, past dark windows and shriveled flowerbeds. Verene's grip on my hand has grown a little bit too tight. Her eyes keep darting around, like she's just waiting for an angry mob to start pouring out of one of the alleys.

Then we reach an intersection. There used to be a fountain here—three beautiful tiers overflowing with water, and an intricate statue of Verene on top. But somebody has destroyed all of that. It's been pummeled into a pile of white rubble and dust.

Theo stops, so we stop, too.

"And?" Verene says, her voice wavering.

Theo gives the remnants of the fountain a significant look, and only then do I see it. Sitting on top of the wreckage, there's one lonely flower. A white rose.

Verene lets go of my hand. Tentatively, she edges onto the rubble and reaches up to grab the rose. Up close, it's obvious that this flower belongs to a city with no water. It's wilted, its petals dangerously close to dropping off, but Verene holds it like it's the most precious thing she's ever touched.

"They want you to come back," Theo says. "For as long as we have."

"But..." Verene says. "They know what I did. They know how far I went. I'm not the Heart of Iris, and I'm definitely not the girl who can magically save them. I have nothing to give them. I'm just..."

"You're a person who lives in this city," Theo says. "And a person who loves it."

Verene hesitates. She looks at the rose again, like she's not quite sure what to do with it. But then, carefully, carefully, she reaches up and tucks it behind her ear.

A flicker of movement in the corner of my eye catches my attention. In the window of one of the nearby manors, the curtains have been pushed aside. There's a woman watching Verene with wary curiosity. At her elbow, barely peeking over the windowsill, is a little girl who's watching Verene with huge dark eyes. She looks positively dazzled.

The older woman's gaze falls on me, and her expression changes in an instant to one of disgust and fear. She puts a protective hand on the child's head.

I take a step back.

Verene turns to me. "Where are you going?"

But we both know the answer to that. I burned this city down once. I don't belong in it.

"I'm just..." I try to speak, and find that my throat is suddenly very tight.

"You can't be alone for this," Verene whispers a bit helplessly.

"I'm already bored of this place," I manage. "If all of your gaudy fountains have finally been destroyed, then there's nothing left for me to do."

Verene's eyes flicker over my face, and when she speaks, her voice is far more tender than it has any right to be. "Well... good riddance."

She doesn't come any closer to me. She doesn't try to touch me again, or kiss me again, and I don't try to touch her. There's no point. We could have each other for an eternity, and it would never be enough.

Instead, Verene turns away. She starts to walk down the nearest street, moving deeper into her city, and I can feel the way she's fighting not to look back. For a moment, Theo and I are left there, hovering in front of each other. His hands are in his pockets, his shoulders slumped. He has the weary look of someone who's tried every solution one person could possibly try, and who has instead ended up back in the same place, standing in a city with no water. And somehow, I know exactly what he's been doing with every spare moment he's had. He's been shutting himself away from the rest of his family and thinking about how it's all his fault.

I turn away and walk in the opposite direction.

"You're really going to leave?" he says to my back, skepticism in his voice. "Just like that?"

He's right to be skeptical. He knows just how hard it is to get rid of me.

I pause just long enough to glance over my shoulder. "You don't have much time. Don't spend it with me."

The last thing I hear, right before I round the corner, is a lot of grumbling about how I have no right to give him orders.

I return to the dark, empty city of Occhia. I don't go back to my house, because if I climb into my bed, it will still smell like Verene. Instead, I wander the streets.

The worst part is that I have no idea what it's going to be like. My throat is parched, and I'm starting to feel weak and dizzy, but I don't have any omens yet. I don't know if it's even going to happen through omens now, or if it's going to be... something else. But I'll find out soon enough.

I don't know how long I've been meandering when I look up and realize I'm in front of the House of Morandi—the real one. It's just as grand as it was in the afterlife, but the walls are dark, and the ivy that used to cover them has long since withered away into dust. Off to one side, there's a pile of melted prayer candles and red roses sitting on the street. That's where the watercrea landed when I pushed her to her death. My people surrounded the gown she left behind with offerings, hoping to bring her back. Later, I snatched up that gown—I can see the spot where I trampled through all the flowers—and took it for myself. That was supposed to be the moment that the people of Occhia realized, once and for all, that I was the only one who could save them.

I turn away from the shrine and walk toward the entrance of the house. I push my way through the double doors with a creak that feels overly loud and invasive. This place has been empty for a year, but somehow, the familiar smell of the life it had is still lingering. For a second, I almost lose my nerve, unable to take it. But something propels me forward. I walk around the foyer, peeking in all the doors. Then I make my way upstairs.

On my way to the study, I pass by the doorway that leads to the sewing room, and I stop. The loveseats inside are empty and covered in dust. My eyes skirt over them and linger on the wardrobe against one wall.

It's not magic. I know it's not. Nothing in this house is magic.

But I'm walking for it anyway. I put my hand on the cold knob of the wardrobe door.

"I just want to know if he's all right," I whisper. "If there's a way for me to know…that's all I want."

I pull open the door.

There's nothing inside but piles of musty fabric. I hover there, staring at them desperately, like I'm going to find some kind of sign in a bunch of abandoned sewing supplies. But I don't. Of course I don't.

I turn to go. I step out of the sewing room and then, one more time, I look back at the wardrobe.

It's gone. I blink once, then twice, and still, all I see is the blank space where it used to be.

There's an explanation for this, of course. The wardrobe was never there in the first place. I'm thirstier than I realize, and weaker than I realize, and I'm imagining things. I want to believe I'm still in a place that has magic, but I can't delude myself any longer.

I stumble back down the stairs and push open the front doors of the House of Morandi. I can't look at this building anymore. I need to disappear into the streets and find somewhere that doesn't remind me of how very alone I am.

"Emanuela?"

I've only taken two steps onto the cobblestone when I hear the voice. I freeze. Then, slowly, certain that I'm imagining this, too, I turn in the direction it came from.

Ale is standing right on the spot where the watercrea died, surrounded by roses and candles. He looks exactly the way he did when I last saw him in the ninth city—dark red clothes, black eyepatch, and untidy hair. His arms are crossed, and he's shivering, like he just came from somewhere cold. He's looking at me with one very wide eye.

"What..." he says. "What did you do?"

Magic.

I did magic. The kind of magic that's far too powerful for any one person to wield. The kind of magic that I've always wanted to be able to do.

"Emanuela." Ale's voice is panicked. "I shouldn't be here. I was—how did you—"

My head feels so light it's practically floating off my body in elation. I don't even care that the wardrobe is gone. I don't care that there are a thousand other things I could have done with it. Because for one moment, I used it to do the most incredible feat I've ever done, and now my best friend is here.

"Emanuela." Ale is trembling so hard I can see it from here. "Say something."

Then the reality of it hits me, and I feel myself stumbling back.

"Oh no," I whisper.

"What?" Ale's voice is getting loud and thick, like he's on the verge of tears. "What did you do? What did it cost?"

"I didn't—" My own voice is shaking, too. "There must have been a little bit of magic left, somehow, but I didn't know it would bring you back. I shouldn't have brought you back. We don't have any water. We're going to die, and I don't want you to go through this again. I didn't mean to, Ale. I just asked it to.... I was just thinking about you, and it must have..."

Ale goes very still. The look he gives me is uncomprehending. My face feels strange and wet, and I realize after a moment there are tears on my cheeks. I don't try to wipe them away. Even though Ale has never seen me cry—not even when we were children—I don't see the point in trying to hide it from him.

"There's no water anywhere?" Ale says.

"No," I say.

He's silent, his face utterly blank. Abruptly, like his knees have given out, he sits down cross-legged on the cobblestone, right in the middle of the shrine. A moment passes in utter stillness. Then he gives me a strangely expectant look, like he's wondering what I'm doing standing all the way over here.

I approach him uncertainly. I step over the dead roses and overturned prayer candles and hover in front of him. Then, after a moment, I sit down. Our knees accidentally touch— I always underestimate the absurd length of his legs—and I quickly scoot back.

"The vide…" I venture. "It's not still…?"

He pulls up his eyepatch to reveal a jagged pink scar.

"Ah," I say. "Much better."

He adjusts the eyepatch so it's sitting properly again. He spends a bit too long on it, like he's not quite sure what else to do.

"Ale—" I start, then cut myself off, because I'm not quite sure what to do, either. I'm not quite sure what I'm trying to say.

The look he gives me is a little bit wary, and I think about how, two minutes ago, I was certain I was never going to see him again. I think about all the people who are already gone, and who are never going to get brought back to life by a magic wardrobe, even for a moment. I think about all the things that are unsaid, and all the things that are going to stay that way forever.

"You were right," I say. "About everything. And you were right about me. I am scared, all the time. I'm scared that nothing I do matters. I'm scared that I don't matter. And I'm scared of dying, even now. I'm scared of feeling it happen. I'm scared of not feeling it happen. I'm scared that—"

"Don't," he says sharply.

I falter.

"Don't apologize to me," he continues. "Not after what I did."

His eye is welling up with tears. A couple of them break loose and run down his cheeks.

"Ale—" I say.

"This is my fault," he says. "It's all my fault. I thought I could handle that magic, but I was wrong. All those people— they suffered for it. I'll never even know how many of them I fed to the vide. There's no way to know. And my mamma—"

He cuts himself off, his voice strangled. "It's good that we have no water. It's good that I'm about to die again. That's what I deserve."

There's a sharp certainty to the way he says the last words. He says them like they're a truth he's believed for a long time, and for a second, I'm so taken aback by it that I can barely breathe. I can't believe he talks about himself so viciously.

But then again, I shouldn't be surprised. I know exactly where he learned how to do that.

I let out a dramatic sigh. "Oh, Ale. I don't care."

He goes very still. He looks up at me, slowly. "What?"

"I don't care what you did," I say. "I don't care how terrible you think it was. You don't deserve to die."

"I do," he says.

"Don't argue with me," I say. "You're incredible, but you're not going to win this one."

He gapes at me, and it's painfully clear how much the compliment means to him. It's painfully clear that it's pierced right into his heart, the way all of my words do. But then, out of nowhere, he gets a steely look on his face. "No. We're not going back to that, Emanuela."

"Going back to what?" I say.

But my voice is small, because I already know.

"The way it's always been," he says. "You don't know who you are without power, but I don't know who I am without you. My life has always revolved around you, even when I was ruling the ninth city. Deep down, the reason I was doing it was to prove myself to you, and I tried to pretend otherwise, but...it just wasn't true. That's who you are. That's what you do. You leave your mark all over people. Especially me." He pauses.

"But I'm going to decide things for myself now. Even if there's no water, and no hope of finding more, I'm going to decide for myself what I deserve to do with this time. I'm going to decide I want to do."

I swallow hard. "And what do you want to do?"

He leans forward, and he takes my face in his hands. His fingers are cold and devastatingly gentle, and when he presses his lips to my forehead, it's somehow even gentler.

"I want to live," he says.

He stands up. He steps carefully over the roses, and he starts to walk down the street. After a moment, he pauses and turns around. He looks at the House of Morandi. He looks at me, sitting in front of it. Then, without a word, he turns away, and he keeps moving on.

I don't try to follow him. I don't try to ask him where he's going. Because he doesn't belong to me, and he never will.

Things shouldn't stay the same forever. They should get better.

I'm lying curled up on the street, right where the watercrea died, when I feel it.

At first, I think it's my omens. There's a tiny, cold pinprick on my skin. A second later, another one touches the side of my face. They keep coming, steadily, and I don't move. I just close my eyes and grit my teeth and try to tell myself that there's nothing I can do, so I just have to accept it.

It doesn't work. I don't want to accept this. I want more, and I always will.

Then I notice something strange. I don't feel the way I usually feel when I get my omens. I feel...cold. And...wet.

I open my eyes.

And I see water.

It's all around me, falling onto the cobblestone in little mysterious drips. I sit up and try to figure out where it's coming from, looking around wildly. Only when I tilt my face up do I realize that it's coming from the swirl of gray and white over my head, which means it's coming from everywhere.

I stagger to my feet as the water starts to fall faster. I expect this to be a fleeting thing—a miracle that's gone in a flash—but the barrage only picks up, hammering onto the roofs of the nearby manors and filling the streets. It feels endless. Like magic.

I'm soaked and shivering. But as I whirl around, taking it all in, I'm also laughing with delight, because it's the most extraordinary thing I've ever seen.

The city of Occhia is drenched. And I'm alive.

ACKNOWLEDGMENTS

Thank you to Carrie Pestritto, who singlehandedly talked me off fifteen different ledges while I was trying to wrestle this unruly book into submission. Thank you to Alex Hightower, the most gracious and patient editor, who brought her A game every single time I made her listen to another one of my "amazing new ideas." A million thanks to the team at Little, Brown, including but not limited to: Alvina Ling, Katie Boni, Bill Grace, Savannah Kennelly (TikTok queen), and Victoria Stapleton. Thank you to Sasha Illingworth and ILOVEDUST for the cover. What a blessing to have not one but two beautiful flowery goth books in the world.

Thank you to my writing friends. It turns out that writing a sequel while also releasing your first book in a pandemic is kind of tricky. To Maddy Colis, Ashley Burdin, Alexis Castellanos, Kat Cho, Amanda Foody, Christine Lynn Herman, Tara Sim, Claribel Ortega, Melody Simpson, Ella Dyson, Meg Kohlmann, Axie Oh, Amanda Haas, Erin Bay, Akshaya Raman, Katy Rose Pool, and Janella Angeles—thank you for being there, and thank you for being you. Thank you to Isabel Sterling, Nina Varela, and Rebecca Kim Wells. Thank you to my family. And thank you also to my Venus flytrap. It didn't do anything to help me write this book, but it still deserves thanks.

And thank you to the readers. One of the most astounding things to me about releasing the first book was the number of people who pushed it into the hands of their friends. Never underestimate the power of that, because to an author, it's the most powerful thing in the world. Thank you for the blog posts and videos, for the memes (!) and the art (!!) and the cosplay (!!!). You are and always will be the most valuable part of this equation. Or, as Emanuela would say: You're welcome for the gift of my presence—now keep showering me with attention, because I deserve it.